TELL ME HOW YOU HATE ME

CALI MELLE

Copyright © 2024 by Cali Melle

All rights reserved.

No part of this book may be reproduced in any form or by any electronic or mechanical means, including information storage and retrieval systems, without written permission from the author, except for the use of brief quotations in a book review.

This book is a work of fiction and any resemblance to any person, living or dead, or any events or occurrences is purely coincidental. The characters and story lines are created purely by the author's imagination and are used fictitiously.

Cover art by darya.mist.art
Edited by Rumi Khan
Proofread by Alexandra Cowell

PLAYLIST

WHAT JUST HAPPENED - The Kid LAROI
run for the hills - Tate McRae
imgonnagetyouback - Taylor Swift
Hate Me - Ellie Goulding, Juice WRLD
Down Bad - Taylor Swift
Bloodline - Ariana Grande
The Take - Tory Lanez, Chris Brown
ETA - Nick Alexandr
No Guidance - Chris Brown, Drake
I GUESS IT'S LOVE? - The Kid LAROI
Eyes On You - SWIM
Nervous - John Legend

This one is for the hopeless romantics who ship every pair of enemies together...
I see I'm in good company.

PROLOGUE
ARIA

"This changes nothing between us," I remind Leo as I lift my blue cashmere sweater up over my head and toss it onto the marble floor. His large hands find my hips and he pulls me flush against his body. "If we do this, it doesn't mean I like you. This doesn't make us friends."

"Likewise," he murmurs, nipping at my bottom lip with his teeth. His leg presses between mine, inching me back until I hit the wall of my foyer. "I never said I liked you, nor did I say I wanted to be your friend."

His lips find the side of my neck as he trails them along my skin. He doesn't kiss me, but I can faintly smell the spearmint on his breath, undoubtedly from the mint he was chewing on after practice. He waited until everyone else had left before approaching me. Heaven forbid Leo Wells gets caught talking to me and being nice.

Leo breaks away from teasing and tasting my skin. I inhale a lungful of oxygen as he stares down at me. His gaze is hooded, his eyes darkening as he rakes them over my face. It's like he can't decide what he wants to do with me. When he kissed me at the rink, he caught me off guard, but it was also something that had been building between us for months.

I don't have to like him to want him.

My chest rises and falls in rapid succession. I'm trapped under his gaze, but I don't find myself wanting to hide from him. I want him to see all of me—to *want* all of me. My hands shake ever so slightly as I reach behind my back and unclasp my bra. Leo's eyes widen, his pupils constrict, and I watch the muscle in his jaw tighten as I drop my bra onto the ground.

"Goddammit, Aria," he groans, closing his eyes as he runs a frustrated hand through his hair. It falls just above his eyebrows in light brown tousled waves. "I could stare at you forever."

A smile dances across my lips as I take a step toward him. "You don't like me, Leo."

"I don't have to like you to admit that you're fucking gorgeous." He pauses while moving closer to me, again backing me up until I'm against the wall. He lifts his hands, planting them beside my head as he cages me in. "It's pure torture, having to constantly see you—to watch you—knowing this is all we'll ever be."

Lifting my own arms, I slide my palms against the nape of his neck. "You watch me?"

"All the damn time," he murmurs, his voice filled with lust. "How could I not? You're everywhere, Aria. Sometimes I wish you would just go away and leave me in peace."

Leo runs his hands down the sides of my torso, his fingers trailing lightly over my flesh. I reach for the hem of his t-shirt and begin to lift it upward. Leo reaches behind his back and pulls the cotton shirt up over his head before he throws it onto the ground. My eyes momentarily drink him in, traveling over the planes of his body as I memorize the curves of the chiseled muscles of his chest and abdomen.

His grip lands on my waist and he lowers his mouth to my ear. His tongue traces the outer shell, his breath warm against my earlobe. Dropping one hand away from the back of his neck, I reach for him, gripping his cock through his pants. He inhales sharply, his breath hitching as his grip tightens on my hips.

"Aria," he growls my name, his voice low and husky, even though there's a warning in his tone. "I can still leave now with your pride intact, and we can pretend this never happened."

"Or," I say slowly as I reach for the waistband of his pants. My hands find his belt and I unbuckle it before pushing the button through the hole. I begin to pull his zipper down. "You can stay and we can still pretend this never happened."

Leo flattens his palms against my hips and slides his fingers beneath the waistband of my leggings. His touch is soft, his hands warming my skin as he begins to push them down my thighs. He trails his lips down my neck, peppering kisses across my collarbone before he starts to work his way down my body. His hands slide my black leggings and lilac-colored panties down to my ankles. He stops as he reaches my chest and lifts his hands to cup my breasts.

His eyes meet mine with a fire burning deep within his golden brown irises. I watch him as his pink, plump lips part, his tongue slipping out, and he slowly circles it around my nipple. My flesh pebbles under his touch and I fight the urge to arch my back. My gaze stays locked with his and he moves over to my other breast. His movements are deliberately and torturously slow. He never breaks eye contact as his tongue flicks at my skin.

He lowers himself onto his knees, sitting back on his heels as his mouth abandons my chest. Grabbing my ankle, he bends my knee and frees my foot from my underwear and leggings. As he sets my foot down, he does the same with the other leg. My feet are both on the marble floor, my back pressed against the light gray wall, and I'm completely naked and exposed under his gaze. Leo sits back, his eyes traveling up and down the length of my body.

"God, you're perfect."

Words fail me as he inches closer. His fingers start at my ankle, skating across my skin, until he reaches my knee. I watch him, completely mesmerized as he begins to lift my leg up. He spreads my legs, hooking my knee over his shoulder. The heel of my foot rests against the bottom of his shoulder blade. Pinning his forearms against my hips, he splays his fingers along the bottom of my stomach.

He lowers his face, his eyes finding mine as his warm breath tickles the apex of my thighs. "Just one taste," he whispers, his lips brushing against my skin. He makes no other movement as he waits. His eyes bounce between mine and the tension in the air is palpable.

My heart pounds erratically in my chest. I pull my bottom lip between my teeth, biting down as I nod. Approval passes through his gaze and the corners of his mouth twitch before he lowers his mouth down to my flesh. His lips are warm and soft like the finest silk. He slides his tongue along my pussy, licking me from the bottom up to my clit.

A shiver of pleasure slides up my spine. My head tips back, the crown of my head pressing against the wall as my back simultaneously arches. Leo holds me in place, not letting me move as he begins his assault on my pussy. His movements are intentional. Every lick, every taste, every tease, every touch. Every single thing he does to me is calculated. Leo Wells knows exactly what he's doing to me and he has no plans of stopping.

He flattens his tongue against my clit and begins to roll it around in circles. The amount of pressure he applies is just enough to cause friction. It is exactly what I'm looking for, exactly what I need for that release I'm so desperate for. Leo keeps one hand pinned against my hip as he drops his other one. His fingertips are soft and featherlight against my skin as they trail between my legs. His mouth pulls away from me for a fraction of a second as he wets his fingers with his tongue.

My body instantly craves his touch. A warmth is

building in the pit of my stomach. His lips suction around my clit once more and my knees almost give out from the relief. It's like a reward after having to go a few moments with his face between my legs without him actually touching me. My breath catches in my throat as he presses his fingers against my center.

"You really don't like me, huh?" he murmurs against my flesh, the sarcasm thick in his tone. He looks up at me from where he is on his knees and flicks my clit with his tongue. Slowly, he pushes two fingers inside me, a soft moan falling from my lips as my eyelids flutter closed.

"Not in the slightest bit." I practically moan the words as he works his tongue against me again. The warmth is spilling into my veins, coursing through my body as a wildfire ignites inside of me. I don't want him to stop. I can't have him stopping and leaving me hanging. "You're undoubtedly the worst person I've ever met in my life."

"Mmm," he hums against me, his fingers slow and deliberate as he pushes them deep inside me and pulls them out. He finds a rhythm and begins to pump his fingers. "Let me show you how bad I can be."

"I won't stop you."

Mischief dances with the lust in his eyes. A groan rumbles in his chest as his tongue finds my clit once more. Instinctively, my hands find his head and I run my fingers through his hair. The messy, tousled waves are soft and silky. He applies more pressure and pumps his fingers harder as my hips buck against his hand that is pinning me to the wall. I grab a fistful of his hair, gripping tightly as my orgasm crashes into my body without any more warning.

It erupts deep inside, quickly consuming me in one swift wave. I cry out, his name falling from my lips as my face screws up and my eyes slam shut. Stars dance in the darkness and my body is on fire, shaking and quivering beneath his touch. Leo's movements become slower as he moves his fingers in and out of me. His mouth doesn't abandon my pussy and he licks and sucks until I'm fully satiated, riding the unbelievable high from him.

Leo pulls his fingers out of me and slips them between his perfect lips, licking my arousal from his skin. My mouth hangs wide open, my chest heaving as I struggle to catch my breath. I can't tear my gaze away from him. The way he just licked me from his fingers. It does something to me that betrays my feelings toward this man.

What we just did goes against everything I feel for him, but I don't even care. I want more of him. I want whatever he wants to give me.

He smirks and his eyes shimmer as he continues to watch me. As he rises to his feet, he wipes his mouth with the back of his hand. He breaks eye contact as he bends down and grabs his t-shirt. Confusion washes over me, my eyebrows pulling together as he takes a step away and puts his shirt on.

"Where are you going?" I ask him, attempting to keep my voice steady, although my body is betraying me with my heart pounding inside my chest. We didn't really talk about our plans for the night, but I'm confused as to why he's ready to leave already.

"I have a flight to catch. I'm going to go spend the weekend with my sister."

Suddenly, I feel extremely exposed under his gaze. There's nothing menacing about the way he looks at me, but his expression is unreadable as he scans my body before landing on my eyes again. "I'm a little confused." I cross my arms over my chest and nod down to his erection in his pants. "What about you?"

"Don't hide yourself from me." Leo reaches for my arms, pulling them away from my chest as he takes a step toward me. "And I'll survive. Consider this a favor from me." He pauses, his lips meeting mine before he pulls away again. I'm left breathless, staring after him as he walks the short distance to the front door and begins to turn the handle.

As he pulls the door open, he pauses at the threshold and glances back at me one last time.

"And now you owe me."

CHAPTER ONE
LEO

I stare out at the glistening surface, feeling the contempt sliding through my veins like ice. She is perfect—flawless, really—with the way she skates effortlessly around the rink. I can't help but stare, even as I want to tear my own eyes away from her. She pays no attention to anyone because she doesn't care what they think of her. I welcome her cold shoulder. It's exactly how I want things between us to be.

Aria Reed only cares about herself and winning.

She moved back to Idyll Cove a few years ago, but I've known her for longer than that. We had spent a majority of our lives competing against one another. And if I am being honest, she is a phenomenal figure skater. I appreciate that because I don't want the competition to be easy. I want to win because I earned my spot by competing against the best skaters.

Aria Reed is one of the best.

And she is the furthest thing from easy.

After giving her one last piece of my attention, I tear my gaze away from her and walk over to the door. As I step out onto the ice, the moment my blades hit the surface, everything around me fades away. The background noise stops. Any negative energy simply dissipates. It is just me and the ice and nothing else. I pop my AirPods into my ears and turn up the music as I begin to skate around the rink.

I don't know what I'm going to do since I don't have my figure skating partner Delaney to skate with anymore. A few months ago, she found out that she was pregnant with her long-time boyfriend. We were originally planning on her skating until she wasn't able to anymore. That was still supposed to be a few months from now. I was supposed to have more time to plan on what I was going to do when she was out.

And then she experienced some complications. Her doctor advised her to stop skating immediately. Delaney wasn't due for another five months and she was planning on taking at least two months after she gave birth off too.

I'm not mad—I want nothing but the best for her. I want her baby to be healthy. I want her and Tim to be able to celebrate this time in their life. I also want to have a partner I can skate with. I wanted to have a little more time to find someone else I could compete with.

To put it mildly—I am fucked.

Delaney's abrupt departure from the competitive skating world threw a bit of a wrench in my plans. Since we're already well into the season, I need to find a new partner, but it's not easy. Partners typically find each other early on in their skating careers. When you find someone that you mesh with, you basically skate with them for the rest of eternity.

Or until situations like this happen.

Delaney and I had been skating together since we were about twelve years old. We went through middle school, high school, and then joined a team that competed worldwide, representing our country. Sixteen years of learning how to move and work together and now I am back at square one. It's a much bigger challenge to find a partner as an adult than it was to find one as a kid.

Aria skates past me, her feet moving swiftly across the ice. The smell of lavender lingers in the air and the scent invades my senses. I can't help myself as my eyelids flutter shut and I take a deep breath, drawing the lingering hints of her perfume into my lungs.

"Let me show you how bad I can be."

"I won't stop you."

Fuck. The memory of her moving under my touch, the way she tasted—goddamn, it was like it just happened, but it didn't. Four months later and I still can't get her out of my head.

After I walked away from her that night, I left with the promise that she owed me. But I promised myself I wouldn't show that same weakness again. I wouldn't give in to the temptation I felt for Aria Reed. I thought at the time that she would feel the same way, but I wasn't going to bring the subject up to her. Aria and I aren't friends and we certainly don't talk to each other if we don't have to.

I never approached her again after that night and she

never spoke another word to me. If anything, the distance between us grew even further. The coldness got colder. She stayed out of my way and I stayed out of hers. Competitions were the worst. It was impossible not to watch her, especially as she skated around the ice with another man's hands touching her where I touched her.

Shaking the thoughts of her from my mind, I start to skate harder around the rink, warming my legs up. My muscles burn as I spin and begin to skate backward. I do an entire lap like that before breaking out into some Lutz jumps. There are more skaters on the ice than I prefer, so I opt out of any axels. The last thing I need is to run into someone when I'm trying to land a jump.

It's bad enough not having Delaney here. I don't know what I would do if I wasn't able to skate either.

Luca Kincaid, one of our coaches, stands over by the door, but he doesn't come out onto the ice. His eyes lock with mine and he waves me over. Bobbing and weaving through other skaters, I head over to where he is. Pointing my toes inward, I shift my weight onto my outside edges and come to a halt, shaving some of the ice as I stop in front of him.

I pluck my AirPods from my ears and the music stops. "What's up?"

"We're going to be having a team meeting after the free skate. The coaching staff has a few things we'd like to go over with everyone."

I resist the urge to frown and keep my face free of any emotion instead. The unplanned meeting has me a little concerned, but I don't let it show and I keep my voice even. "Is everything okay?"

Luca nods. "I think we may have found a partner for you. Someone of your caliber."

Delaney had to inform them when her doctors insisted that she take a leave of absence. It brought my lack of a partner to the coaching staff's attention, so they had all been trying to help in any way they were able to. Not only is it difficult to find someone because most skaters are already bonded, but it is especially hard to find someone who has a similar skill level.

I didn't expect them to succeed.

"Really? When did this happen?" I ask him as I step off the ice. "No one said anything to me."

"It literally just happened half an hour ago. It's nothing concrete, but there's another skater who has also lost a partner." He pauses for a moment, looking out at the rink before he looks at me again. "I think Loren mentioned something to her, but it hasn't been confirmed. Get your skates off and come with me. We can go talk before the meeting starts."

Luca calls out to everyone else on the ice to let them know about the meeting before he disappears into the warm room. There's only five minutes until the free skate is over. I find my things on the bench and take a seat before removing my skates. I grab the towel from my bag and dry off the blades and put the skate protectors back on. Grabbing my bag beside me, I put my skates inside and secure the zipper before sliding my feet into my sneakers.

Everyone else is still on the ice but there's only about two minutes left and I want to go talk to Luca and the other coaches before everyone else gets there. I'm not going to get blindsided and caught off guard. I want to know who the skater is. The thought of them setting something up for me without my input makes me a little unsettled. It has to be a good fit. It has to be someone who I have chemistry with.

When two skaters aren't in sync, it is very apparent. The way they move together isn't fluid, it isn't like a melody of its own. It just doesn't look good. That's when accidents happen. The performances that create an emotional pull are the ones that score very well. If you're skating with someone that you don't have that chemistry with, you won't be able to create that emotion you can feel in the air. That's when you lose, and I didn't get into this sport to lose. I didn't get this far to compete at such a high level to have it all go to shit.

Anything less than excellence wouldn't be acceptable.

When I walk into the warm room, I see Luca sitting with Coach Davis and Coach Sinclair. Eva Davis and Alanna Sinclair are two of our other professional coaches. The three of them work together with all of the skaters who compete for our country. Luca was the one Delaney and I worked with the most and he was the one I had more of a friendship with. He tends to look out for me and provide a bit of guidance when I need it in life.

"Hey, Leo," Luca says when he sees me in the room. The three of them are seated in the sitting area where there's a sectional couch and two armchairs. Luca sits in one of the chairs, Eva to his left on the chaise lounge and Alanna on the arm of the couch. "Come sit."

I follow his instructions and sit down on the couch across from them. I look at Eva and Alanna. "Coach Kincaid told me that you guys found another skater?"

Alanna nods, her blonde bob shifting with the movement. "We actually have another pair that has been recently separated. The one skater has some private medical issues that he doesn't wish to have disclosed to everyone. Unfortunately, he's been required to take an indefinite leave of absence."

It must have been something that just happened because I hadn't heard anyone talking about something happening to their partner. Since it's just an open skate and not a practice, there are a few skaters who didn't come, so it's hard for me to judge who it is. And it doesn't seem like they're going to make an announcement just yet.

"Who is the skater looking for a new partner then?"

Luca looks a little concerned and there's a crease on his forehead as he purses his lips. The door behind me opens and Luca looks past me. I look at Eva and Alanna who are both grinning.

"Well, this is perfect timing," Eva says, smiling brightly as she claps her hands together. I slowly turn around, immediately feeling the tension and anticipation hanging heavily in the air. My eyes meet her gray irises and dread instantly fills the pit of my stomach.

The muscle in my jaw tics and she stops just inside the door. Her eyes widen slightly and those perfect lips part. I remember how they tasted. How soft they felt as they melt against my own lips.

"Leo," Luca says softly, breaking through my thoughts and grabbing my attention. I turn back around to look at him, my jaw clenched so tightly it feels like my molars are going to crack. "You know Aria Reed."

I stare at him and don't speak a single word. I know exactly where this is going and I don't like it one bit.

"Meet your new partner."

CHAPTER TWO
ARIA

Well, shit.

This is not what I was expecting.

Leo doesn't turn back around to look at me. He continues to stare at Luca as he explains everything to Leo. I overheard about Delaney this morning, but I didn't put two and two together at the time. I honestly didn't give it much thought when Eva told me about it and then the thought really left my brain when I got my own dreaded phone call earlier.

Preston had been having some muscle fatigue issues for a while and it was progressively getting worse. He was constantly tired and growing weaker, which was making it harder for him to lift me into the air. It was affecting the way we skated together, but I didn't want to make him feel bad about it. I did what I could to modify our routines and he did everything he could do to make himself stronger.

And then it kind of stopped working. Preston's doctors were running tests and looking into every aspect of his health. They determined it was some kind of autoimmune disorder but they needed to run more tests to determine what it was and what they could do for it. Preston had to make the impossible decision to take a break from skating. He was at risk from his health and it was also proving to be dangerous for both of us.

He didn't tell me the severity of things until earlier today and I'm still trying to process it all. I went from thinking my partner was having some minimal issues to being without a partner completely. Preston reached out to the coaches after he dropped the bomb on me. I didn't really say much to any of them, but Alanna told me earlier that they had some ideas for a new partner for me.

Like I said, I didn't put two and two together at the time.

Leo and I both need a partner... and they want us to skate together.

I literally want to crawl into a hole and die right now. Of all people, why does it have to be him? Hell, at this point, I will take someone who doesn't skate as well. Okay, that's a lie.

This isn't an ideal situation, but it could work. Leo is an exceptional skater. The two of us have been in a silent competition with one another for years. Even though we skate on the same team, we still compete against each other. I want to win and I know Leo has the same drive. He's one of the sorest losers I've ever met. If we can put our differences aside, we might be able to make this work.

"No."

Every ounce of hope I have falls to the ground as soon

as the word leaves Leo's lips. He rises to his feet in a haste. He runs a frustrated hand through his hair and I remember exactly how silky his locks felt running between my fingers. My tongue darts out to wet my lips. I nervously shift my weight on my feet as Leo crosses his arms over his chest.

"What are you talking about?" Eva questions him, her eyebrows pulling together.

"Leo, you don't have any other options," Luca chimes in at the same time.

Alanna looks at me with a sympathetic look on her face. I shrug and take a deep breath as I step farther into the room. I don't want this any more than he does. Hell, he left me feeling more rejected than anyone else ever had. I'd never had someone come to my house, give me an orgasm, and then never speak to me again. He didn't even get anything pleasurable out of it, which stung more than anything.

I wasn't good enough for him to collect on the debt I owed.

"Can I talk to Leo in private?" I ask the three coaches. Leo avoids my gaze and stalks over to the window and stares out at the ice. This isn't really what I want to do, but he's not being receptive right now. I don't know if talking to him will make any difference, but I have to try.

There has to be some way that we can come to an agreement. It's either that or we are both stuck without a partner and neither of us will be able to skate in any of the pair skating competitions.

Luca nods and rises to his feet as Alanna and Eva

follow him. "We'll give you two a few minutes. We'll start the meeting in the lobby instead."

I thank them silently as they leave the room. Leo doesn't look at them, he doesn't look at me. He just stares out the window. The small smile that was on my face instantly falls and an exasperated sigh escapes me as I walk over to where he is.

"If it makes you feel any better, I don't want to be your partner either."

Leo snorts and I see him roll his eyes as he continues to look out at the ice. "It doesn't make me feel any better because I never would have expected you to want to be my partner."

"Fair enough," I agree with a shrug. He's not wrong. Leo has his reasons for not liking me and I have my reasons for not liking him. They're all petty and ones that developed when we were younger, but it drove a wedge between us that we never seemed to get over. It was pretty stupid. "We seem to both be at the same crossroads right now."

"That's where you're wrong," he says, his words slicing through me like sharpened blades of steel. "You may be at a crossroads, but I already know my answer. I will not skate with you."

I try to ignore the sting that he leaves behind. His words have always been his weapon. "You like to win, don't you?"

He slowly turns his head to look at me and gives me a knowing look. "Get to the point, Reed. I don't feel like playing games."

"You know that we are equally skilled and we are both at the top. What else could happen if you put two of the best skaters together? It's a sure bet that we will win."

There is no guarantee like that, but it is basic math at this point. We skated together many years ago, but not in a competition. It was one fluke moment when we were both in high school.

I wasn't as fortunate as the other kids. My parents were separated and both worked, so sometimes it was hard for me to get to the rink on time. One night, I ended up being late to practice. Our coach said I had to sit out and watch everyone else as I did off-ice exercises. It was brutal and also humiliating.

Leo told me he needed my help with something after everyone was finished. He was working at the rink at the time, running the Zamboni and working at the front desk. He was supposed to close up after practice was over, but he didn't.

He waited until everyone was gone and locked the door with both of us inside. He told me that I could skate as long as I wanted to. Free ice time was next to impossible to come by and considering the fact that I had missed the entirety of practice, I was not going to pass up the opportunity to skate.

What I wasn't expecting was for him to ask me to skate with him. We had never done that before, we didn't have a routine. We made it up as we went... and I never had a moment skating with someone like that again. We were in perfect harmony together, absolutely flawless. He whispered sweet words of how he never wanted to skate with anyone but me.

Leo went back to pretending I didn't exist after that, like he never said those words, and I started dating his rival, who I ended up partnering with for a few years. Things couldn't have gone any further south between Leo and I. For whatever reason, I hung on to that memory of us together that night. It meant something to me.

"We've never skated together before." He narrows his eyes on mine. "There's no way you can be sure we will win together."

Hearing those words cuts deep. He has to remember or else I've been holding on to nothing. It was a pivotal moment in my life. He extended a kindness that no one else would understand. "Yes, we did."

Leo looks at me—really looks at me—and the rug is pulled out from under my feet as he smiles. "Are you talking about that time in high school?" He pauses, shaking his head. "Aria, that wasn't anything choreographed. We were just messing around on the ice. There's no guarantee it would be the same now. You know there has to be chemistry, there has to be emotion woven into the performance."

He's doing this on purpose, either because he doesn't want to skate together or he doesn't want to admit the truth. We do have chemistry. We've *always* had chemistry. There has always been a magnetic pull between us. Or that's what I thought. After the past few months of silence, I wasn't so sure. Perhaps I'm delusional. Perhaps there never was anything there.

"You're right," I agree, nodding as I take a step away from him. "It's fine. I'm sure we will both be able to find someone else."

He stares at me, the smile falling from his face as he sets his lips in a straight line. "You don't like me, Aria. Why are you acting like this?"

"Because I like to win, Leo. I don't have to like you to skate with you. I just want to win and you might be my best shot at it."

It's the truth. He's an emotionally unavailable, avoidant man. He's not the type of person I would ever want to get involved with. Leo Wells is too much work for me. I need a partner that will help me win. I need someone that will help me stay at the top. He's the one, but if he doesn't want it, I can't force him.

"That's all you've ever cared about."

I recoil a bit at the harshness of his tone. My spine straightens and I push my shoulders back. "If you're not winning, what are you doing?"

He sets his jaw as he stands as still as a statue with his gaze trained on mine. His eyes shimmer under the fluorescent lights above. Moments like this are the ones where I find myself cursing the universe for how damn good this man looks. I don't know if I would call him grumpy, but he definitely has some tendencies. "Fine."

I cock my head to the side as confusion washes over me. For a second, I'm not sure if I heard him correctly, or if I'm hallucinating. "What?"

"I said fine," he huffs, uncrossing his arms. They hang down at his sides and he carefully tucks them in the front pockets of his joggers. His face softens a bit as he stares down at me. The coldness around him defrosts a fraction. "I'll skate with you."

I straighten my head and lift my chin. "As my partner?"

"As in, we do a trial skate together and see if it will work or not."

It will. I know it will, and so does he. He doesn't want to admit it, so of course he has to make it more difficult.

"So, you don't want to commit to anything without knowing it will be a good fit," I say, looking for clarification from him.

The corners of his mouth twitch. "I'm not a huge fan of commitments."

I'm not going to bring up the fact that he was committed to skating with Delaney for years. That was a different type of commitment. This is an unusual situation we've both found ourselves in. We have the chemistry, I just need to remind him of that electricity that crackles between us.

"You have yourself a deal."

I hold my hand out for him. His gaze drops down to my hand and he looks at it for a moment before dragging his gaze slowly up my torso. Heat creeps up my neck and spreads across my cheeks as his eyes finally find mine again. I absolutely hate the effect he has on me. He blinks twice, his breathing increasing a bit, before his warm palm slides against mine. It's a stark contrast to the cold that radiates from him.

His hand wraps around mine and he holds it firmly. "Just one skate and then we will decide what happens."

"Just one taste," he whispers, his lips brushing against my skin...

I swallow roughly. "Just one skate," I echo as I push the memory of him on his knees for me from my mind.

Leo Wells shakes my hand.

"Deal."

CHAPTER THREE
LEO

Austin is waiting for me at the bar when I arrive and I take a seat beside him. Austin and I have been best friends since we were in elementary school. His family moved to Idyll Cove after his mother left his father when he was seven. He was the new kid in town and we met on the playground one afternoon. A group of kids had him cornered along the side of an old brick building. I couldn't see what was happening at first and then I saw Austin throwing punches at each kid that towered over him. They never messed with him again after that day.

His white t-shirt was torn on the shoulder and I gave him my black lightweight jacket to block out the cool air that day. I had brought a basketball to the playground and asked him if he wanted to shoot hoops with me. The rest was history after that.

Fast-forward two decades and we're still best friends,

even if life didn't always make it the easiest for us to see each other, especially since Austin moved to New York. He still has his place here in Idyll Cove, but he's been spending more time in the city than he has been here lately.

Austin glances over at me, his almost black hair shifting on top of his head. He unbuttons the sleeves of his white dress shirt and begins to roll them up his forearms, revealing the ink that's etched on his skin. His left arm is covered in a mural of ocean-themed tattoos, all colored in black and white. "So, you and Ari, huh?"

"She told you, didn't she?" I pause for a second, pushing the bar menu out of my way as I fold my arms on the cool wooden bar top. Of course she told him. He is her brother, after all. "I can't believe I'm really stuck with her."

Austin lifts his glass of bourbon and takes a slow sip as he narrows his eyes on me. His throat bobs as he swallows the mouthful of liquid. "I feel like I should warn you to tread lightly with how you talk about my sister." He rolls his dark gray eyes and shakes his head. "You know you couldn't find a better partner than her. She is literally one of the best skaters in the entire world. Can it really be that terrible?"

I rake a hand through my hair as the bartender approaches. I pause our conversation and order whatever it is that Austin is drinking. Knowing him, the drink probably costs more than my mortgage payment. "You're right."

"I know I am."

The bartender brings me my drink and I take a sip of it,

feeling the burn of the bourbon as it slides down my throat. Aria is my best shot at staying at the top. As much as I hate admitting it, it's the truth. I've been an asshole to her, acting like we don't have any chemistry when we both know we do. That damn woman has been under my skin for years. She's an itch I can't scratch. A delicacy I won't allow myself the pleasure of indulging in.

"Are you really still pissed off at her because she dated Griffin Carr in high school?"

My posture stiffens momentarily and I shrug. "I never cared about that," I lie through my teeth as Austin toys with the gold AP watch on his wrist. "She has the ability to beat me. I don't like that."

"Which is exactly why you should want her as your partner, you damn idiot."

An exasperated sigh escapes me and my shoulders momentarily sag. "I know. I'm supposed to meet her tomorrow morning to see how we skate together."

He levels his gaze on mine and his gray eyes look like molten steel. "Don't fuck it up." He pauses for a moment, his tone sharpening like the blade of a knife. "Don't make me have to fuck *you* up. You being my best friend does not give you a free pass. Ari is my sister first."

"I'm literally shaking in my boots right now." I stare back at him before my face finally cracks. Laughter spills from my lips and I shake my head at him, feeling the lightness in my chest. The tension dissipates and a slow smile creeps onto Austin's lips. "You do know I have a tendency to fuck things up, right?"

"Well, duh." He chuckles as he rests his arms on the

bar. "I'm just saying... fuck up your own career and not my sister's."

"I mean, I'll try my hardest," I tell him with sarcasm in my voice and laughter still lingering in the air.

"That's all I can ask for." Austin lifts his glass for me to tap mine against. "Cheers. To trying not to fuck things up."

And working with the one person you've been trying to avoid.

"Cheers," I say as I clink my glass against his, and we both drain our glasses. "Another one?"

Austin smiles, flashing his bright white teeth. "Abso-fucking-lutely."

***

My head is pounding.

I didn't plan on drinking as much as I did with Austin last night. The two of us sat at the bar until it was closing time. And then we both had to get an Uber because neither of us were in any condition to drive. I barely remember stumbling into my house a few hours ago. The only thing I remember is my cats being slightly pissed off that I shut them out of my bedroom.

When my alarm went off this morning, I instantly regretted telling Aria I could meet her at nine o'clock. There was a part of me that wanted to cancel, and another part of me that felt extremely guilty about doing that. I wasn't sure why I cared if it bothered her or not, but I did.

As I open the door to the rink and step inside, the cold air sweeps over my body, sending a shiver down my spine. I welcome the sensation, closing my eyes for a breath as I breathe deeply. The smell is familiar and comforting, although it has a hint of chemicals lingering through it. It's really indescribable, more like one of those 'if you've smelled it before, you get it' kind of smells.

Aria is already here and I catch sight of her as I round the corner of the arena. She bends over, her black leggings stretching around her taut muscles as she gathers her long midnight-colored hair in her hands. My feet stop moving and I'm momentarily cemented to the floor as I let my eyes roam over her body. She's literal perfection. She secures a hair tie around her thick hair and swings it back as she stands back upright.

I can't get caught looking at her.

Quickly, I divert my gaze down to the black rubber flooring as I turn and drop down onto one of the benches along the boards. As I pull on the zipper of my bag, I see Aria moving from the corner of my eye. It takes everything in me to ignore her presence as I take out my skates and kick my sneakers off my feet.

"Hey," Aria says quietly as she steps over to me. Her voice is soft and warm. I hate how much I love the sound of it. "I wasn't sure if you were going to show up."

I lift my gaze to hers, finding her steel-colored eyes trained on mine. "I wasn't sure I was going to either."

It's not a lie. It still feels weird, the thought of skating with her. We've spent years in silent competition with one another. Years of avoiding each other after she started dating my rival in high school. Years of this fucking tension between us that you could practically reach out and pluck from the air. Something about her has always been like a thorn in my side.

Probably the fact that I've never been able to get her out of my head.

"Well, I appreciate the honesty." She smiles and nods. I direct my attention back to my feet and finish tying my skates as she watches me. "Did you have a preference for music?"

Shaking my head, I stand up. Aria's already well over a foot shorter than me, but standing on skates, she appears that much shorter. "Just put on whatever you like."

She tilts her head to the side ever so slightly that if I weren't studying her, I would have missed the moment. I see the unreadable look pass through her expression before it disappears. She gives nothing away, holding her cards close to her chest. Add that to the list of things about Aria Reed that drive me fucking insane.

"I'll meet you on the ice," she tells me with a bright smile before she walks past me. I catch a whiff of her perfume again and I can't help myself as I inhale deeply. That smell has been etched in my memory since the night I had her against the wall in the foyer of her house. I want to go back to that night. I should have fucked her then so I could have gotten her out of my system.

I'm not sure how avoiding her is going to work anymore since we're stuck together indefinitely.

I get on the ice while Aria goes to the sound system and connects her phone to the speakers. A classical song starts playing, one I don't recognize. My blades slide across the surface and I use the muscles in my thighs to generate power as I bend my knees. I move swiftly around the rink, warming up my legs while tuning out the world around me. The music is background noise and my mind is finally in a state of nothingness. I breeze past Aria, who is slowly moving around, going through her own warm-up routine.

We skate separately for the duration of the song, both of us ending up at opposite sides of the rink from one another. The song shifts into another, the sound of the cello and piano melting together through the speakers. Aria's eyes meet mine from across the ice. I swallow hard as her gaze holds mine and she begins to skate toward me. My breath hitches and I start to move, following her lead.

We meet in the face-off circle in the center of the ice. Our toes just barely touch each other as we lock our gazes, listening to the tempo of the music beginning to pick up. Aria moves first, positioning herself so her hips are facing me as she begins to skate around me. Pushing off with the inside edge of my skate, I move in synchrony with her, both of us circling around each other. The way we move together, there's a subtle push and then a magnetic pull, drawing us back to one another.

Aria moves in front of me as she does a mohawk so her back is facing me. She comes toward me with her arms stretched out to the sides. I hook my hands under her arms and lift her into the air in one swift movement. Her legs stay straight and I skate backward for a few strides before slowly spinning her in a circle. I set her down on the ice, sliding my hands out to hers, and we begin to skate together, moving across the rink.

The pounding sensation is gone from my head. My muscles are warm and pliable. My heart beats hard and strong in my chest, my breathing picking up. Nothing else matters in this moment except the perfect harmony that is being created between Aria and I.

I hate it so much.

I hate that I fucking love this.

Releasing her, we break apart, skating separately before we come together again. This isn't a planned routine or anything we've done before. We're simply moving together, making it up as we go. We're doing whatever feels right in the moment.

I spin to face Aria, my hands instinctively grabbing hers. I start to skate backward, pulling her with me as she skates forward. "Do you trust me?" I ask her, my eyes searching hers as we round the corner of the rink.

Aria's pink lips part and her gaze is trained on mine. "At this moment? Yes."

"Good answer," I say, pulling her along. It's a risky move, especially since we've never done it together before, but the adrenaline rushing through my body has me ready to do it now. If we're going to be a pair, this is something we will have to do together. "I'm going to spin you around and throw you into a jump."

She nods as she folds her lips in between her teeth and then releases them. "I'll do a triple toe loop."

"Perfect. Are you ready?"

As we come back around the opposite side of the rink,

Aria's gloved hands leave mine and she spins around to face the other direction. She glances over her shoulder, extending her hand back to me as we both begin to skate backward. I pull her along and she does a few crossovers as we skate past the benches. When we pass through the neutral zone, I reach for her hips and she keeps her feet crossed over one another.

Bending my knees, I press my weight into my feet and grip her hips harder as I begin to lift her into the air. It all happens so quickly and she doesn't miss a beat. I spring up, spinning to face the other direction. Her body leaves my hands as I throw her upward. I watch her spin and I'm completely captivated at how effortless she looks spinning through the air. I skate forward as she lands the jump perfectly, coming down on one skate with her other foot out behind her.

Her eyes quickly meet mine. Her chest heaves with a rushed breath, cheeks tinted pink. My mouth is instantly dry and the depth of my own breathing matches hers. My heart pounds erratically in my chest and I meet her again on the ice. My hands instinctively drop down to her hips and I pull her closer to me.

"Leo," she murmurs, her voice like velvet as we slow to a stop. Our skates shave the ice, creating a dusting of snow. Aria tips her head back to look up at me as she holds on to my biceps. Her chest rises and falls with every breath that escapes her. My gaze drops down to her lips.

I shouldn't do it.

Do not do it.

My face begins to dip down to hers. There isn't a single

coherent thought inside my head. I'm too caught up in the moment, lost in the euphoria after skating with her like that. We connect on a level I've never felt with anyone else before, not even with Delaney. I'd be a fucking idiot if I turned down being her partner.

Clearly I am a fucking idiot because I'm about to fuck it all up in one second.

My lips are mere millimeters from hers. Her warm breath fans across my face, smelling faintly of her strawberry lip gloss. Her eyelids flutter shut, her long black lashes resting against her skin. I let my own eyes shut. Just as I'm about to kiss her, someone starts to clap. It's like a slap in the face and reality comes crashing down around us.

Aria quickly pulls away from me, her hands abandoning my biceps as she inhales sharply. I instantly feel her absence and also want to kick myself for being such an idiot. I told myself not to do it and what did I do? I started to do it anyway. Her eyes are wide, her face flushed, and she blinks three times. The music shifts into a different song and things just feel off-balance now.

"Um, I'm sorry," she says in a rush as she glances around me. My back is to the door and I'm shielding her with my height. My jaw clenches and I slowly turn around to see who the hell is clapping for us.

It's Coach Kincaid.

A part of me is relieved, but I also want to put my fist through his face. He came at the perfect time, yet I also wanted to be catapulted back into the moment he ruined.

Luca pushes open the door that leads onto the ice and

he stands there as Aria and I begin to skate toward him. "I only caught the tail end of that performance, but holy shit. The two of you are meant to skate together."

Aria smiles at Luca and nods. "It felt really good," she tells him before turning to look at me. "How about you, Leo?"

It was unlike anything I'd ever experienced before...

Well, except maybe that one time many years ago, but we're more skilled skaters now. More experienced in life. More experienced with each other.

"It was good."

Luca moves out of the way as Aria steps through the door, and I follow after her. We fall into step together as we head over to the bench where our things are.

Aria stops beside me, a shy smile sliding onto her lips as she looks up at me through her lashes. "So, what do you say, Leo?" She pauses for a moment, not looking at Luca as she keeps her eyes glued to mine. "Do you want to be my partner?"

Luca is still standing with us and he's waiting for an answer just like Aria is. She's acting like I didn't almost kiss her. She certainly wasn't making any move to stop me when I did. It was a moment of weakness and I'll gladly pretend it didn't happen.

I can't believe I'm actually going to agree to this. Austin told me not to fuck it up and saying no would most likely fuck up my entire career. I don't have any options other than Aria Reed. If I want to win, I need her, and after skating with her, I know we can do this together. It doesn't mean I have to like her and I certainly won't develop any type of attachment to her.

It's strictly business and nothing more.

"Yes."

Aria's smile doesn't reach her eyes and her expression is unreadable as she nods.

She doesn't want this either.

CHAPTER FOUR
ARIA

Grabbing my latte, I turn around inside the coffee shop looking for my best friend Brynn just as my phone starts ringing in my purse. I pull it out and see my brother's name on the screen at the same time I spot Brynn. She's across the room, sitting at one of the tables along the wall made of windows. I catch her gaze and hold my hand up to show her my phone before I answer the call.

"Hey," I say as I step out of the way of a group who steps up to the counter. My brother and I talk regularly, so his call isn't completely unexpected.

"What are you doing?" Austin asks me in greeting.

"Getting coffee with Brynn. What's up?"

"I went out with Leo last night," he tells me. I can't tell if he's in a bad mood or what, but his tone is a bit clipped. "He's not happy about skating with you."

"Yeah." I laugh softly, shaking my head. "I already told you that."

"If he's an asshole in any way, I need you to tell me."

I roll my eyes as I hold my phone against my ear. "I'm a big girl, Austin. I don't need you to fight my battles for me."

"Well, you're still my sister. I don't care if we're in a nursing home and someone is an asshole to you then. I'll still defend you."

My brother has always been there for me. When we were young, our mother left our father and it made the two of us form a close bond. We moved to a brand-new town and didn't know anyone. Austin is only a year older than me, but he doesn't treat me like I am any different. He always treats me like his equal and always looks out for me.

"Did you really call me to tell me to snitch on your best friend if he's mean to me?" I can't help but laugh. "Please, Austin. You need to get a hobby or find something better to do."

"Leo can be a dick sometimes."

"And so can you. Like right now, interrupting my coffee date with Brynn." I pull my phone away and glance at the time before holding it up to my ear again. "So, I'm going to go now."

"How is she?" Austin asks with a hint of amusement in his voice. "I haven't seen her in quite some time. Does her ass still look as good—"

"I'm hanging up now."

Austin laughs and I pull the phone away from my ear as I abruptly end the call. He's absolutely ridiculous, but I love him all the same.

Brynn is staring out the window, like she's lost in thought when I walk over to the table. On the other side of the glass, you can see people walking down the street. Idyll Cove isn't a very busy place. It's more of a sleepy little town where people move at their own pace.

It's comfortable. It's home.

Brynn and I met five years ago on the night we both turned twenty-one. I was living in Charleston at the time and we were both out with our separate group of friends. Brynn and I have the same birthday and we ran into each other outside of a bar when we both got separated from our friends. We ended up stumbling down the street, barhopping through a row of dive bars. Things got a little fuzzy by the end of the night. We ended up back at Brynn's apartment where she ended up getting sick. Brynn fell asleep on the bathroom floor, hugging the toilet, and I woke up in the bathtub.

It was quite the night, but it was what started our friendship. Brynn and I instantly hit it off that night and we've been close friends ever since.

"Okay, I need the details immediately," Brynn says as I sit down across from her. She props her elbows on the table and rests her chin on her balled-up fists. Her brunette hair hangs in curls past her shoulders and her bright blue eyes meet mine with an expectant look on her face.

I take a sip of my latte and set it down on the table. "There's not much to tell. We skated together this morning and agreed to be partners."

"But how was it?"

Brynn is my best friend, so naturally she knows everything there is to know about Leo Wells.

I shrug with indifference and adjust myself in my seat. My feet are planted on the floor and I shift and cross one leg over the other instead. If she wasn't my best friend, I would be embarrassed at how much I've talked to her about Leo. She knows that I'm not particularly fond of him, yet I still can't seem to keep my thoughts about him to myself. Thankfully, she's the only one I've confided in about him.

"It was good."

Brynn purses her lips and lifts her head as she folds her arms and rests them on the table. She doesn't look convinced. She looks like she doesn't believe a single word I said. "You're a terrible liar, Ari."

A sigh escapes me and I circle both of my hands around the warm cup. "It was like we had been skating together for years. I don't even know how to explain it. We were completely in sync." I pause for a moment, contemplating whether or not I should tell her the whole truth. "He almost kissed me after we finished."

Her eyes widen and her lips part slowly until her mouth forms an O and she covers it with her hand. She drops her hand and plants them both on the table. "No fucking way. What do you mean *almost*? What happened that he didn't kiss you?"

"One of the coaches came in while we were in the middle of skating and neither of us realized it. Leo's lips were literally about to touch mine when Coach Kincaid started clapping." I let out a deep exhale and shake my head as I play over the whole thing that happened a few hours ago. "I don't think he saw anything other than the two of us standing close. You know how some of the performances end, so I think it looked normal."

"Thank God," she lets out a breath of relief before her soft laughter floats through the air. Freckles cover the bridge of her nose and are peppered over the tops of her high cheekbones. "I told you, girl. He might act like he doesn't have a thing for you, but he totally does."

I shake my head in disagreement. With the exception of the one night we shared together, there's no way he feels anything for me other than dislike. "I promise you he doesn't. We both got caught up in the moment, which is easy to do when you have adrenaline and emotion mixing together like that. I didn't even attempt to stop him."

Brynn laughs again and sits back in her seat as she picks up her drink and takes a sip. "You didn't stop him because you wanted him to kiss you."

I raise my eyebrows at her and I feel the heat prickling my skin as it threatens to travel across my cheeks. "Maybe," I admit, dropping my voice to a quieter tone. "It doesn't change the fact that he ignored me the past few months after we hooked up."

"Oh, totally," she agrees, nodding as she crosses her arms over her chest while holding her cup in one hand. "He's a complete douchebag for ghosting you. Not cool and unforgivable, unless he does some apologizing and makes it up to you. Honestly, it's probably a good thing he didn't kiss you."

"You're right," I tell her as I have an enlightened

moment, like a whole damn epiphany. "Who knows where it would have gone, and then that's just showing him he can do whatever he wants. Like I'm just here for whenever he wants something from me."

Brynn leans forward, setting down her coffee as she nods again eagerly. "We don't reward ghosting behavior with sexual favors. I swear to God, Ari, you better not give in to this man." She gives me a knowing look. "If you guys are going to skate together, you're going to have a lot of moments like this one. You cannot hook up with him or sleep with him until he makes it up to you. You're not just here for him to fuck around with when it pleases him. We only accept queen treatment here. He can go fuck himself with that fuck boy shit."

I can't help but laugh after she finishes her entire pep talk. I'll give it to her, she made some really good points. I don't know if I consider Leo a fuck boy, but I get what she's saying. And she's right. I can't let him think that any of this is okay. "The thing is, I don't even like him, Brynn. Like, he annoys me and pisses me off more than anyone else."

She tries to fight a smile and rolls her eyes. "Right. Whatever you say, girl. If you want to be delusional today, I can do that too."

Tilting my head to the side, I purse my lips and raise an eyebrow. Brynn is definitely a ride-or-die type of friend, but I'm not being delusional. "Seriously, it's so stupid. I'm not being delusional. I'll admit that I'm attracted to him, but that doesn't change how I feel about him personally.

He has the good looks, he just doesn't have the right personality."

"Yes, girl, be shallow," she encourages, laughing softly. Brynn's entire face lights up as she smiles brightly. "You're not lying, though. He is hot."

"Aria Reed?"

Brynn lifts her gaze to look behind me at the deep voice that just spoke my name. I slowly turn around, following the direction of her eyes until I see the person standing behind me.

"Well, if it isn't Griffin Carr."

I rise to my feet as a smile creeps across my lips. Griffin closes the distance between us and sweeps me into his arms as he half swings me around. Griffin and I dated while we were in high school, but that was almost ten years ago now. We broke up the summer before my senior year. Griffin had graduated and was going to university in England and we agreed we were better off as friends. We kept in touch at first after he moved, but then our contact kind of dissipated.

He smells like pine trees and he hugs me tightly before we break apart. Griffin's dirty blond hair is combed to the side and he's wearing a black crewneck sweatshirt with a pair of gray washed pants and loafers. He always had a good taste in fashion and was always well put together. I see not much has changed in the past ten years since we last saw each other.

"How the hell are you?"

Griffin smiles, revealing his pearly white teeth. "I am great. How about you?"

"I'm really good," I tell him before sweeping my arm to Brynn. "This is my friend, Brynn. Brynn, this is Griffin. I think I told you about her before?"

"You guys are birthday twins, right?"

Brynn nods and holds her hand out to Griffin. "Nice to meet you. I've heard a few things about you."

"Good things, I hope?" he says as I sit back down across from Brynn. She motions to the other seat at the table and Griffin pulls it out before sitting down with us.

"Of course," I assure him with a warm smile. There wasn't anything bad anyone could say about Griffin Carr. Everyone loved him—except for Leo. "What brings you back to Idyll Cove? Are you still skating?"

Griffin was one of the best figure skaters in our area back in high school. He and Leo were always swapping places of who was winning the gold medal. Leo was a poor sport, so Griffin naturally became his rival. I personally think he hated how likable Griffin was. He was at the top of his class and graduated with honors. Even though he was an exceptional figure skater, he never wanted to do it professionally.

"I came back to visit family. My grandmother had a little health scare, so I figured it was time to come back." He pauses for a moment, folding his hands on his lap. "I don't skate anymore, unfortunately. I didn't have the time to keep up with it, and you know it was always just a hobby for me."

"It looks like you've been doing really well for yourself."

Griffin smiles and raises his eyebrows at me. "So have

you, Ari. Look at you, living your literal dream right now. It's so amazing, I'm so proud of you."

He's nothing short of genuine and it warms my heart. "Thank you, Griffin. I wasn't sure it would happen, but here we are."

Brynn is sitting in silence, watching the entire interaction happening between us. She knows about Griffin, although there wasn't a whole lot to say. Our relationship was your typical happy high school relationship. It wasn't anything deep or long-lasting. There was never any drama or fights. We shared a few sweet moments together and a few kisses, but it never went any further than that.

"So, Griffin," Brynn breaks into the conversation as there's an elongated pause. "How long will you be staying in Idyll Cove?"

He looks at her with a soft expression. "I'll be here for about a month and then I have to get back to England."

She nods with a look of understanding as I take a sip of my lukewarm latte. "I'm sure your girlfriend is probably waiting for you to come home."

I half choke on my drink and break into a coughing fit. Brynn raises an eyebrow at me, silently telling me to get my shit together. Griffin looks extremely amused and I'm not sure if it's from me almost inhaling my drink into my lungs or from Brynn and her forward statement.

"Actually, I don't have a girlfriend waiting for me at home," Griffin admits with a chuckle. He's not uncomfortable with any part of the conversation and I'm grateful for that. Brynn isn't exactly afraid to be forward with people and she tends to lack a filter.

Brynn tilts her head to the side. "Boyfriend?"

I fight the urge to kick her under the table as Griffin laughs a little louder and shakes his head.

"Nope. There's no one at home waiting for me, other than my cat who is currently staying with my neighbor."

"Interesting," Brynn says with a mischievous smile as she looks back at me. "Would you believe that Aria is also single?"

This time I do kick her under the table. She jumps in her seat as she winces and cuts her eyes to me. She mouths *What the hell?* and I glare at her. She's meddling and needs to knock it off. That ship with Griffin sailed many moons ago. I don't have any interest in dating anyone right now. I'm better off being single. Griffin has an entire life across the ocean. My life is here and I will not be doing long distance with anyone.

"That is very hard to believe," Griffin agrees with her before he turns his attention back to me. "Have you lost your charm, Aria?"

Now I look at him with my eyebrows pulled together, half glaring at him before I relax my facial features. "Never. I don't have the time to date anyone right now."

"Do you have time to maybe get dinner with an old friend sometime?"

A small smile pulls on my lips. "Are you asking me out, Griffin Carr?"

"Not on a date," he says with a wink.

"Well, in that case, I would love to have dinner with you."

Brynn laughs quietly to herself, but she doesn't say

anything as she pulls her phone out of her purse and pretends to be busy on it.

"Perfect." Griffin glances at his watch and his mouth turns downward into a frown. "Shit. I'm sorry, Ari. I hate to run, but I'm meeting my mother at Freckled Hen for a late lunch."

"You don't have to apologize," I assure him as I rise to my feet as well. Griffin is about half a foot taller than me, so I still have to tilt my head back a bit to be able to look him in the eye. "Brynn and I were getting ready to leave anyway."

Brynn lifts her head up to us after she hears me say her name. For a moment, she looks confused, like she has no idea what is going on. I silently try to send her a message from my own brain, but obviously that doesn't work. I motion with my eyes instead and kind of tilt my head toward the door.

"Oh, yeah, right," Brynn says quickly as she ducks her head to hide her grin and collects herself. She straightens up, grabs her coffee, and then pushes her chair in. "I forgot we were planning on going shopping."

We weren't. We didn't talk about going shopping. I'm relieved she picked up on my hints and is going along with it. Brynn is usually good with that. If I ever need to get out of a situation, she always has a way out. Brynn is a problem solver—she usually has a solution for everything.

"What's your number?" Griffin asks me as the three of us walk to the door together. The sun ducks behind a cluster of puffy white clouds that hang above in the bright blue sky. Griffin stops on the sidewalk and turns to face me and Brynn. "I'll text you, that way you have my number and we can figure out what evening would work for dinner."

I tell him my number and he taps the digits on his phone screen. My own device vibrates in my purse and I pull it out to check the screen.

UNKNOWN
Hey, it's Griffin.

"Got it," I smile at him before I save his number with his contact information. I lock my screen and put my phone back into my purse. "It was good seeing you, Griffin. I'm glad you stopped to talk to us."

Griffin nods. "Until next time." He grins sheepishly and looks at Brynn. "It was nice meeting you."

Brynn and I both bid him farewell and we stay by the front of the coffee shop as we watch him disappear down the street. He stops beside a sleek white sports car and drops down into the driver's seat.

"Looks like we have some shopping to do," Brynn says in a chipper tone as she links her arm through mine. "You need something cute to wear for your date."

"It's not a date, Brynn," I remind her at the tail end of a sigh. We fall in step beside each other and walk around the corner of the building as we make our way closer to where we both parked. "I'm not interested in him like that."

"Oh, I know," she says with a sly grin as she turns to look at me as we reach my car. She's parked in the parking spot directly behind me. "That doesn't mean you can't make this fun. Think about it... you've been all flustered because of Leo. This is the perfect opportunity for a distraction."

I frown as I slip my arm from hers and fetch my keys out of my purse. "I feel kind of bad. Almost like I'm using him."

"Girl, you're not using him if he's on the same page." She pauses for a beat, grabs her own keys, and unlocks her car door. "You were upfront with him. You told him you don't have time to date anyone. Go to dinner with him, have fun, and just see where it goes. He's leaving in a month, so I don't think he's looking for anything long term either."

I stare at her for a moment as I realize what she's suggesting without coming out and saying it. "I don't know, Brynn…"

She puts her hand up. "Stop it right there. You're already overthinking it." She locks her car again and walks over to my passenger's side door and pulls it open. "We're going shopping. You're going to make plans with him and you're going to have a great time. You don't have to commit to anything other than dinner."

"Okay, no more overthinking," I agree as I offer her a smile and walk up to the driver's side. I get into the car and Brynn follows suit, both of us meeting inside. "I'm just going to go and have fun."

"That sounds like the perfect plan."

I turn the car on and put it in drive before pulling away from the curb. Brynn rattles off a few stores in the mall that she thinks we should stop at, but I'm only half paying attention to what she's saying. I'm driving on autopilot, heading in the direction of the mall, except I'm not thinking about shopping. I'm not thinking about dinner with Griffin.

I'm thinking about Leo.

And I fucking hate it.

CHAPTER FIVE
LEO

Aria looks at me with a perplexed expression. "Is this the routine you and Delaney did together?"

I shake my head at her, attempting to conceal the contentment that settles over me. There's a bite in her tone. If I didn't know she didn't like me, I'd question whether or not that was jealousy I hear in her voice. "Why would I do the same routine over again?"

She narrows her gray eyes. "I meant if this was the one you two were working on this year."

"Oh." I knew exactly what she meant. That didn't mean I wasn't going to poke harder. If we are going to be forced to work together, I'm not going to make it easy on her. "No. This was one I asked her if she wanted to do, but the throw triple Axel made her a little nervous."

"I want to do it."

I bite back the smile that threatens to form on my lips. It's kind of fucked up, but I like seeing her like this. The determination is set on her facial features as she stares me down. She knows it was a routine Delaney and I were working on, so she wants to perfect it. She wants to rise to the challenge and be better. She's acting like she has something to prove and I admire that.

Aria knows she's one of the best figure skaters in the world, yet she doesn't let herself get comfortable with that position. It's something you have to constantly work on if you want to stay at the top. It's very easy to fall into the habit of thinking you will always remain at the top. That's not how things work in this sport. One competition could make or break your career. Aria Reed wasn't going to let anything get in the way of her and a gold medal.

"Can I make a small suggestion?"

Deciding not to be difficult, I shrug and nod. "Sure, let's hear it."

Aria begins to skate in slow motion, working through the things I showed her. I watch her and slowly move behind her. "When we get to this part in the routine, we skate together instead of in unison separately." She spins around to face me. "Follow my lead."

I'm a bit reluctant, but I do as she asks and I jump into the skating routine with her. We skate together, our hands clasped as we come around the turn. The way Delaney and I had practiced was without any jumps and we skated together during this part. I pull Aria close to me, before pushing her away. My hands slip from hers until just our fingertips are linked together. She slides her hand into mine and I use my body weight to generate momentum as I spin, swinging her around me.

Aria gets low to the ice, spinning around me. The

tension is palpable in the air and Aria's long hair whips around her head. I pull her up and we both straighten out, skating together again with our arms outstretched. "I think we should add in a twist lift here," she tells me.

Excitement licks at my veins. I have no intention of stopping her from exploring her ideas for our routine. It was Delaney's and mine, but it isn't anymore. Now it belongs to Aria and me and she's intent on making it her own. The adrenaline courses through me, flooding my veins. My spine straightens and I nod as she looks back at me once more. We begin to skate around one end of the rink. We're moving in perfect unison. I drop my hands from hers and grab her hips.

"Are you ready?" I ask her as we set up the movement for the lift.

Aria nods. "Do it."

We move faster, still skating backward as I generate speed and lift her into the air. Aria crosses her ankles, drawing her arms into her body as she twists in the air. Her body is tight and firm, rolling three times before gravity begins to pull her back down to earth. I effortlessly catch her and drop her back down onto her skates. We don't miss a beat as we work through the rest of the routine, ending up in the center of the ice, both of our chests heaving as she wraps her arms around the back of my neck and we melt into each other.

The faint smell of her perfume invades my senses as I breathe her in. My chest rises and falls with every shallow breath. My lungs scream for oxygen but my body screams for something entirely different. Having her this close is literal torture. She's the one person I shouldn't want, yet my cock is constantly betraying me. That's all it is—lust. There's nothing more and there never will be. Aria is undoubtedly beautiful. I'm not blind, but I also know I can't let myself travel down that road with her again.

The music comes to an end and I abruptly let her go. Aria's eyes meet mine as she straightens herself, but the disappointment in her expression quickly vanishes. She gives me a small smile. "So, what did you think? Can we add that modification to the routine?"

My jaw clenches and my nostrils flare. It's perfect. It's exactly what the routine needs, which is why it can't happen. If I give in to her, it's only going to chip away at my resolve. How long until I'm giving her everything?

"I think it's better the way I showed you."

Anger flares in her irises as I turn, no longer facing her. "You can't be serious."

I skate away, choosing to not engage. It was a dick move and I instantly regret it, but I can't give in now. Doing our routine with the twist lift made it much better. I can't admit that to her, because if I do, I would essentially be saying she is a better skater than me and my pride will never let me do that. She might help me stay on top, but I won't let her pass me.

"Leo, wait," she calls out as she skates after me. She's quick and I'm not moving that fast, so it doesn't take much effort for her to catch up to me. Her soft, delicate hand reaches for my wrist and she pulls me back. "Stop being a fucking asshole."

I slowly turn around to face her, my head slightly tilting to the side. "Excuse me?"

"You heard me," she snaps at me. Her grip tightens on my wrist and I don't bother removing her hand. I like how it feels there. "You know the routine is better with the twist lift. Do you want to say you came up with the idea? Is that what this is about?"

"I'm sorry?"

She rolls her eyes. "It's no secret you don't like me. I'm not exactly fond of you either, so the feeling's mutual." She pauses, shaking her head as she purses her lips. Disappointment washes over her expression as she lets go of my wrist. "I thought maybe you could put this petty bullshit aside so we could work together, but I was wrong. I don't think this is going to work."

I shouldn't be surprised, but her words feel like a slap to the face. She brushes past me as she exits the ice rink and leaves me out there alone. I watch her as she disappears into the locker room without another look in my direction. As I finally force myself off the ice, she's coming back out of the room with her bag slung over her shoulder.

"Aria," I start, my voice hoarse and low. I can't let her walk away, not when I need her. Without her, I'm back to where I was. Without a partner. I'm fucked without her.

She looks at me over her shoulder with a warning written in her expression. "Don't, Leo."

I let it go and allow her to walk out of the rink without another word.

I fucked up.

***

My footsteps are heavy as I follow the paved path around the park. It snakes through trees and shrubs, circling the pond in the middle with a bubbling fountain. The sun has since set and the moon hangs in the night sky. It's full tonight, so it illuminates the walkway and casts its light across the surface of the pond. The park's now vacant, but I'm still here after it technically closed. I can't eradicate the guilt that continues to flood me in waves. As soon as I think I've forgiven myself, I see the image of her face flash through my mind again.

The disappointment hits me like a knife in my chest. Aria was right. Goddamn, she was right about so many things. We skate so well together and what she added to the routine made it perfect. It was exactly what it was missing. I was being childish and letting our past rivalry get in the way of our future. I didn't want to skate against Aria. I wanted to skate with her. I was just too stubborn and too fucking hardheaded to see it at first.

And now she's gone.

I have to get her back.

Pulling my phone out of my pocket, I open my messages and tap on Coach Kincaid's name. I type a message to him and I head out of the park. I step onto the sidewalk and follow the path into the small town of Idyll Cove. It's a sleepy town where everyone moves on island time. Given that it's a Thursday evening, the street is relatively empty. Most of the shops are closed and the only thing open are two restaurants and a bar.

As I walk past Davino's, I glance to the right and look

through the window. The glass is tinted, but I can see her as clear as day. She's sitting alone at a table as she lifts a glass of wine to her lips. I watch as she tilts her head back, the liquid sliding down her throat. Her long black hair is pulled back from her face and hangs down her back in loose curls. I stand outside the window, watching her as she directs her gaze in the opposite direction.

A smile pulls on her lips and I glance to where she's looking. She isn't there alone. Griffin steps into the main room of the restaurant and takes a seat across from her at the table. Griffin fucking Carr. The asshole she ended up dating in high school. The asshole who took home the gold medal from regionals after I fell during a jump and fucked up my score.

Anger spreads through my body like wildfire. My feet are cemented in place, my entire body paralyzed with irritation as I watch the two of them. Griffin settles in the seat across from her with his gaze trained on hers as they fall into what appears to be a comfortable conversation. I watch them for another minute before I'm able to regain control over my legs again. Griffin is not getting the girl this time.

"Fuck this."

Abandoning my spot by the window, my movements are purposeful as I stride over to the door of the restaurant. I pull it open gently and I'm careful to not draw any attention to myself as I enter. My footsteps are light, yet there's a heaviness in my limbs. Only two other tables are occupied in the dimly lit space. Soft classical music plays in the background. I step around the other tables with my sights set directly on Aria fucking Reed. She doesn't notice me at first as she laughs at something Griffin says to her.

As I get closer to the two of them, she lifts her gaze from his, her eyes widening as she sees me. My strides are long and I cover a lot of space in no time until I stop directly behind Griffin. Aria's lips part slightly and I watch the pink tint wash over her cheeks. She's surprised to see me, but she doesn't look like she's not pleased with me.

Good.

"Leo?"

Griffin slowly turns around, his lips lifting into a smile as his eyes settle on me. "Well, if it isn't the infamous Leo Wells."

I resist the urge to drive my fist into his face. No one would ever let me live something like that down considering Griffin is practically God's gift to everyone. He was always known for being a kind, gentle person. I knew there was more to Griffin Carr than what he showed the rest of the world, but I was never one to throw someone under the bus… unless he gave me a reason to.

I force the fakest, most plastic-looking smile onto my face. "Griffin."

"What brings you here?" Griffin asks me, the sweetness in his tone sickening. He tears his gaze from mine as he grabs his glass of wine and takes a sip. "I'm sorry we don't have another seat for you at the table."

I shrug with indifference as I grab an empty glass from the table behind me. Aria's eyebrows pull together as she watches me pick up the decanter of wine and pour some into my own glass. "That's okay. I'll just take yours instead."

"I'm sorry, what?"

"Leo," Aria scolds me at the same time Griffin asks his stupid question.

I turn my attention to her, instead of wasting any more of my time on her date. "Aria. We need to talk."

Her chin dips slightly, her eyes widening as a wave of worry passes through her irises. "Can this wait until later?"

"No," I tell her with a stern tone. One of us will be leaving this restaurant alone and it will not be me. I will not be leaving until I speak directly with Aria and I'm not going to do that with Griffin present. "It's a time-sensitive matter and it would be best if we discuss it now."

Her tongue slips out as she wets her lips and nods. She looks back at Griffin, a frown pulling her lips downward. "I'm terribly sorry, Griffin. Something has clearly come up that needs my attention. Can we reschedule this for another time?"

Griffin glances at me from the corner of his eye and I don't miss the look on his face that quickly disappears before Aria sees it. He isn't happy about this situation, but he doesn't let Aria know. Of course, Griffin has to be the most agreeable and accommodating person. "Of course. We can reschedule for whenever is good for you." He pushes his chair back and rises to his feet. "Please, you stay," he tells her and nods. "Just give me a call later tonight."

She won't be calling you, dickhead.

Aria reaches for Griffin's hand and gives it a gentle squeeze. "Thank you. I appreciate you being so understanding."

Griffin gives her his award-winning smile before bidding her farewell. He nods at me before exiting the restaurant. I grab his wine glass and set it on the empty table beside us before I sit down. Aria looks flustered as hell, her neck and cheeks a perfect shade of pink. Her eyes are wide with her jaw set as she stares at me for a moment.

"You're something else, you know."

I flash a grin at her, this time a genuine one laced with amusement. "I'm well aware. I have a tendency to get what I want."

"What is it that you want?" she questions me.

The server walks up to the table with two plates of food. She gives me a quizzical look before she turns her attention to Aria and sets a plate in front of her. Aria offers her a smile. "You can put the other plate in front of him. My other friend had to leave."

She doesn't respond to Aria and gives her a smile while setting Griffin's food in front of me. I don't want to be rude, since I've already fully covered that base. I have no intention of eating the food that another man ordered.

"I want you."

Aria's fork clatters onto her plate as it slips from her hand. She gasps and recovers as she picks it back up. Her eyes flash to mine. "What?"

"I can't do this without you, Aria," I tell her as I fold my arms on the table in front of me. "We will do whatever you want to do with the routine. Hell, we can choreograph a new one if you'd rather do that." I pause for a second, letting out a deep breath. "Please skate with me."

Her lips part and she clamps them shut before trying again. "You interrupted dinner for that?"

"It was an urgent matter," I explain as I shrug sheepishly. "I need to know that you'll do it. I don't want to skate with anyone else. I don't want to have to find another partner. We both know we have chemistry and the skills. It has to be you."

She studies me as she slides her fork between her teeth. I watch, mesmerized, as she pulls the food from the tines and begins to chew. Her jaw moves in a delicate motion and the silence stretches between us. The electricity bounces off the molecules floating in the air. Her throat bobs, a slender movement as she swallows her food. She still doesn't speak a single word as she lifts her glass to her lips. She kisses the rim, tipping her head back as she pours some of the liquid into her mouth.

Aria swallows the wine and lifts her napkin from her lap to blot the corners of her mouth. Red lipstick stains the white cloth as she lowers it back to her lap. The anticipation is killing me. Amusement dances in her irises.

"Well?"

A slow smile pulls on her lips. "This is unusual. Let me enjoy the moment a minute longer."

I tilt my head to the side in question, not following what she is implying.

"I like watching you squirm like this, Leo."

A chuckle rumbles in my chest and I shake my head at her. "I'm begging you to put me out of my misery."

"Okay," she says with a grin. Her eyes shimmer as the light from the candle on the table catches them. "I'll skate with you."

CHAPTER SIX
ARIA

Leo visibly relaxes in his seat and a slow smile creeps across his lips. The butterflies in my stomach flutter to life. Earning a smile from Leo Wells feels like a goddamn reward. He's pleasant enough with most people, but it isn't often that I see him genuinely smile. He's really good at faking it.

"Are you going to eat?" I ask him as I point to the food Griffin ordered that Leo moved to the other table.

Leo takes a sip of his wine and shakes his head at me. "I don't want that."

"Well, if you don't want it, I'll take it home in a box if there isn't any meat in it," I tell him as I motion for him to move it back to our table. Leo's movements are hesitant but he reaches for it and sets it down by my plate.

"Are you going to take it to Griffin?"

I look up at him as I move the plate to the side. "No. Although, I probably should. What you did was pretty rude."

It wasn't a lie. Leo was rude as hell for showing up like that. What he needed to talk to me about could have waited. He didn't have to come in and insert himself. I'm not sure what his motive really was or if he was even thinking about any of that. It all seemed very impulsive, yet there was an underlying tension between Griffin and him. I don't know what happened between them when we were younger, but it was clear that neither of them had moved past it.

"I would say I'm sorry, but I'm not." Leo shrugs with indifference as he sets his wineglass down on the table. "He's not a good guy, Ari."

My eyebrows draw together. "Says who?"

"Me." He pauses, his nostrils flaring as he lets out a deep breath. "Just trust me, please. You only see what he wants you to see."

I want to question him, but I don't want to pry. I want to know what evidence he has to support his claims about Griffin. He has never been anything but nice to me and from what I know, that's how he is to everyone. There's something that Leo knows that he isn't openly offering. This might be the most civil conversation I've ever had with him, so the last thing I want to do is chase him away now. I want him to be like this with me—easy and comfortable.

I'm not going to argue with him and I'm not going to press the issue. I'll let it go… for now.

Instead of commenting on what he said, I shift the conversation in another direction. "So, since you decided to crash my date tonight, what are you going to do to make it up to me?"

Leo cocks his head to the side as a smirk lifts one side of his mouth. "I already made it up to you. I agreed to skate with you."

Clicking my tongue, I shake my head at him. "Nope, that won't do. That was something we already planned on doing, so just because you finally decided to be on board doesn't mean that counts as a way to make it up to me."

"What would you propose I do then?"

The server comes back and I break the conversation with Leo to tell her that I need two boxes to take the rest of the food home with me. She sets the check down on the table before walking away. I extend my arm, reaching for the small black folder, but Leo beats me to it.

"All you drank was wine. Let me have it."

Leo narrows his eyes at me and leans to the side in his chair as he pulls his wallet from his back pocket. "Absolutely not, and don't you dare argue with me, Aria." He takes out a credit card and slides it into the folder while he continues to stare at me. He holds the check in his hand instead of setting it back down on the table.

A sigh escapes me and I slouch back into my chair as I cross my arms over my chest. "If that's your way of making it up to me, that doesn't count."

A chuckle rumbles in his chest and he rolls his eyes. "I didn't say it was. I asked you to tell me what I can do to make it up to you."

"I want to go dancing."

His lips part and he stares at me like I have two heads. "Just because I skate, doesn't mean I dance, Aria."

"Well, tonight you do," I tell him with a smile as the server comes back to the table. She takes the folder from Leo and hands me two boxes. I can feel Leo's eyes on me as I begin to shovel the food into the two containers. As I finish, I look back up at him just as the girl returns with his credit card. The smile is still on my lips as Leo slides his card back into his wallet and rises to his feet.

He pushes his wallet into his back pocket and he picks up his wineglass. I watch him as he tilts his head back and drains the liquid before setting the glass back on the table. He holds his hand out to me as I shrug my jacket on. "Let's go, tiny dancer."

I place my hand in his and he pulls me to my feet as I get up from my seat. He releases my hand and I half expect him to leave me to follow him, but instead he bends his elbow and holds it out to me. I look down at his arm and back at his eyes before I gently slide my own through his. My forearm presses against his and I can feel the warmth of his flesh through his long-sleeve shirt and my jacket. Leo grabs the food containers from the table and begins to walk, shortening his stride as I fall in step beside him.

He walks up to the door and holds it open for me, but he doesn't move his arm from mine as I step through the threshold. My car is parked in the parking lot that is situated along the right side of the building. Leo turns to the left and I walk with him. "My car is in the parking lot," I tell him as I stay beside him. "I can follow you wherever we're going."

Leo shakes his head. "We're not going far. Just down the street to The King's Inn."

Turning my head to the side, I look up at him, but he continues to walk. When I said I wanted to go dancing, I didn't plan on going to the local dive bar. Leo stares straight ahead, confidence dripping from him as he walks. He pays me no attention, so I don't bother questioning him. A sigh escapes me and I let him lead me down the street.

The bar isn't far away from Davino's. It's only about a two-minute walk and we find ourselves standing outside the door. It's noisy inside and I'm surprised with it being a Thursday evening. Leo pulls open the door and we step into the dark room. Lights flash from above and I feel like I've stepped into a club instead of the local bar. They tend to get a lot of locals here and I know some nights they try to make it a little more exciting than people just sitting around getting drunk.

On the weekends they tend to showcase different DJs who want to come to the small coastal town. When it's not off-season, we get a lot of tourists that come to Idyll Cove. This is a different vibe for tonight, but I'm not going to question it. It saves us from driving into the actual city tonight for a similar scene.

The music is loud and the bass pounds throughout the building as Leo unlinks his arm from mine. Instead, he drops his hand down to hold mine and he leads the way as he pulls me through the crowded room. He stops when he reaches the bar and I almost collide into his back. I let go of his hand and place it on his shoulder as I lift myself onto my toes to speak into his ear. Instinctively, Leo dips his shoulder, lowering himself so I can reach him better.

"What are all these people doing out tonight?"

Leo turns to face me, dropping his mouth down to my ear as he speaks. "There was some kind of a beer fest at The Garden tonight, so I imagine a lot of the people came here afterward." He pulls back and looks at me, shrugging. "We can leave if you want to."

I shake my head at him. "No, this is fine."

Leo turns back to the bar and I watch him as he leans across it to yell something to the bartender. Turning my back to him, I glance around the room, watching everyone dancing. A popular song sounds through the speaker that there is an actual dance to. I look and see that everyone is dancing in synchrony, following the rehearsed moves. Now it makes sense why there aren't many people sitting down.

There's a tap on my shoulder and I turn back to Leo. He sets the containers of food down and hands me a beer. I don't comment on the drink choice and I don't tell him I actually hate the taste of beer. Instead, I smile and take it. Leo takes a swig of his and his hand finds mine again. The song shifts to a new one and the floor clears off a bit. Leo leads me onto the dance floor, his hand leaving mine as he turns to face me. I'm a few feet away from him and I take the opportunity to drink him in.

Goddamn him for being so good-looking.

He begins to move his body to the beat as he throws

back another mouthful of his beer. My fingers circle around the neck of my bottle and I hold on to it as I begin to move. Closing my eyes, I let the music slide through my veins and just begin to mindlessly dance. My hips sway back and forth and I hold my arms up as I begin to turn around. All the thoughts fade away from my mind. Suddenly my problems seem fairly insignificant. I forget about Griffin and how he may have been feeling with the way Leo interrupted us.

And then I feel his hands gripping my waist.

He hauls me backward until my back is pressed flush against his chest. His hands drop down to my hips and his fingers splay across the front of them as he holds me tight to him. His body feels firm and warm behind me. I melt into his touch, feeling myself relax against him. Tilting my head back, I take a sip of my beer and make a face at the gross taste of it. Leo starts to move with me, both of our bodies moving in perfect harmony together.

The song shifts, the tempo slowing down as it shifts into a slow song. Leo's hands are on my hips turning me around to face him as the music continues to play. It's some old school R&B song that is definitely meant for slow dancing. I lift my arms and hook my wrists behind the back of his neck as his hands settle again on my hips. We begin to move back and forth together, swaying side to side as he begins to slowly rock us around in circles on the dance floor.

I haven't been paying attention to anyone else and I don't bother looking around as we continue to move. I don't care who else is on the dance floor. I don't care if anyone is watching us. The only thing that matters right now is this moment with Leo. And I know it is one I need to hold on to because I already know this will never happen again.

It's just like that time we skated together in high school. This is what Leo does. He shows a softer side of himself and lets his guard down just enough to give me a peek inside. It makes my insides warm and fuzzy and I find myself melting into him. I'm sure it won't be long before he's putting his guard back up again and shutting me out. It may not happen tonight, but that just means I need to savor this moment and his warmth.

When we meet on the ice again, he will undoubtedly be just as cold as the surface beneath our skates.

It's Leo's MO.

"What are you thinking about?" Leo asks me, his voice soft and almost hard to hear over the sound of the music echoing throughout the room.

I tilt my head back to look at him. I can't tell him the truth—I can't tell him I was thinking about how it's only going to be a matter of time before he's shutting me out again. "I was thinking about our trip to Germany that is coming up soon."

Leo nods. "We leave in two weeks," he reminds me as his expression becomes unreadable. "Did you book a room and everything yet?"

Shit. Shit. Shit.

"No," I admit as I purse my lips. "It was supposed to be handled for me and then we canceled the reservation after Preston decided to take a leave of absence." I pause, feeling my shoulders deflate as I let out a sigh. "I didn't even think to try and rebook it."

"If you need a place to stay, you can stay in my room," Leo offers, completely catching me off guard. Who is this man and what did he do with the Leo I've known for years?

"I appreciate that, but I don't want to impose," I tell him. I appreciate his generosity, but I'm sure he'd rather not have me in his room. "I'll figure something out before we have to go."

Leo stares at me for a moment and I can't quite make out the emotions in his eyes before they abruptly vanish. He shrugs with indifference again. "If anything changes, just let me know. I'm here for whatever you need, *partner*."

We both fall silent as the sound of the music playing envelops us. The scent of his cologne tickles my nose and I inhale the smell. He smells like teakwood and the ocean. I don't know how to explain it. I'm not sure he's managed to find a cologne that has that smell bottled up, but he smells like a spa on the ocean shore. I find myself enjoying it a lot more than I should.

I need to come to my damn senses.

This is Leo Wells. He's a broody asshole who only really cares about himself and winning. He has the temper of a teenager who doesn't know how to control their emotions yet. I can't be thinking of him like this. I can't be reveling in the way he feels and the way he smells. Every moment with him is fleeting. We agreed to skate together and nothing more. I need to separate the two inside my mind. This is all things can ever be between us.

He was being nice. He interrupted my date and this night of dancing was his way of making it up to me. I asked him to take me dancing and he was simply complying.

I couldn't help but feel slightly deflated at the realization. I let myself get lost in the moment. I let myself be fucking delusional.

This meant nothing to Leo and I couldn't let him know it affected me in any way.

As the song comes to an end, I release my wrists from around the back of his neck and take a step away from him. Instantly, I feel his absence and miss his warmth. I resist the urge to step back into his space. His eyebrows scrunch and he gives me a perplexed look as his hands hang by his sides, one still clutching the neck of his beer bottle.

"Thanks for the dance," I tell him with a smile as I curtsey. I lift the rim of the beer bottle to my lips and tip my head back as I drain the beer. I chug what's left from the one sip I took earlier. It tastes bitter and disgusting, but I manage to keep a straight face as I momentarily block out the taste. I straighten myself as the bottle is empty and hold it up for Leo to see. "I think I'm going to call it a night."

He cocks his head to the side, blinking like he's trying to figure out what the hell is going on. I spin on my heel and march back over to the bar as Leo follows behind me. He stops beside me and I set the empty bottle down on the bar top. Leo looks at me. "Are you okay?"

I nod. "I'm good." I slowly turn my head to look at him.

"Today has been a long day, so I'd better get home and get some sleep." I grab the containers of food and hold them up. "I need to get these in my fridge before the food goes bad."

Leo's silent for a beat before he finishes his own beer and leaves it beside mine. "I'll walk you to your car."

"That's okay, you don't have to do that." I can't help it but there's a part of me that wants to get as far away from him as I can.

"I know I don't but I want to."

Leo and I walk back through the bar until we're stepping out onto the sidewalk out front. He falls in step beside me, his legs moving slower than normal so he's not walking ahead of me. With our height difference, his stride is naturally longer than mine. The silence stretches between us and I'm afraid to speak a single word to him, as I don't know what the hell I'll say. I can't let Leo in—I can't let him in because I know he'll never stay.

It's a short walk back to the parking lot and I walk over to my car. "This is me," I tell him with a smile as I look back at him. "Thanks for tonight, even though you did interrupt my dinner with Griffin."

"I'll never apologize for that, Aria," he tells me, his voice hoarse. His eyes burn holes through mine. "I'll see you tomorrow morning."

"See you then," I tell him, my words coming out in a rush as I unlock my door and climb inside. Leo takes a few steps back as I turn on the engine. He stays where he is, watching me as I back my car out of the parking spot. My eyes meet his as I push down on the brakes and put my car in drive.

His expression is unreadable as he tucks his hands in the front pockets of his pants, his gaze never leaving mine. His lips part, almost like he wants to say something to me, but I can't hear him. I ease my foot off the brake pedal and push down on the gas pedal before pulling away. As I head out onto the empty street, I glance in my rearview mirror and see Leo as he begins to walk down the sidewalk in the opposite direction. There's an unsettled feeling inside of me as I drive away from him. I know I'll see him in the morning, but I can't quite dissect these emotions that are rippling through my body.

Leo Wells will always be the greatest mystery in my life.

I just hope one day I'll be able to figure him out.

CHAPTER SEVEN
LEO

Aria and I are both silent as we go through our routine again. It's the twelfth time we've gone through it and for some reason, we can't get it right. It's not a technical issue, but more of a unison issue. Our timing is off when we break apart. Something is just off between us right now, and I can't quite put my finger on what the issue is. The tension hanging in the air is so damn thick you couldn't even cut it with a knife. A chainsaw would be the most appropriate tool to cut through the thickness right now.

As we skate around the end of the rink again, Aria glances over her shoulder as I grab her hips. She gets into position and I lower my knees as I hurl her up into the air. She spins three times before she begins to drop down toward the ice. Aria lands the jump perfectly and instantly begins to skate without missing a beat. I lose an edge and stumble as I skate after her. It throws off the entire routine and I'm a few fractions of a second behind her as we both begin to spin in spirals.

Aria comes out of her spiral before me and I see her from the corner of my eye as I begin to slow down. She isn't moving and instead, she's standing there staring at me as I come out of my spin. My chest heaves as I suck in a mouthful of oxygen and stop skating. Disappointment is written across her face and she purses her lips slightly.

"What's wrong?" I ask her breathlessly. I already know the answer, but I want to hear what she has to say about it.

She lets out an exasperated sigh. "You tell me. Why are we off right now?"

I shrug because I genuinely don't have the answer to that question. We hadn't been skating together for long but this was the first time either of us had experienced this disconnect together. So far every time we had skated, it was nothing short of perfection. I don't know if there's some kind of pressure that is hidden beneath everything. We both know we have to perform at an elite level. "I don't know," I tell her honestly. "Maybe it's just an off day. Our timing isn't right."

"We can't have off days." There's nothing playful in her voice. Aria's spine is rigid and her jaw is set. It almost takes me by surprise with how she's acting. I know how she's feeling right now, but we're not in a competition. Mistakes will be made and that's okay. She's clearly under a lot of stress, but we both are.

I tilt my head to the side as I let my arms hang loosely at my sides. "Aria, it's okay. Everyone has days where they are off a little bit. We're still new in the process of skating together, so I think this is normal. We will get it right."

"We have to," she says with irritation in her tone. She closes her eyes and takes a deep breath before she opens them again. Her shoulders fall as she exhales and looks back at me with a softer expression. "I'm sorry. I'm stressed, I'm anxious. We have less than two weeks now to perfect this if we want to have a chance at winning. We just have to get this right by then and we cannot fuck it up at the competition."

"I promise you, the competition will be fine. Everything will work out and we will do great, okay?"

She shakes her head at me, like she's refusing to believe the words I'm speaking to her. "You don't get it, Leo. It has to be perfect. *We* have to be perfect."

There it is.

She's a perfectionist. I didn't realize the extent of it until now. I always used to notice how much time she spent on the ice practicing the same things over and over again. I thought it was just because she liked to win and she wanted to be the best at what she was doing. I didn't know it had to do with her having to have everything perfect.

"Things aren't always perfect, Aria. They don't always have to be."

Her eyes widen slightly and she stares at me like I have three heads. She swiftly shakes her own head as she uncomfortably shifts her weight on her feet. "It's better if they are."

"Let's take a break?" I suggest as I motion toward the door. This isn't good for either of us right now. A break would be better, mentally and physically. That way we can almost do a bit of a reset before we get back on the ice. "We have unlimited ice time to practice, so it isn't going to hurt us if we just take a little bit of time to collect ourselves."

"I don't need to take a break."

I stare at her, the muscle in my jaw twitching. She's incredibly stubborn and her perfectionism isn't helping in this moment. "Forget I asked you then. We are taking a break, Aria. It's not up for debate."

A worried look passes through her expression. "We need to use this time sensibly. If we're not on the ice practicing every second that we can, what are we even doing this for?"

"Aria." Her name feels good rolling off my tongue, but I don't like the stern way I say it. "Get off the ice. This isn't going to be productive for anyone."

She stares me down in a challenging way. I don't back down and I don't falter. Instead, I close the distance between us, half blocking her from skating anywhere else in the rink. Aria huffs and she's visibly irritated. It rolls off her in waves and she gives me a dirty look before finally caving. "Fine. I'm not going to argue with you, but that doesn't mean I agree with you or like this at all."

"I don't care," I tell her as she turns away from me and skates over to the door. "You're not thinking straight and this is what we both need whether you want to admit it or not."

She looks at me over her shoulder as I follow her off the ice. "You don't know what I need, Leo."

I don't respond and instead walk past her as I head

over to the bench. Aria is purposely slow, like she's dragging her feet to make a point. The silence is deafening as we sit side by side and I begin to take my skates off. Aria doesn't move to unlace hers. Instead, she sits there with her hands in her lap and stares out at the rink.

"Take your skates off," I tell her as I put my skate guards on mine and put them in my bag. "We're going to go get some food and then we will come back."

She sighs and complies without challenging me. It's almost as if she's defeated, yet the annoyance is still radiating from her. I can't help it as the corners of my lips lift in the slightest as I watch her untie her skates and take them off. She wipes the snow and ice from the blades before putting on her skate guards and placing them in her own bag. I slide my feet into my sneakers and wait for her to finish up.

Aria puts on her shoes and stands up before she looks up at me. "You're buying."

A chuckle rumbles in my chest and I don't bother fighting the smile as I look into the swirling gray hues of her eyes. "Come on," I nod my head toward the exit, "I'll even drive too."

"Good," she says, her voice warm and soft. She's still clearly annoyed with me, but she has softened a bit.

Her struggle with being perfect is something that seemed to cause her a bit of distress. The anxiety was evident in her face when I told her that we were taking a break. It's not my business and I shouldn't care, but for some reason, it bothers me seeing her like that. If she's going to be my partner, whether I like her or not, part of my responsibility is making sure she's safe.

Even if it means keeping her safe from herself.

We head out into the parking lot and Aria follows me to my car. There were a few other skaters at the rink, all practicing to get ready for the upcoming competition. Figure skating is the type of sport that requires hours upon hours of practice. Aria and I really need to make sure we get in as much ice time right now as we can. We are at a slight disadvantage considering the fact that we're a new pair. Most of the other skaters have been skating together for years.

Aria and I have the chemistry and all the right tools to make this partnership work, but we still have a lot of work to do.

"Your car is abnormally clean," Aria muses out loud as she sits down in the passenger's seat and shuts her door. I look over at her as she buckles her seat belt. "Did you just get it or something?"

I raise an eyebrow as I glance at her while securing my own seat belt. "No. I just make sure I clean it regularly."

"Weird," she mumbles before looking out the window. She's in a weird mood now and I'm not sure how to play this. It's like her anxiety has made her irritable.

I'm genuinely curious now. "Is yours not clean?"

"No, it is," she tells me as she looks back at me. I turn on the engine and pull my car out of the parking spot. She leans forward and wipes her finger along the dashboard. I watch her from the corner of my eye as she inspects her fingertip for any dust. "It's just a little more lived-in than yours."

I don't bother saying anything else to her about the car. She's not happy with me right now, and that's okay. She doesn't realize it, but everything will be okay. I don't like losing any more than she does. I also know that stress has the ability to leave you crippled. When you're under an immense amount of pressure and stress, that's when you're more likely to fuck up. I need Aria to be at her best, and the woman I was skating with not long ago was not at her best.

I don't want to be the cause of Aria's anxiety. I don't want to be the cause of her stress. As much as I like getting a rise out of her and pissing her off, this isn't how I want it to be.

We drive into the heart of town and I pull my car up along the curb in front of the local coffee shop. Freckled Hen is the only one on this side of town and in my opinion, they have some of the best brunch food. They also have a lot of vegetarian options and I know Aria doesn't eat meat. She's distant, almost as if she's lost in her own mind as I put the car in park and kill the engine. I watch her for a moment as she drops her gaze down to her lap and undoes her seat belt.

As she reaches for the door, I reach out to grab her arm. She looks down at my hand on her forearm before her gaze meets mine. "Hey. If you don't want to eat here, we can get our food to go." I pause for a second. "I can go in and order for you if you'd rather that. They have a lot of vegetarian options here."

Her eyes soften and she shakes her head. "No, I want to eat here."

I nod, quickly releasing her arm before I undo my own seat belt. Aria doesn't give me a chance to open her door for her and a part of me is glad. My grandmother would have scolded me up and down for not being a gentleman and opening it for her. I didn't want Aria to get the impression that this was some kind of a date. We're not friends. We're just two people stuck working together who decided to come get some food.

Nothing more, nothing less.

Aria and I walk up to the front door and the bell dings as I pull it open and hold it for her to walk in first. Her perfume invades my senses as she steps past me and I instinctively take a deep breath, breathing her smell in. I fall in step behind her and we walk up to the counter. Aria looks up at the menu on the wall behind the baristas and I do the same. There are two other people in line and the smell of fresh coffee fills the entire shop. I glance around, looking for an empty table, when I find one over in the back corner. It's pretty busy, but that's to be expected at this time of day.

We both order and I pay for our food before grabbing one of the small signs with the number eight on it. I point to the table in the back and Aria heads in that direction. As we approach it, I lengthen my stride so I can get to the table before her. Extending my arm, I wrap my fingers around the top of the chair and pull it back for her. Aria pauses and raises a curious eyebrow at me. She doesn't say anything as she sits down, but I notice the pink tint creeping across the tops of her cheekbones as she ducks her head.

I step to the other side and take a seat across from her. Aria folds her hands in her lap and her gaze meets mine. Her face is free of any makeup, her hair pulled up in a tight bun on top of her head. She looks absolutely beautiful. I could stare at her all fucking day.

"I'm sorry for being bitchy," she says, her voice quiet. "When things don't go the right way, it makes me really anxious and I get irritable. It's better if I keep my distance from people when I'm feeling like that."

My eyes slowly search her face before settling back on hers. "You don't have to apologize, Ari. Believe it or not, I understand." I take a deep breath, exhaling before I start to talk again. "We're both under a lot of pressure right now, but stress is never good for anyone. You know as well as anyone else that in this sport, your physical health isn't the only thing that is important. Your mental health is equally as important."

"My mental health is fine," she tells me, her voice a bit clipped. "It was just a moment I was having."

Her guard is up and there's no breaching the walls right now. I don't want to piss her off any more, so I simply nod. "I wasn't saying your mental health is not good. I just don't want to see your need for things to be perfect to be an added stressor."

Aria chokes out a laugh as someone walks up to our table with our drinks and food. Aria ordered a garden salad and I got a cup of soup and half a sandwich. She waits until the girl disappears from our table before she starts to talk again. "That's easier said than done." She pauses for a moment and takes a sip of her drink before her eyes search mine. Vulnerability etches itself in her facial features. "What if I don't know how to not be perfect?"

Hearing her ask that question has my chest and throat tightening. I don't like how it feels. I don't like the way her eyes are glossier than normal. I shouldn't care—I *can't* care. Aria is in my life for one reason and one reason only —so we can win.

But I can't not help her, not when she's looking at me like that with those big gray eyes.

Goddamn her. I'm not supposed to like her. I'm not supposed to be growing soft for her.

"No one is perfect, Aria. We all have flaws and we all fuck up from time to time." I pause, trying to search for the right words. I don't know how to respond to her question because I don't have the magic answer for her. "You can't live your life under the assumption that you have to be perfect in every aspect of your life. All it will do is bring you disappointment. It will destroy you over time."

"I don't know how to be okay with that," she admits, her voice barely audible. "I am my biggest critic. No one is harder on me than myself."

I may not be a perfectionist like she is, but I used to be the same way. When it came to skating, if I didn't perform well, I would literally beat myself up for it. Especially that time I fell and Griffin won. I snuck into the rink that night and skated for hours, practicing the same jump over and over until I eventually threw up. As I got older, I realized this wasn't healthy and it wasn't benefiting me at all. It wasn't a change that happened overnight, but I learned that we all make mistakes and there is no sense in harping on them. All we can do is do better the next time.

That didn't always apply to competitions, but that was a different beast. I still allowed myself to be frustrated if I fucked up during a competition, but eventually I would move on from it. I had to.

"We are all our biggest critics, but if you can quiet that voice a little bit, you'll be able to see how good you actually are."

Her lips part and she quickly clamps them shut before ducking her head again. Her expression is unreadable when she looks back up at me. She takes a deep breath, exhaling it slowly as she nods. "Thank you, Leo." A nervous laugh escapes her. "I didn't know you could be this nice to people."

The corners of my mouth twitch and I blow air out through my nose. "This moment is just a glitch in the matrix. Don't get used to it."

Aria's face is bright as she smiles at me and laughs more comfortably. The sound is like music to my ears and I want to hear it on repeat, playing just for me. "Noted."

"I'm going to be bold here for a second," I tell her as I finally pick up my spoon and slide it into my soup. The liquid sloshes along the sides of the cup but it doesn't spill out. "I promise you we will get in sync before the competition. We will get our routine down and we will skate better than any other pair there."

"You really think so?" she asks me as she lifts up her fork and spears the lettuce on her plate with it.

I take a bite of my food and swallow it as I watch her eat her own. Her lips wrap around her fork and she slides it out of her mouth. "Do you trust me?"

She doesn't break eye contact as she stares at me for a beat. There's a pregnant pause before she finally nods. "I do."

"Then trust me when I say, I know so." My gaze penetrates hers with the same intensity. "We won't be perfect, but we will be the closest thing to it."

CHAPTER EIGHT
ARIA

The sun is just barely cresting the horizon as Leo pulls his car into the parking lot at the airport. It was about a half hour drive from Idyll Cove to the closest international airport. I originally planned on driving myself, but yesterday after we finished practice, Leo asked if I wanted to ride with him. Since we had to be at the airport by five o'clock in the morning, it seemed like the better option.

Neither of us talked the entire drive. It was way too early to have any type of conversation. Leo doesn't really strike me as a morning person anyway. The rest of the skaters from our team were supposed to be meeting us here. We're all flying on the same plane to Germany and we are supposed to be there for the next week for our competition.

There's a part of me that still feels a little unsure about all of this. Leo was right when he said we would finally click and things would work. For the past week and a half, we worked around the clock, skating together and perfecting our routine. I feel much more confident skating with him now, but I still have my reservations.

Thinking about the two of us being in perfect harmony almost seemed like it was too good to be true. There was a part of me that tended to air on the pessimistic side of things. Anything that could go wrong, would go wrong. Lately it felt like the universe was working against me. Things were going great and then I was without a partner. The odds were in my favor by ending up with Leo, although I still feel like I'm waiting for the other shoe to drop.

Leo finds a spot and pulls his car into it before putting it in park. He pops the trunk and turns off the engine as I unbuckle my seat belt and let myself out. The air has a chill to it and I pull the zipper of my coat farther up my neck until it's resting just beneath my chin.

Leo beats me to the trunk and he hoists my suitcase out and sets it on the ground in front of me. I grab the handle and adjust my bag on my shoulder as he gets out his own suitcase. I'm sure I overpacked, but it's okay. I don't particularly want to be in a different country with not many options for different outfits.

We're still silent as we walk through the parking garage and into the airport. It's not that busy given the time, but there's still a good amount of people checking in. We go through the line, check our bags and make sure we have our digital boarding passes ready to go before we get in line for security. Leo steps out of the way for me to go first and we funnel through the line before we make our way past the security check.

"I'm going to stop and get a coffee," Leo finally says as we're grabbing our personal bags and shoes from the conveyor belt. "Did you want one too?"

I slip my feet into my soft slipper shoes and direct my attention back to him as I position my bag on my shoulder. "Sure. I can get it, though."

Leo shakes his head at me as we begin to walk together toward our terminal. "I got it."

There's a small coffee shop just across the hall and I see all the people we're flying with standing off to the side. Leo nods his head at them all in acknowledgement as he walks past and goes over to the small stand. I stare after him for a second and then go over to where everyone is.

"Good morning, Ari," Alanna says to me with a bright smile. "Are you ready to go to Germany?"

I smile back and nod at her. "I am," I admit. "I think I'm more excited to fall asleep on the plane, though."

She laughs quietly. "Not me. I don't do well with jet lag, so I want to be able to go to sleep at a decent time there tonight."

I laugh with her. "Well, thankfully we have a few days to acclimate."

Any time we traveled into a different time zone, we always flew a few days before any of the competitions so we could adjust. It's a lot of stress on the body to have a significant time difference and to still be able to perform without being exhausted. Going early also gives us the time to get used to the arena we will be skating in and to get used to the ice. Even though it is a frozen surface with an entire cooling system, conditions still vary from one rink to the other. The extra practice is always welcomed too.

"Are you guys ready to head to our gate?" Coach Kincaid asks everyone. They all speak in unison and I involuntarily yawn. "The plane starts boarding soon, I think."

I nod and everyone starts heading in the same direction down the hall. I begin to walk over to the coffee shop and see Leo turning to face me with both of our drinks and a brown paper bag with the shop's logo on it. I stop a few feet away from him and he hands me the bag when he reaches me.

"What's this?" I ask him as I start to open it and look inside. There's a chocolate croissant and a cheese Danish.

He shrugs and looks down the hall where everyone went. "I got you some pastries."

"Thank you," I say softly, as I lift my gaze from the bag. He isn't even standing in front of me anymore. I look and see him a few feet from me, walking toward our gate. I half roll my eyes and let out a huff as I close the bag and shuffle after him.

I'm not far behind him, but I don't bother trying to catch up to him right away. He reaches the gate first and sits at the end of the group in a seat that's facing the window. I walk over to the window and look outside. Our plane is already out there and they're getting it ready for us to begin boarding.

Leo appears beside me, handing me the warm drink he

bought me. "Here," he says quietly as my hands wrap around the cup. My fingers brush against his and he inhales sharply at the contact. His hand abruptly leaves the cup and I fumble with it, putting my other hand beneath it in an effort to prevent it from falling onto the floor.

I look over at Leo and he's staring back out the window. His jaw tenses and I leave him standing there as I walk back over to our group and sit down.

This is going to be one hell of an exhausting trip.

We all sit and wait until they begin boarding our plane. Leo hasn't moved from where he's standing by the window and I make no attempt to walk over to him. If he wants to be a grouch this morning, then he can enjoy his own company. I have no desire to interact with him until he's in a better mood.

Maybe he didn't get enough sleep and after we get in the air, he can get a nap in and be in a better mood when we touch down in Germany. I've never really seen Leo like this in the morning, so I can't tell if this is normal for him or not.

The girl by the counter at our gate finally calls our seating group and we all head over to the line to board the plane. I fall in step behind Alanna and end up being in the middle of the pack. Glancing over my shoulder, I see Leo still standing by the window. I swear to all things holy, if this man does not get on this plane, we are going to have some serious problems.

Like me having to hide a body kind of problems.

"Don't worry about him," Luca says to me quietly as he

notices me watching Leo. "He's not a big fan of flying, but he'll get on the plane. He might be an idiot, but he's not that much of an idiot."

The line begins to shift and I start to move forward before I get the chance to say anything in response to Luca. I play over his words in my head as I show my boarding pass to the woman and she scans it before motioning for me to keep walking. Perhaps I wasn't giving Leo the benefit of the doubt like I should have.

This whole time I thought he was just being a grump because it was too early for him. Not once did I consider the fact that he was feeling anxious about the flight. If he doesn't like flying, that would make complete sense. I know when I'm feeling anxious, I tend to get snippy with people and become extremely irritable.

Maybe this is just how Leo is dealing with the anxiety he has about flying. It's a common fear. I guess there really is a lot about Leo that I don't know.

We head down the tunnel to the plane and one by one, we step onto the aircraft and find our seats. I wasn't able to get a seat with Eva and Alanna since the flight booking system just randomly selected a seat for me when I booked my ticket.

Looking down at my ticket, I see that the row I am in is closer to the back of the aircraft. The line is moving slowly and it takes a solid ten minutes before I reach my row. I had to wait for everyone to get their carry-on bags into the overhead bins. It's like trying to play Tetris with the way everyone has their bags shoved in there.

There's one person sitting in my row when I reach it.

It's an older woman who is in the seat that is along the aisle. I got lucky and my seat is the one next to the window. The woman smiles as she stands up for a moment and lets me scoot past her.

As I sit down, she turns to face me. "I hope there's no one in the middle seat," she says in a hushed voice. "I like having the extra space."

"So do I," I agree with her while giving her a small smile as I pull my headphones from my personal bag. "I plan on getting some sleep, so I'm not too worried if we end up with another person."

She doesn't look as thrilled about the idea but leaves the conversation at that. I make sure my headphones are connected to my phone and I slide them up over my head. I've always preferred over-the-ear headphones. Earbuds make my ears sore and they're uncomfortable for me.

I select the music app on my phone and settle on the playlist of classical music I have on there. It's the one I typically listen to while I'm skating and I find it helpful to listen to it when I'm not on the ice. It's like it embeds the melody and the sound of the music into my mind and it becomes second nature to move to those particular songs.

There's a rolled-up blanket in my backpack and I pull it out before storing my bag under the seat. I grab the neck pillow I brought along, although I don't wear it around my neck. I position it like it's a pillow before I recline my seat.

There weren't any first-class seats so I ended up having to fly coach. Thankfully the seats do recline a little and there's a decent amount of legroom. It's not ideal but the flight to Germany isn't too long so these accommodations will suffice. I'm not picky, but I do enjoy the finer things in life too.

Laying back in my seat, I pull my blanket over my body and try to find a comfortable position. It's not the most pleasant seat, so it's a little difficult for me since I'm half sitting, half trying to lay. Turning my head to the left toward the window, I settle against the wall and lift the blanket even higher until it's just beneath my chin. My eyelids flutter shut and I let the sound of my music lull me into a state of just being. My body begins to relax and I start to feel more at ease than I did when I first got into this position.

A few minutes pass and I can feel myself about to drift off to sleep. The plane hasn't left yet, most likely because we were still boarding passengers after I got on. It isn't unusual for me to fall asleep before takeoff. I'm one of those fortunate people who could fall asleep anywhere. I don't know if my anxiety is more on the side of "everything will be fine if you just go to sleep". It's almost as if I am handing everything over once I step foot on a plane. If something bad happens, there isn't anything I can do about it. It is beyond my control, so I'm not going to stress about it. I am just going to sleep through every part of it that I can.

And then I feel the other woman and I are no longer alone. Someone moves into the middle seat and is now sitting directly between both of us. Our guest's arm accidentally bumps into mine and I resist the urge to let out a long, exasperated sigh. The thought of no one sitting in the center was honestly wishful thinking. I overheard someone at the airport talking about how it was going to be a pretty full flight, but I was a little hopeful.

I slowly sit up as I open my eyes and turn to look at my new neighbor. Much to my surprise, it's none other than Leo Wells sitting next to me. He's staring at me and my heart pounds erratically in my chest as I pull my headphones off and let them rest around my neck. Leo's eyes are slightly wide and I watch his throat bob as he swallows roughly.

"I wasn't sure you were getting on the plane," I admit to him as I turn down my music on my phone, letting it be background noise as I stare back at Leo.

"I'm here," he says gruffly as he adjusts in his seat. He directs his attention away from me as he slides his backpack under the seat and sits back upright to buckle his seat belt. One of the flight attendant's voices comes across the speakers as she announces that everyone is on the plane and begins to go through the safety information. Leo's body is tense as the woman drones on about what to do if there is a plane crash.

I'm pretty sure none of the things they tell us to do would actually come in handy if we were to go down. I don't think my chances of survival are very high.

The plane begins to move along the runway and you can feel the movement of the aircraft as the pilot gets ready to take off. We wait for a few moments and I see Leo as he grabs both armrests on either side of him. I can't help myself as I watch him for a moment, studying his actions. His jaw is tense and he stares straight ahead like he's trying to block everything out. The plane shifts again and we begin to move forward. It isn't long before we're picking up speed, racing down the runway for takeoff.

The wheels of the plane hit a few bumps and I sit with my own hands on my armrests as I look around. Leo's now sitting there with his head pressed back against his seat and his eyes are closed. I feel a bit invasive staring at him, so I direct my attention elsewhere. I stare at the stitching of the headrest of the seat in front of me. This is my least favorite part of a plane ride other than when there is turbulence. This is exactly why I make it a habit to fall asleep before we take off. This shit feels sketchy as hell, even though it lasts less than a minute.

We're picking up even more speed and I feel the wheels of the plane begin to lift from the ground. Leo suddenly reaches out, his hand warm against mine as he tightly wraps his fingers around mine. I don't look at him. Instead, I turn my wrist so my palm is facing up and Leo laces his fingers within mine. I didn't realize how scared he actually was. He doesn't dare to open his eyes, so I simply sit there in silence next to him, holding his hand to comfort him as the plane soars up into the sky. Leo's knee begins to bounce and he looks uncomfortable as we hit a pocket of air. His grip tightens on my hand and he doesn't let go.

The music plays from my headphones, filling the empty space between us. A minute or two passes before we're settled in the air and it smooths out. I see Leo from the corner of my eye as he straightens his head and his gaze drops down to our hands clasped together. I look over at him and he begins to unweave his fingers from mine and slowly pulls his hand away. His lips part like he's about to say something, but he clamps them shut again.

"I didn't know you were afraid of flying."

Leo levels his gaze on mine. There isn't a hint of amusement in his expression. Instead, he looks irritated as hell. "I'm not."

I'm about to challenge him on that when I decide to let it go. With the way Leo typically presents himself, this is a stark contrast to the way he acts. You would think there wasn't a single thing that bothered this man. Him being afraid of flying comes as a shock. The fact that he grabbed my hand surprised me even more. He needed comfort in that moment and he sought it from me. Perhaps he doesn't hate me the way he acts like he does… or I was the closest thing for him to cling to.

"If you tell anyone about that, I'll deny it until the day I'm dead."

I can't help myself as I laugh and roll my eyes at him. "Your secret is safe with me, Leo."

And it is.

Any of his secrets would be safe with me.

CHAPTER NINE
LEO

Germany is beautiful. It's the middle of spring and flowers are beginning to bloom along the streets. I walk down the cobblestone road, my head looking up and down the street as I make my way back to the hotel. I love visiting here, even if I hate the process of getting here. It's where I'd like to live eventually. I've spent a lot of time traveling with this career and for some reason Germany has always been enticing to me. There's just something warm and comforting about it that makes me never want to leave.

I imagine when I retire one day, this is where I will be. I'll buy a little house on the hillside, not far from town, but far enough that I can have my own peace and quiet.

It's just a different vibe. I do like Idyll Cove. It's all I've really known in terms of my permanent residence, although I'm a little tired of the sleepy little town. I want more. I want to wake up every morning and feel like my life has more purpose. This life of traveling and competing can be tiresome and lonely. It's easy to feel like you're not really living when you're caught in the continuous cycle of hustling and busting your ass off.

I will never ever admit it out loud… but sometimes, I just want a break from it all.

But I do like winning more, so as long as I keep doing that, I'll keep living this insane life.

The hotel is less than a mile away from where I wandered off tonight. I ended up in a little German restaurant where I sat at a table by myself and had dinner. It wasn't any different than how I normally lived my life, but it circles back to being lonely. It's not easy to find a partner in life with the demanding schedule I have. I tried dating before and it didn't work out. There was one woman, Amanda, who lasted a little longer than the others. We dated exclusively for about two years before she decided she wanted more from me. She was waiting for me to propose and I am not a fan of committing to another person.

My life revolves around one huge commitment and I don't think I could commit to anything more than that.

I thought she would have been happy that we lived together, and things seemed to be good. We spent time together when we could and she had her own job that kept her busy. I was mistaken. She wasn't happy and she wasn't content. Amanda complained occasionally about me being gone. She didn't like to be alone for long, so most times she ended up staying at her sister's apartment. We had a pretty big fight when it finally came out that she wanted more and I wasn't ready to give that to her. I had to leave for another competition and when I got back home, she was gone. All of her things were out of my place and she changed her number so I couldn't even get in contact with her.

I'd be lying if I said I didn't feel a bit of relief.

I didn't have to try to live up to someone else's expectations anymore. I was free to be me and to come and go like I pleased. Or like my career demanded.

After Amanda and I broke up, I kept things casual. I never went on more than three dates with a woman, although I'd end up in her bed on more occasions than that if she understood the deal. There was no room or time for relationships or commitments. I just needed someone every now and then to make me feel good and feel a little less alone.

There aren't many people on the street as I walk up to the front of the hotel. It's already getting close to midnight and my body is exhausted. The time difference really took a toll on me, especially since I wasn't able to sleep on the plane. They always made me too nervous and my anxiety was too high for me to be able to get enough rest. Aria, on the other hand, had no trouble falling asleep. After I stupidly grabbed her hand and finally let it go, she smiled at me and put her headphones back on before getting comfortable in her seat. At one point during her nap, she shifted my way and ended up with her head against my shoulder.

I didn't want to move her. She was too peaceful, her face so relaxed and her lips parted slightly as she snored softly.

She turned the other way before she woke up, so I'm certain she didn't realize she spent some of her time sleeping against me. I'm also certain she didn't notice my fingers as I instinctively brushed the hair from her face and tucked it back behind the band of her headphones. I was finding there were a lot of things I couldn't help myself with when it came to Aria Reed. Having her this close, deeply embedded in my life, was beginning to feel like more of a problem than I thought it would be.

It's getting harder to keep my guard in place and harder still to keep her out.

She's working her way under my skin and I don't like it.

The hotel lobby isn't busy as I walk inside the doors. There are two people at the front desk and they glance up at me before returning their attention back to their phones in front of them. Their voices are hushed and low. I mind my own business as I walk past them, heading straight for the hall to the elevators. I press the up button and pull out my own phone to check my messages.

I asked Austin if he could stop by and take care of my cats while I'm out of the country. He's not a huge fan of cats, but he reluctantly agreed. They're both slight menaces, so I'm sure he's having a great time cleaning up after them.

The elevator reaches the lobby and I step inside after the doors slide open. As I slide my phone back into my pocket, I pull out my room key. To reach the seventeenth floor, you have to swipe your key card. We were all given our own suites, but those floors are restricted from other guests.

It takes about a minute to get up to the seventeenth floor since the elevator doesn't stop at any other floors. I'm surprised with how quiet the hotel is right now. It's a bit shocking, but then again, it is the beginning of the week, so maybe there aren't that many people staying here, or people are already sleeping. Maybe some of them are out, I don't know. I don't know why I'm even putting this much time into thinking about what anyone is doing here.

I'm trying to keep my mind off the one thing it keeps drifting back to.

Aria fucking Reed.

And as I step off the elevator, she almost runs into me.

She lets out a loud gasp and drops the bottle of water she was holding. "Oh my god, I'm so sorry!" She says the words a little too loudly as she tries to collect herself. She still hasn't even looked at my face, but I look at hers. Her cheeks are red with embarrassment. Her hair is pulled back in a French braid and she's wearing a robe and slippers. I have no idea if she's wearing anything under the plush, white garment, but I'm curious.

We both bend down at the same time to pick up the water bottle she had dropped. It was completely accidental as we both reached for it. My hand brushes against hers, sending a wave of electricity through my fingers. Aria gasps and instinctively jumps. I didn't realize how close I was to her until her head bumps against mine.

"Oh no," she says under her breath as we both stand up right. I have the water bottle in my hand and I go to offer it to her, ignoring the twinge of pain in my forehead from where her head hit mine. Aria rubs the back of her head momentarily as her gaze collides with mine. "Leo."

"Ari."

A wave of nervousness passes through her expression and she laughs apologetically as she takes the water bottle from me, careful to avoid her fingers coming in contact with mine again. "I'm sorry, on both counts. I didn't even realize anyone was coming off the elevator and I didn't mean to bump your head."

"Stop," I tell her as I stare down into the swirling hues of gray. Standing this close, I can pick out the small flecks of dark blue in her irises. She's fucking beautiful. "You don't have to apologize to me for anything, ever. You got that?"

She pulls her bottom lip in between her teeth and nods. "It's just a habit, I guess." She pauses with a shrug. "And I kind of owe you an apology for all of that."

I shake my head at her. "I don't want any apologies from you." There's something about her doing it that doesn't sit well with me. I don't care if she runs me over with her goddamn car. The last thing I want to hear is the regret in her voice as she profusely apologizes as if she's going to be in trouble if she doesn't.

She's under my skin. I want her out. But I don't want her to ever feel like she's small. I don't want her to ever feel as if she's beneath anyone.

Aria Reed deserves to sit upon the highest fucking pedestal.

"What were you doing?" I question her as I glance behind me at the little room she must have come from.

A smile spreads across her lips and she pulls a bag of pretzels and a chocolate bar from the pocket of her robe and shows them to me. I've seen what Aria normally eats during the day and she isn't one who seems to indulge in junk food often. "These are my guilty little pleasures. Don't tell anyone."

The corners of my mouth twitch. "We all have our secrets."

She stares up at me, shifting her weight on her feet as her eyes shimmer beneath the lights in the hallway. "We do, don't we?"

"I want to know yours."

I can't stop the words and they just fall from my lips. Any logical or irrational thoughts I once had are completely gone. I don't even possess the ability to control the things I'm saying. Aria stares back at me, her eyes widening slightly, but she recovers. Instead, a fire begins to burn deep within her irises. She tilts her head to the side, almost as if she isn't sure what to do next or how to respond.

And then she surprises me.

"I'll tell you mine if you tell me yours."

Goddamn her. As much as I want her to play along, a part of me wishes she would have told me to fuck off or chose to not respond. Instead, she just opened a door that I know I don't have enough self-control to close.

My feet move and I close the distance between us. Aria doesn't take a step away from me. The soft hint of her perfume invades my senses and I breathe her in. Aria tucks her snacks back into her pocket as I lift my hand and run my fingertips along the seam of her plush robe that crosses over her chest. "Are you sure that's what you want to do?"

"Don't question me like I don't know what I want, Wells," she says in warning, straightening her spine as she lifts her chin more to look at me. I can't fight the smirk that lifts my lips. This is the side of Aria that brings me immense amusement along with frustration. She's confident and isn't going to back down from a challenge.

And I can't be the one to make her fucking bend.

"What is it you want, Aria?"

She levels her gaze on mine. "I want you to stop talking," she admits as she smiles sweetly at me. "I want you to finally collect on your debt, unless you're too afraid to do that."

A chuckle escapes me. "You think I haven't collected because I'm scared?" I shake my head as I cup the side of her face and run the pad of my thumb along her bottom lip. "I haven't collected it because I'm not sure you can handle it."

She narrows her eyes on mine and her lip moves against my finger as she talks. "You don't know me that well then, do you?" She nips at the tip of my finger, her teeth grazing my skin.

"Perhaps I don't," I muse out loud as I stare down at her. She's beautiful and I like her worked up like this. Her body deceives her, although I don't think she's actively trying to hide any reaction. Her chest rises and falls in every shallow breath she takes. "Do you think you might want to show me?"

"Show you what?" she breathes as she instinctively takes a step closer. Her body is almost flush against mine and I want to know what the fuck is under that goddamn robe. Her heat radiates from her body. Abandoning her lips, I slide my hand around the back of her head, pushing my fingers through her hair as I tilt her head back even farther. Her neck elongates and it can't be comfortable in that position as she maintains eye contact with me.

My face slowly inches closer to hers until I can feel her breath across my face. It smells faintly of chocolate and I smile. That chocolate bar in her pocket isn't the first one she's snuck from the vending machine. My lips brush against hers but I don't kiss her. Her hands reach for my waist and she holds on to my hips in an effort to keep herself upright as I don't let up the pressure on the back of her head.

"Prove me wrong. Show me you can handle it."

"Done."

That's all I need for my mouth to end up crashing into hers. The tension between us is so goddamn thick, it swirls in the air around us, encapsulating us as I slide my tongue along the seam of her mouth. Aria doesn't hesitate and parts her lips to let me in. My tongue slides against hers, soft like silk, tasting like rich milk chocolate. Jesus Christ, she's fucking divine. Her fingers dig into my skin and I kiss her slowly, drawing out every sweep of my tongue. She doesn't rush it, instead matching my energy. She doesn't mind the slow torture.

Instead, she does the same, nipping and tasting, touching and teasing.

She drives me fucking insane and she doesn't even know it.

Abruptly, I pull away from her, both of us breathless as my eyes search hers. The flames lick her irises and I want to fucking burn in her. "Your room or mine?"

"Yours. I can't get the temperature to turn up, so it's an icebox in my room."

Bending forward slightly, I lean close to her and hook my hands behind her thighs, sweeping her into the air. Her breath leaves her in a rush as I lift her up. My hands are under her robe and her bare skin is warm beneath my hands as she wraps her legs around the small of my back. She doesn't say anything as her hands go around the back of my neck and she holds on to me as I carry her down the hall. This isn't the first time I've ever carried her, but every other time has been on the ice. This is different and intimate. I love the way she feels in my arms, the way her slender legs feel wrapped around my body. The way her hands wrap around the nape of my neck.

My footsteps are light and it doesn't take long before we reach the door to my suite. I press her back against the door and my one hand drops away from her thigh. "Hold on to me, Ari. I need to get my key from my pocket."

"Okay," she says softly as I push my hand into my pocket and retrieve the key.

I pull her back away from the door and she holds on to me as I use one hand to unlock and push it open. My heart pounds to its own beat inside my chest, but it rattles against my rib cage. Warmth is spreading through my body like wildfire and I have a deep-seated need to be inside her. We've been toeing this line for far too long–it's time. I don't know what happens after this and I don't even care anymore. If I can just have one more taste of her, I'll have had my fill and then I can close the door on whatever the hell this is.

The tension will dissipate and we can resume life like this never happened.

As we step inside the suite and the door closes behind me, Aria's lips find mine in the darkness of the room. My feet move us across the space and I struggle to not run into or trip over anything as I carry her to the bedroom. Aria's fingers slide up my scalp, her nails raking my skin as she runs her fingers through my hair. I fucking love her like this. She's just as greedy for my touch as I am for hers.

My thighs hit the bed and I slowly lower her down onto the mattress. We don't need any of the lights on with the way the moon shines through the window. It's big and full and it casts its light across the bed and across her body. Aria's hair splays out around her head, creating the illusion of a halo. She stares up at me as I reach for the sash of her robe and pull on it. It undoes the knot and I toss it to the side as I grab the lapels of her robe and begin to push them open.

My breath catches in my throat as I find out what she's wearing beneath that damned robe…

CHAPTER TEN
ARIA

Leo's eyes are burning with a deep desire, the swirls of brown mixing in his dark irises. I watch the way his Adam's apple bobs as he swallows roughly. The robe I'm wearing is now pushed to the sides, resting on the bed on either side of my torso. I'm left completely bare and exposed for him to feast upon with his gaze. His eyes glaze over a bit as they begin to roam across my body and his fingertips follow suit. He drags the tips of his fingers across my collarbone and down my sternum, stopping as he reaches the top of my stomach. My breathing hitches as goosebumps break out and cover my skin. My nipples are instantly hard and his gaze drops to them.

"You are so fucking perfect, I hate it," he murmurs as he reaches for my shoulders and lifts me up before pushing the robe down my arms. He strips me from it and discards it onto the floor without a single care. I'm wearing a pair of lilac underwear that are cut like bikini bottoms. His touch is tender as he pushes me back down onto the plush mattress. He's still wearing all his clothes, but the expression on his face leaves him completely exposed.

He's vulnerable and I like him this way. It's like he doesn't know how he's supposed to act. It's a stark contrast to the typical cold exterior he shows to the rest of the world. Instead, he's a fire burning brightly under the full moon. Something shifts within him and his eyes darken a bit as a smirk slides across his lips.

"I can't wait to have my way with you," he says softly as he grabs the hem of his shirt and pulls it over his head. He tosses it down onto the floor as my eyes begin to roam over his body. His torso looks like it was hand-carved and sculpted by an artist. The defined muscles and the way his skin is taut across them. I resist the urge to reach out and touch him, as I'm still waiting for him to be the first to make a move. He grabs my ankles and pulls swiftly, dragging my ass to the end of the bed so my legs are dangling off the edge. "I look forward to thoroughly fucking you out of my system."

I regain my breath and my heart races inside my chest, thumping hard against my rib cage. "I hope it works."

"So do I," he says as he begins to spread my knees apart and steps into the space between my thighs. He plants his hands on my legs and begins to lower himself to his knees. I lift my head to look at him as his fingers hook beneath the waistband of my panties. He slowly begins to drag them down toward my feet until he leaves me completely naked on the bed. "I know I said just one taste last time, but I'm failing to remember how good it was."

Leo settles between my legs, his fingers splaying out on the insides of my thighs as he holds them open for himself. He smiles at me with lust dancing in his irises as he begins to lower his mouth to the apex of my thighs. His lips brush against my center and I swear, I almost die right there on the spot. I forgot how much I craved his touch and how good it actually was. His mouth is warm and wet as he parts his lips and begins to slide his tongue along my pussy. He licks me in one lap, applying pressure to my clit as he brushes past it. My hips instinctively buck and I pull my bottom lip between my teeth and bite down, resisting the urge to cry out.

"I remember now," he groans as he adjusts himself between my legs.

My body is already humming and my nerve endings are tingling. Somehow this man has become like a drug to me. I haven't had a full dose of him, but I've been chasing that high from him since the first time I felt pleasure from Leo a few months ago. I've slept with a total of zero people since then because for whatever reason, I couldn't get this man out of my head. I've been on dates, I've entertained the idea of messing around with someone else, but when it actually came to hooking up, I couldn't go through with it. None of them kissed me or touched me quite like he did, so I've been spending my days in a sexually frustrated haze. Even my own toys weren't scratching the itch for me. They don't compare to the way Leo knows how to play me like a fiddle with the tips of his fingers and his tongue.

He continues to work his mouth against me. Every now and then he slides his tongue deep inside me before suctioning his lips around my clit. I'm coming undone, bursting apart at the seams with just this little amount of contact with him. His fingertips dig into my flesh as he eats me like a starved man. Alternating between teasing and going full force, my body doesn't know what to do anymore. All I'm doing at this point is hanging on for dear life as I wait for that inevitable plunge that is going to leave me soaring to unmatched heights of ecstasy.

"I could spend the rest of my life eating this sweet pussy," he murmurs against my flesh before flicking my clit again. He rolls it around, applying the perfect amount of pressure that has my eyes rolling into the back of my head. I'm so close and I don't want him to stop. I try to lift my hips and he chuckles as he pulls his mouth away from me. "You want to come, don't you?"

Lifting my head, I look at him and nod before closing my eyes as I inhale deeply.

Slap.

His hand comes in contact with my pussy, sending a hot stinging feeling across my flesh that has me crying out in pleasure. My eyelids fly open and my lips are parted as my mind registers what just happened. He just slapped my pussy and it may have been one of the hottest things I've ever experienced.

"Words, Aria."

Jesus Christ.

"Yes," I breathe out, nodding with a desperation I've never recognized in myself before. "Please, Leo. Please let me come."

"You beg so well. I think you deserve to be rewarded

for that." His mouth suctions around my clit once more. A moan escapes me as my head drops back down onto the bed. He holds me down and begins to move his tongue against me, showing no mercy. My mind can't even decipher what is going on anymore. All I know is I'm chasing after that high and that's the only thing that matters.

Leo doesn't stop as he continues to fuck me with his mouth. He knows exactly what he's doing. My hands grip his hair, pulling on the locks while still pushing his head between my thighs. I think I feel him smile against my pussy, but I'm not sure. He flicks his tongue once more before flattening it against my clit, working it in circles until I'm completely coming undone.

My orgasm hits me like a fucking freight train. His name spills from my lips in a moaning chant. I don't even bother trying to compose myself as my body writhes beneath his touch. My legs shake, my hips bucking. He pins me down and feasts upon me until I'm drifting into the abyss. My body feels like I've been doused in kerosene and lit on fire. And it's the sweetest, most euphoric inferno I've ever experienced in my life. I'll gladly stay like this, floating in and out of ecstasy as the warmth consumes my body.

This is borderline addicting.

As he lifts himself away from between my legs, I lift my gaze to meet his. The flames in his eyes mimic the feeling that's still spreading throughout my body. Leo's chin is damp from my pleasure and he smirks as he wipes it away with the back of his hand. His hands drop down to the waistband of his pants and he hesitates as his eyes search mine. "Is this what you want?"

"Yes," I tell him without a second thought. It's not a lie. I want him. I want to feel him everywhere. I appreciate him asking and needing verbal consent rather than just doing whatever he wanted to me.

Leo unbuttons and unzips his pants. My eyes follow his movements as he begins to push his pants and his boxer briefs down his thighs. He bends forward, pushing them down to his feet, and steps out of them as he straightens his body. His cock is hard and I swear it looks like it has its own heartbeat as it throbs. My eyes widen slightly as I take in the sight of him. He's literal perfection. He is the type of man you want to keep you safe and give you babies. I can't help but stare at his dick as I try to measure it with my eyes. It's big. Like *big* big. Like *I don't know if it's going to fit inside me* big.

"Fuck. I love seeing you like this," he groans as he fists his cock and pumps it twice with his hand. "Look at the way your pussy's glistening. You're so ready for me, aren't you?"

"Yes," I breathe as I lift my hands to reach for him. He moves closer and motions for me to move farther up the bed. He follows after me, crawling onto the mattress. It dips beneath his weight and he settles between my legs as he plants his hands on either side of my head. A soft gasp escapes me as he presses the tip of his cock against my entrance.

He hesitates, his eyes bouncing back and forth between

mine. "Shit," he mutters, his eyebrows pulling together. "I don't have a condom."

His words irritate me. He's so fucking close to me right now and I just need to feel him inside me. Shaking my head, I hook my ankles around the small of his back and urge him forward. "I'm clean and I have an IUD."

"Thank fuck." He lets out a sigh of relief. A smile dances across his lips and the fire in his eyes burns deep. "You have no idea how badly I need to be inside you right now."

"I think I have an idea," I assure him as he begins to ease himself into me. I can't help myself as my eyelids flutter shut and a moan slips from my lips. Leo matches me, a low moan rumbling in his chest as he fills me to the hilt. His girth stretches me in a way I didn't think was possible. His length literally takes my breath away as he situates himself completely inside me. I struggle to catch my breath.

Leo slides one hand beneath my ass, holding up my hips as he lowers himself down onto his forearm. He strokes the side of my face, brushing hair from my cheek. "Just breathe, baby," he murmurs as his fingertips dance across the side of my face and trail across my lips. "You can take all of me."

He begins to shift his hips, slowly stroking my insides as he pulls out and pushes back in. He never fully pulls his cock out the whole way. Instead, he just pulls back until it's only the tip inside before sliding back into me. His movements are deliberately slow as he continues to work my body, stretching me out to accommodate his size. I swear, I've never been with someone built like him. At first, there is a bit of discomfort since I'm not used to him, but as he continues to move, it's only getting better. My pussy clenches around him, holding him tightly as he pistons his hips.

"You take my cock so well," he breathes before his lips find mine. They sweep across my mouth, his tongue pushing between my lips as it finds my own. Our tongues tangle together as he continues to thrust into me slowly. I want more. I want it all. I want him to fuck me into oblivion until there's nothing left.

Leo pulls away from my face and moves his hand away from my ass as he pushes himself off the bed. I immediately feel his absence. He stares down at me for a moment, his gaze raking over my body. I love the way he's looking at me right now. I never want him to stop. He grabs my hips as his eyes meet mine. "I want to fuck you from behind."

"So what are you waiting for?"

Leo chuckles softly and shakes his head. "You're something else, pretty girl." He abruptly grabs my hips and flips me over so I'm lying face down on the bed. His hands are still on my hips and he lifts them up into the air, positioning me as he pulls my ass back toward him. "If I didn't plan on being alone forever, I'd consider making you mine."

He takes my breath away again as he thrusts his cock into me without warning. My body lurches forward, but he holds me in place by my hips so I don't fall onto the bed. His movements are a bit more rushed than they were before, like there's an urgency to the way he fucks me. His fingertips bite into my flesh as he moves faster and harder, each thrust more powerful than the one before. He slows to a stop out of nowhere. Abandoning my left hip, he slides his hand along my spine, leaning into me until his palm reaches the back of my neck. He's not forceful, but he pushes me down toward the bed until my chest and the side of my face are against the mattress. My hands fist the bedsheets as he starts to move again.

"God, you're so perfect with your ass in the air like this." He moves his hand to the top of my back and holds it between my shoulder blades as he keeps me in place for a moment. He moves slowly as he removes his hand and brings it back to my hip. Both of his hands move to my ass cheeks and he parts them as he begins to slide in and out of me. "One day I'm going to fuck this ass."

A moan escapes me, my eyes screwing shut at the thought of him inside me there. It's something I've never done with anyone before and excitement licks at my veins. I don't comment on how this is supposed to be a one-time thing. He's supposed to be fucking me out of his system, not making plans of how he's going to fuck me in the future and the different ways he's going to do it.

Leo begins to move again, thrusting in rapid succession as he fucks me even harder. His fingers are digging into my skin as he holds me firmly. My own knuckles are turning white with how tightly I'm gripping the sheets. I can feel myself getting closer and closer to the edge as he pounds into me. He strokes my insides with every thrust, hitting that sweet spot that has me curling my toes. He lets go of one of my ass cheeks and slides his hand in front of me until his fingers are between my legs, brushing against my clit.

"I want to feel you come on my cock," he moans as his balls slap against me. He rolls his fingers over my clit again and again. "I want to hear you screaming my name as you shatter into a million pieces."

He applies more pressure, his fingers circling me, and I can feel it coming. I'm so close and with the way he's moving, I think he's right there with me. He groans, his hand gripping my ass tighter. His cock fills me deeply with every thrust, undoubtedly bruising my insides. The pain mixes with the pleasure and I fucking love it. I've never been one to like pain, but this is so different than anything else I've ever had with someone. He's tender, yet he knows exactly what he wants. He wants my pleasure and I'll gladly give it all to him if he has me soaring through the clouds like this.

"That's it, Aria," he groans as he thrusts again, simultaneously rolling his fingers over my clit. "Come for me."

That's all it takes for me to fall over the edge. My orgasm tears through my body and he's coming with me, spilling his warmth deep inside me. His thrusts slow and he murmurs my name as he releases my ass and his hands are suddenly all over my body, softly stroking my skin in the most tender, featherlight touches. He continues to rock into me, each thrust longer and slower until we're both riding the high of each other. I collapse onto the bed as he pulls out of me. I feel the bed dip as he leaves me there on the mattress alone, but he isn't gone for long. Leo comes back to the room and I roll onto my side as he sits down beside me. He parts my legs, his gaze landing on my pussy as he slides his finger through our cum.

"I like you like this, with my cum dripping out of you." He pushes his finger inside me and slowly pulls it back out again before he places a warm washcloth against my center.

"What are you doing?" He catches me off guard by his actions—this isn't something anyone has ever done for me after having sex—so I go to reach for his hand. "I can do that."

His eyes find mine and he pushes my hand away. "Shut up and let me take care of you."

My lips part and I watch him for a beat as he cleans me up and disappears back into the bathroom to leave the washcloth in there. While he's gone, I quickly climb off his bed and pick up my robe and underwear. I don't want to be the one to ruin the moment, but I can't help but feel like it's already over. Leo reappears, still completely naked as he leans against the doorway and watches me.

"Running away so soon?"

I lift my gaze to his as I stand upright, holding my robe in one hand and my panties in the other. "I should probably get back to my room. We have to be up early to skate."

His expression is unreadable as he pushes off the door frame and walks over to me. He closes the distance between us, and he reaches out to take my robe from me. "Stay here tonight."

I stare up at him, swallowing roughly. "This was just a one-time thing."

Leo drops my robe onto the floor and cups my face as his body moves flush against mine. His face drops down to mine, his lips brushing against my own. "I changed my mind. It's more of a one-night kind of thing now."

"We'd better make the most of it then." I smile as my hands reach for his waist.

"My thoughts exactly."

Leo pushes me back toward the bed, falling onto it with me as his lips crash into mine.

CHAPTER ELEVEN
LEO

Standing on the ice, I stare across the rink at Aria as she stands and talks to one of the coaches. Irritation pricks my skin while I continue to watch her for a moment. I'm the last one to get here, which isn't usual for me, and it wouldn't have happened if I would have remembered to set my alarm last night. When I fell asleep, Aria was still in my bed, although the two of us were fairly exhausted from going three different rounds throughout the night. I practically passed out and completely forgot to make sure my alarm was set for six o'clock. We were expected to be at the rink by seven thirty and it's currently seven forty-five.

This isn't a good look for me.

I don't pride myself on being late. If anything, I'm usually one of the first to arrive.

I don't know what time Aria left. All I know is she wasn't in my bed when she woke up and the side she fell asleep on was cold. She made sure not to disturb me or wake me up when she snuck out. I wasn't pissed that she left. We agreed it was a necessary evil last night, even if it was pretty fucking spectacular. I'd be lying if I said I wouldn't fuck her again. Although, I'd only do it if she knew nothing more would ever come of it. I also don't want to mess up this business relationship we now have. When partners start seeing each other and their relationships go to shit, it usually affects their working relationships too.

At this point in my career, that's something I cannot afford and neither can Aria.

"You're late," Luca says as he skates up behind me. As I turn around to face him, he smiles and doesn't look annoyed like I expected him to be. "I think everyone's having a little bit of trouble adjusting to the time difference."

"We both know that's no excuse," I tell him, my voice flat as I begin to skate away.

He doesn't follow after me or say anything else. I assume that was essentially my warning: *don't let it happen again.* Even if I did let it happen again, I don't know what they would really do. All the coaches have their own pride issues and drive to win. If our country doesn't win, it's a bad reflection on them. They want me here skating, so me being late doesn't jeopardize anything when it comes to that.

Although, there's a part of me that blames Aria for it. All she had to do was wake me up when she left and I wouldn't have been late this morning.

I skate directly over to where she is, abruptly coming to

a stop in front of her. Aria doesn't look at me at first. Eva glances at me over Aria's shoulder and she kind of nods toward me and gives her a smile.

"Hey, Leo," she says to me before looking back at Ari. "We'll talk later and figure it out."

Aria nods at her and then turns around to look at me, her smile falling when she sees my mouth set in a straight line. "Hey," she says softly as a pink tint creeps across her cheeks. I can't help but feel a touch of satisfaction knowing that her mind probably traveled back in time to the numerous times I made her come last night.

"You didn't wake me up when you left."

Her eyebrows pull together and she tilts her head to the side. "Why would I have woken you up? It was early, you were snoring, and I didn't want to disturb you."

My nostrils flare as I let out a breath. Perhaps the anger I was directing toward her was unwarranted. "What time did you leave?"

"It was, like, four o'clock, maybe four thirty."

Well, now I'm even more curious. We had to have been asleep for a few hours before she woke up and decided to leave. It would have made more sense for her to wake up when it was time to get ready, but she left long before that. It wasn't her fault that I didn't set an alarm and it wasn't her fault I didn't wake up on time. I still wish she would have checked to see why I wasn't ready to go, but I'm also not her responsibility. Just because we slept together, and we skated together didn't mean she needed to keep tabs on me like she was my keeper.

"Why'd you leave?"

Aria's eyes widen slightly, almost as if she wasn't expecting me to question her on it. "I don't know. I just figured I should go back to my room."

I shake my head at her, not accepting that as an answer. "You don't wake up in the middle of the night and head back to your own room for no reason. Why did you leave, Aria?"

There's a pregnant pause and the silence stretches between us as she shifts her weight on her skates. She's uncomfortable, but I'm not sure why. I asked her to stay last night, so it wasn't like she overstayed her welcome. Everything we did together, she gave consent to. Is she regretting it now? Did she wake up in the middle of the night and wish none of it ever happened?

I'm not an insecure person, but I feel so fucking insecure right now.

Aria finally shrugs. "I didn't want to give you the wrong impression by still being in your bed in the morning. We agreed to a one-night situation, so when I woke up, it just felt like I shouldn't be there."

I'm at a loss for words. We fucked. Multiple times. And she felt like she shouldn't be in my bed. What the hell is going on?

This is a first for me with anyone I'd ever been with.

"I wouldn't have asked you to stay if I didn't want you there."

Her cheeks puff up as she lets out a deep exhale. "I just didn't want it to seem like it was something it wasn't, you know?"

And I thought I had commitment issues...

I can't help myself as a chuckle rumbles in my chest and fills the air. A few of the other skaters turn to look at the two of us as they skate by, but no one bothers to interrupt. I know we're wasting time. We should be practicing together, but I'm not doing anything with Aria until this is resolved.

"Trust me, I will never get the wrong impression," I assure her with a smirk as I shake my head in disbelief that she would even think that was a possibility. "You staying in my bed doesn't make me think it's something it isn't. It's exactly what I want." I pause and mirror the same shrug she gave me. "Plus, it's done and over with now."

Aria nods and smiles back at me, although it doesn't quite reach her eyes. "Good to know. Since we've cleared that up, can we do what we're actually supposed to do together?"

Her tone is a bit abrasive and there's a coldness that lingers in her words. Gone is the warmth she offered me last night, but I know it is my own doing. It doesn't matter now. Whatever that was between us has passed and now we can get back to skating without having anything clouding the air between us.

"That might be the best idea you've had so far."

Aria winks at me. "Sleeping with you certainly wasn't," she mumbles under her breath as she begins to skate toward the center of the rink, leaving me standing by the boards.

What the fuck?

"Aria and Leo," Eva speaks both of our names from where she is standing by the benches. Everyone else is beginning to line up over there and the song Aria picked for us to skate to begins to sound through the speaker system. "The two of you can go first."

I turn around and find Aria waiting for me as she gets into position. A sigh escapes me and irritation slides through my veins as I quickly skate to meet her in the middle of the rink. The melody of the song is still soft and slow. I move behind Aria, wrapping my arms around her waist. She reaches back, sliding her hands around the back of my neck as she tilts her head back against my shoulder. I revel in her warmth and resist the urge to pull her closer.

Goddammit.

Shaking my head, I push the thoughts away. That ship has already sailed. We had our time together and nothing more would ever come of it. I fucked her out of my system and that was that. It can never happen between us again and we already both agreed that it wouldn't.

I'd be lying if I said I didn't thoroughly enjoy it, though...

The music shifts and we both skate away from one another before simultaneously spinning. We're in perfect sync and Aria flashes me a painstakingly beautiful smile as we meet again, joining hands as we begin to move backward around the rink. I really believe we are supposed to skate together. Nothing has ever felt quite as right as this partnership does.

We run through our entire routine, both of us skating to the melody, hitting every single move the exact way we are supposed to. It's a perfect performance and exactly what we need to do in three days when it really counts.

We meet again in the middle of the ice as the music begins to slow and my hands clasp the sides of her face as our bodies bend together. We're both breathless and we fold into one another, me supporting her and holding her away from the ice as the music comes to a stop.

Aria's face is so close to mine, her breath dancing across my lips. All I have to do is shift forward, just an inch, and our mouths would touch. Her eyes bounce back and forth between mine, but she doesn't dare to be the one to break contact. She's waiting for me to kiss her, and fuck me for wanting to do it.

Everyone in the rink that was watching us begins to clap loudly, the sound filling the entire building. It's enough to break Aria and I from our trance. We both stand up together, quickly breaking apart as she steadies herself on her feet. I swallow roughly, running a hand through my hair as I let out a deep breath. I'm frustrated and it has nothing to do with Aria and everything to do with me. My self-control is severely lacking and I need to remind myself of the bigger picture here.

Aria and I need each other to skate and we can't cross that line again. We both allowed ourselves that moment of weakness, to give in to the lust that was burning between us. My mind needs to get its shit together and learn to separate from her. We need to be able to skate together, maintain a healthy level of professionalism that we've finally found together, and ensure the emotional pull and chemistry is still there without giving in to any of that.

Jesus, this is going to be much harder than I imagined it would be.

It was a lot easier when I didn't like her at all...

Aria skates over to where our waters are and I meet her over there, taking one of the bottles as she hands it to me. "That felt really good," she says with a bright smile and a nod as the next two skaters head to the center of the ice. Her face is slightly flushed and I count the freckles peppered across the bridge of her nose.

I take a sip of my water and nod. "I told you we would get it as close to perfect as possible."

Her smile falters. "Friday is the performance that counts. This is just practice."

Whenever she gets pessimistic, it always throws me off-kilter a bit.

"Practice supposedly makes perfect."

Aria's face cracks and soft laughter spills from her lips as her face lights up, and I feel another section of my wall crumbling. The lilt of her laughter dances across my eardrums and I want to memorize the sound and store it there forever. I push open the door to the benches and she steps up. I follow after her, both of us sitting down next to one another as we wait for our next time to go back on the ice and run through our routine again. Aria folds her hands in her lap and her thigh presses against mine.

She leans into me, bumping me with her shoulder. "You know, you might not be so bad, after all, Wells."

Turning my head to her, my gaze meets hers as she continues to smile at me. "I wish I could say the same about you."

"You don't mean that," she says with another laugh as

she rolls her eyes. "Dare I say what I think might be the actual truth?"

I bite back a smirk. "Enlighten me."

"I think you're growing fond of me, Leo Wells."

I choke out a laugh and shake my head at her dismissively. "Don't get ahead of yourself, Reed. I promise that will never happen."

Aria simply chuckles to herself and turns to look out at the other pair as they move around the rink. She smiles to herself like she knows my secret. She knows that promise is a goddamn lie, and she's right. I have started to *tolerate* her company.

She's chipping away at my walls, but it will be a cold day in hell before I actually let her in.

CHAPTER TWELVE
ARIA

I stare at the woman at the front desk, a bit in disbelief, while also feeling the defeat settling in my bones. "Are you sure you don't have any other rooms available?" I'm trying my hardest to keep my voice as even as possible, though I feel like I'm on the verge of having a panic attack. I'm still exhausted from traveling and having to get right onto a strict skating schedule. It has me feeling a little emotional with my anxiety heightened. The thought of having to sleep in that freezing room again might be enough to send me over the edge.

After practice, Leo and I both came back here. I went to my room and discovered it was even colder than it was when I left this morning. It turns out, for whatever reason, it's stuck on air conditioning instead of heat, and as of right now, there is no immediate short-term fix. The only thing they could do was turn it off, but that did nothing to make it any warmer. If anything, it was just going to keep the cold temperature stable instead of having it go any lower. I came down to the front desk in the hope of being able to change to a different room, but it turns out that isn't an option for me now.

"I'm sorry, Miss Reed. Unfortunately, we are completely booked and have nothing open while you are here. If you would like, we could potentially issue a refund and you would be able to stay at a neighboring hotel."

A sigh escapes me and my shoulders hang heavily. I have two options. Either I ask for a refund, take all of my things from my room, and cross my fingers and toes that there is a hotel within walking distance that has a room available. Or, my other option is to stay in a freezing cold room. I don't have to be in the same place as the rest of the people from our team, but I don't like the idea of being in a foreign country staying away from everyone. It's not that I can't navigate and figure things out on my own, I just feel a little bit uncomfortable as it's not something I've ever done before. The thought alone is enough to trigger my anxiety.

My lips part and I'm about to just tell her I'll keep the room. I'll stay there and bundle up with extra clothing and blankets. I can make it work if I have to. I won't let this be the reason I have a breakdown right now. There are far more important things I need to be focusing on instead of having to sleep in a freezer.

"Aria."

The sound of his voice has my spine straightening as warmth spreads across my lower abdomen. It's an extremely conflicting feeling and I hate it. I turn around, my gaze finding his. His eyebrows are drawn together just a fraction. I don't know how long he's been standing there or what he has heard, but judging by the expression on his face, I think he's heard enough. His eyes soften as they search mine, his face visibly relaxing, but his expression becomes unreadable.

"Stay in my room with me."

My eyes widen as I stare at him for a moment. It takes a second for his words to sink in. "What? No, it's okay. I don't mind staying in mine."

He looks displeased and frowns while shaking his head as if he doesn't accept that as a response. "You can't stay in there. You know how bad it is for your muscles to be in a cold environment for a prolonged period of time." His nostrils flare as he lets out a deep breath and his tongue darts out to wet his lips. I find myself staring, watching him. Embarrassment creeps in and my cheeks grow hot.

He has a very valid point, though. Flexibility is a huge requirement for being able to do what we do. I need my muscles to be warm and soft and supple, not stiff and tight. The cold is good for cooling down, but not for a long amount of time.

"There's only one bed in your room."

I don't know why I say it, but I do. The words tumble from my lips and the heat blossoms down my neck. I know for a fact that there's only one bed in his room because I've been in there. There's a loveseat in the sitting area of his suite, but if I remember correctly, it didn't look that big last night. It would be fairly cramped to sleep on something like that, but at the same time, his room is warmer than mine. It's a better alternative. I'm small enough, I could curl up on it with no problem. It's really the most logical option...

"I think we know how to be adults, don't we?" he questions me as he tilts his head to the side, a sly smirk drifting across his lips. "Let's not make this more difficult than it needs to be. You come stay in my room and all of your problems are solved."

Wrong.

The only problem that isn't solved is getting Leo Wells out of my fucking head.

Sharing a room with him certainly isn't going to solve that.

"Fine, but I'm sleeping on the loveseat," I tell him, squaring my shoulders as I lift my chin. There's no way in hell I'm going to put myself in a situation where I'm stuck sharing a bed with him.

Leo chuckles and nods his head, as if he is telling his own little private joke in his head. "I don't care where you sleep, Ari. I just don't need my partner fucking up our entire routine because she was too stubborn and wanted to sleep in the Arctic tundra instead."

His words settle in my brain, creating a scenario that leaves me feeling uncomfortable. Losing isn't something I do and I will not be the reason this goes to shit. I'm not going to be the one who brings our team down. I know when to put my stubbornness aside and do things I might not want to do. We all have to make sacrifices in life, especially in this type of sport. It's not a foreign concept to me at all.

I turn back to face the woman at the front desk and smile at her as I decide my fate. "I'm going to stay in a room with a friend." Now, that felt foreign on my tongue. "I'll bring my keys down after I move my stuff from the room, if that's okay."

She smiles back at me. "Of course. Take your time and just return them whenever you're ready. That will actually be extremely helpful for us so we can get the thermostat fixed in the room."

Leaving the woman at her desk, I turn to face Leo who's watching me with a touch of amusement dancing in his eyes. We fall in step as we head toward the elevators. The doors of one of them slid open after Leo presses the button and we step inside, waiting as the doors close again. Leo swipes his card and pushes the number for our floor as he turns to look at me over his shoulder. He raises an eyebrow, the corners of his mouth twitching. "Did I hear you tell her you're staying with a friend?"

I level my gaze on his. "Don't push your luck, Wells. What was I supposed to tell her? I'm going to stay with my insufferable partner who I actually can't stand but I'm stuck being paired up with?"

"When you put it that way, it sounds like you mean the exact opposite of what you're saying."

I choke back my laugh, snorting as I cock my head to the side. My eyebrows pull together. "It sounds like you want it to be the opposite of what I said. Are you insinuating that you want to be my friend, Leo?"

A laugh rumbles in his chest just as the doors slide open. He winks and steps ahead of me, moving out into the hall. "I could never be your friend." I think I hear him mumble the words under his breath, but I can't be certain what he said exactly. I don't question him on it as Leo leads the way to my suite and pauses outside of the door, waiting for me. Rolling my eyes at him, I wave him to the side and he takes a step out of the way as I scan my key card and the lock clicks. I open the door and Leo pushes it open farther, holding it for me as I step inside.

"Jesus, you weren't lying about how cold it is in here," he muses out loud as he follows me into the main part of the suite. He glances at the thermostat that is on the wall in the small hallway. "It's fucking sixty degrees in here. This is absolute bullshit. How do they put someone in a room with a broken thermostat and expect you to stay in here for a week?"

I turn and give him a knowing look. "Calm down. I already agreed to sleep in your room."

He crosses his arms over his chest, mumbling something under his breath again as he walks across the room and stands by the window. His body is tense as he stares out at the city as I begin to pack my things. "Do you need any help?" he asks without looking at me.

"I'm fine, but thank you," I say softly as I start packing my stuff back into my bags. It's bad enough that I made the mistake of sleeping with him the first night we were here. I don't need him going through my underwear as I shove them into my suitcase. It's unfortunate that he's going to be stuck with me in his space now. I finish packing all my stuff and zip up the suitcase before I start to pull it off the bed. Leo doesn't interrupt but I can see the irritation written across his face as he watches me struggle to lift the heavy object. I told him I didn't need his help and I'm quite certain not helping is killing him.

As I grab my other two bags, Leo lets out the most exaggerated, exasperated sigh. "Can I please carry something for you?"

Turning my body, I face him head-on as I pull my bag over my shoulder. "I think I should be able to get it all myself."

"Aria," he groans, his voice low, almost like a warning. His eyelids fall shut, his chest rising as he inhales deeply and rakes a frustrated hand through his hair. "Please just let me get it."

"I don't need your help, Leo," I tell him as I try to brush off the irritation that laces inside me. He's done more than enough for me already. I grab my other bag and set it on top of my suitcase. Leo's brown eyes meet mine as I begin to walk in his direction and go to move around him. "I am perfectly capable of getting everything myself. I'm already imposing enough by coming to stay in your room, so please, just let me do this."

Leo reaches out, his hand grabbing my wrist as he pulls me around to look at him. "You are not imposing. I told you to come stay with me. I wouldn't have offered my room if I didn't want you in there."

His comment is a little unexpected. He made it clear

that last night was a one-night thing, and I'm fine with that. It's better if we keep things that way, even if I do catch myself thinking of him. It just confuses me, the fact that he offered his room because he wants me in there, not just to be nice. I swallow roughly. "Why would you want me in there?"

He slowly brushes his thumb back and forth along the underside of my wrist. His voice drops to an even softer tone, one that reaches deep inside me and soothes my soul. "Because then I don't have to worry about you."

I can't help myself as a soft laugh escapes me. Part of it is from the nervousness he awakens inside me, along with how caught off guard I am right now. I shake my head at him in disbelief. "Since when do you worry about what I'm doing?"

There's a significant shift in Leo. His body grows rigid and his hand drops my wrist. The muscle in his jaw tightens and he shakes his head as he fixes his lips into an indifferent smile. "I don't."

"Leo," I start, guilt instantly sliding through my veins as I see him becoming detached. He was being vulnerable with me and I fucking ruined it.

He doesn't even look at me as he directs his own gaze down to the floor. "Come on, let's go," he mutters as he takes my suitcase from me and begins to wheel it out of my room.

I follow after him, the guilt cloaking me as I give my room one more glance before following him out into the hall and down to his room. Leo's already there, but he doesn't bother to hold the door open for me. He has it propped open with the doorstop. I watch him as he lifts my suitcase into the air, the muscles in his arms rippling as he sets it down on the bed. He slowly turns, his face void of any emotion. His eyes meet mine for the briefest second. "There's room in the closet and half of the dresser is empty. You can take the bed, I'll sleep on the couch."

"Leo, stop," I call out as he moves past, careful not to brush against me. He walks three more steps, putting as much distance between us before finally turning back to face me. "Where are you going?"

He stares at me for a moment, like he's trying to decide what move he should make next. I watch as his shoulders fall ever so slightly. If I weren't studying him, if I didn't know the way his body moved, I would have missed it. A sigh escapes him, his body relaxing even more. "I'm going to go get dinner. Do you want to come with me?"

I want to, but I don't know if it's wise. Things are already getting blurry between the two of us. It feels like I'm staring at the rest of the world with my eyes open underwater. When I look at him, everything comes back into focus. I can see him clearly, while everything else appears muddled. This is a business arrangement. We aren't friends, and we'll certainly never be anything more than this. I can't live my life hanging on to the hope that lingers in his tone and his gaze. We gave in to our temptation and it isn't something that will ever blossom. There is no room between us for it to grow.

All there is, is tension and lingering gazes.

I shake my head at him. "Thanks for the offer, but I think I'm just going to order room service."

Leo nods, half rolling his eyes as he gives me a bored look like he doesn't care. "Order whatever you'd like, it will be charged to the room."

"I'll pay for whatever charges are incurred while I'm staying with you."

He stares at me for a moment, his lips parting like he's going to say something, but he doesn't. Instead, he clamps them shut and turns back around, walking directly to the door. As he pulls it open, he looks back at me one last time. "The other key is on the dresser if you go out. I'll be back sometime tonight."

I nod but don't say anything more to him. He doesn't need to tell me where he is going or when he'll be back. None of that concerns me. I turn back to the bed, listening as the door closes behind him, and he's suddenly gone. It feels strange being in his space, even if this isn't where he lives. This is still his home for the week while we're over here and I can't help but feel like I really have inserted myself where I don't belong.

Unzipping my suitcase, I begin to unpack my stuff and organize it all in the closet and the empty dresser drawers. I look around the room and notice how orderly Leo keeps everything. He doesn't have clothes lying on the floor and everything seems to have its own designated place in his suite. The bed is made and the room almost doesn't even seem like it's occupied by anyone. I step into the walk-in closet and find a place for all of my things before heading into the bathroom. I tuck my things inside the vanity cabinet and head back into the suite.

I stare at the bed for a second and frown as I head over

to the other closet. I can't sleep in Leo's bed and I'm not going to make him sleep on the couch. Pulling out the pillows and blankets, I carry them over to the loveseat before setting them down on top of it. It's not going to be a comfortable place to sleep, but not a single part of this is comfortable anymore.

Not only am I skating with my enemy, but now I'm sleeping with him...

Literally.

***

The evening passes quickly and I find myself starting to fall asleep on the couch as I watch some drama show that is on. The last time I looked at my phone, it was approaching midnight. The day has me feeling exhausted and struggling to keep my eyes open any longer. I haven't been waiting for Leo to come back, but I think subconsciously, that's why I haven't been able to fully fall asleep. I doze off and then wake up about twenty minutes later, only to find the suite still empty.

I shouldn't care where he is or when he'll be back, but I do.

I can't help but think the worst, that something bad happened to him. I could text him or call him, but I won't. It's not my place to do that. If he's not back when I wake up in the morning, then I'll let myself worry.

Nestling into the cushions of the couch, I pull the blanket up under my chin and get settled in. I make sure my alarm is set on my phone and turn to face the back of the loveseat. I'm relatively cramped, although it's not so terrible. It beats freezing and shivering until I finally fall asleep. Instead, I'm warm and comfortable enough that I let my eyelids fall shut and begin to finally succumb to sleep with the hope of being able to rest peacefully this time.

I don't know how long I'm asleep for when I feel the warmth of his arms sliding under my body. He smells like cedar and sandalwood and I let my head instinctively fall against his chest as I tuck in closer to him, reveling in his warmth. He rocks my body back and forth as he walks across the suite. I'm half asleep, although I could very well be dreaming. Leo's holding me in his arms tightly against his body as he begins to lower me down until I'm resting on the plush mattress of his bed.

"You're not supposed to be on the couch," he murmurs softly as he makes sure I'm settled on the pillows. He pulls the comforter up over my body, tucking me in as his lips gently press against my temple. Leo's fingertips brush against the side of my face and I can't help myself as I reach up and grab his hand. "You're awake," he whispers.

I shake my head, which isn't the truth nor is it a lie. "Stay."

"I am," he says quietly, almost as if he doesn't fully trust his voice. "I'll sleep on the couch."

"Stay," I repeat, my voice laced with sleep. "Sleep in the bed."

He's silent for a moment. "Are you sure?"

No, I'm not.

I nod as I try to pull him closer. Leo gives in and pushes back the blankets as I scoot toward the center of the bed. He crawls under the covers with me, instinctively wrapping his arms around me as he pulls me flush against him. I don't bother trying to stop myself as I melt against his side and nuzzle my face in his chest. Sleep is pulling me back under and I begin to drift off into the darkness as I hear his voice in the distance whispering against my hair.

"This is where you're supposed to be."

CHAPTER THIRTEEN
LEO

My alarm begins to ring from where it's sitting on my nightstand beside me. My body begins to stir awake and I groan as I realize just how exhausted I actually am. I wouldn't mind sleeping in for an extra few hours, but I don't have a choice. Our competition is in a few days. Now is crunch time. We need to get as much time on the ice as humanly possible.

My eyelids are heavy as I try to peel them open and begin to move to turn off my alarm. My arm is pinned to the bed and I turn my head to the side as her warmth registers in my mind. Aria is laying pressed against my side, her head resting in the crook of my arm as I hold her against me with my hand wrapped around her bicep.

Fuck.

I forgot she asked me to sleep with her last night. Instead of being strong and telling her no, I caved without a second thought. There was no hesitation.

"Aria," I say softly, attempting to wiggle my arm out from under her. "We have to get up."

She stirs in her sleep, mumbling something under her breath that doesn't make sense. Hell, I don't know if she's even speaking a language or if it was just gibberish. Instead of waking up or moving away from me, she rolls onto her other side, pressing her back against me. Her ass presses against my hip and I find myself cursing under my breath. My cock has a mind of its own and instantly grows hard at the contact.

"Aria," I say a little louder, this time pushing against her back with my other hand. I need to get out of this bed or we'll be spending the rest of the fucking day right here with me buried deep inside her. "Get up."

I don't know if this is typical for her or what, but she's sleeping like the damned dead. If she wouldn't have made any movements or noises, I would have been checking to see if she was breathing. I'm a bit annoyed as I stare at her and it's such a contradiction. She looks perfect and peaceful. I want to wrap my arms around her and fall back asleep with her. My cock wants me to wake her up and slide inside her. I know neither of those are viable options and I also know what is riding on our performance. We both have to get up and go skate instead.

My alarm is still going off in the background and it feels like it's becoming even louder. I try one last time, giving Aria a gentle shake, but even that doesn't wake her up. I let out a deep breath and finally just pull my arm out from under her, completely jostling her on the bed. Her eyelids fly open and she gives me a look of bewilderment as she abruptly sits up with me. I grab my phone and turn off the alarm.

"What the hell?"

I look at Aria over my shoulder. "Time to wake up."

"You couldn't have been a little nicer about it?" she questions me with sleep and irritation in her tone. I can see she's going to be a joy this morning.

I get up from the bed and walk over to open the curtains. As I pull them back, I half expect her to hiss at me like a vampire. Instead, she groans and squints her eyes. "Maybe if you didn't sleep like the dead and would have woken up one of the three other times I tried, it would have been a more peaceful wake-up."

"You're a dick."

She never struck me as someone who wasn't a morning person since she always seemed pleasant at the rink in the mornings. I'd never seen her when she first woke up before today, though.

I roll my eyes as I grab the clothes she had laid out last night. "And you're annoying." I toss the pile onto the bed in front of her. "Get up."

Aria huffs but doesn't say anything else as I grab my things and head into the bathroom. I take my time using the restroom and brushing my teeth before I get dressed. I pull my hoodie over my head and give myself a once-over in the mirror before opening the door again. I find Aria already dressed, wearing a pair of black skating pants and a cream-colored sweater that hangs off one shoulder.

Standing in the doorway, I watch her for a moment as she finishes making the bed. I didn't ask her to do it, but I can't help but feel a sense of appreciation for her doing something as small and insignificant as that.

She fluffs the last down feather pillow and sets it in place beside the matching one. She slowly turns around to face me and lifts her arms to cross them over her chest. "Are you finally done in the bathroom?"

I smile brightly at her, stepping to the side as I wave my arm in the direction of the restroom. It isn't often that we trade roles where she's the one who is being grumpy and I'm being the bright and cheery person.

"It's all yours."

Aria walks past me and closes the door behind herself after she enters the bathroom. Leaving her to do whatever she needs in there, I move through the suite over to the small kitchen area. I open the fridge and reach inside for two water bottles for Aria and I. I pull one of the bananas from the bunch and peel it open and lean against the counter as I wait for her. When she finally emerges, she looks a little more alive than she did when she walked in there. She walks over to me and I wordlessly hand her a bottle of water. She leans forward, her chest brushing against me as she gets a banana for herself. I watch her as she peels it open and slides it between her lips. She carefully chews a mouthful of the fruit before swallowing.

"Do you always watch people?"

No, just you.

"Do you always wake up in a bad mood?" I counter, ignoring her question.

She narrows her eyes on me. "It's all dependent upon how I wake up and who I wake up with."

I can't help myself as I smile at her. She's fucking feisty and I can't help but love it when she's like this. I like when she claps back without any hesitation. Her words should sting, but they don't. She can wake up with whoever she wants to. I don't care about her past and there's no reason for me to be jealous of any man who comes after me.

I had her first.

The thought of Griffin pricks the back of my mind. It's like lighter fluid, spreading through my veins. My spine stiffens and I struggle to push the thought of him and her together from my brain.

"We should get going," she reminds me, breaking through my thoughts. "We don't want to be late."

I can't argue with her as we both finish our bananas and toss the peels into the trash can. Aria grabs her skating bag that is sitting next to mine by the front door and I follow suit. We step out into the hallway in silence, both of us wheeling our bags along with us. Aria walks over to the elevator and I step up beside her as we wait for the car to get to our floor. When the doors slide open, she steps in and I move into the space with her.

The scent of her perfume infiltrates my senses and I can't help myself as I inhale. I love the smell of her, but I loved the smell of her sleeping next to me even more. Last night, I tried to stay away from her. I went out to the damn bar and had only one drink. I sat there for God knows how long until I finally gave in and came back to the room. There was a part of me that was trying hard to avoid coming back because I needed the space. She's clouding my thoughts. I'm finding myself caring about things I normally don't give a shit about.

I shouldn't care about whether or not Aria Reed has fresh fucking towels and that her fucking pillows are fluffed.

Inviting her to stay in my room was a terrible decision. I should have just let her sleep in her own room instead.

***

The next couple of days go the same way as the first night Aria was in my room. We wake up and argue, go to the rink, and skate for hours on end, head back to the hotel room to shower, and go our separate ways after that. Aria's always back in the room before me and I make it a point to stay out until after she's asleep. If we're not in there together, there's no way I can fuck up and end up fucking her again.

It's the same each night. I find her sleeping on the damn couch and I carry her to bed, only to crawl in under the covers beside her.

We don't talk about it.

There's *nothing* to talk about.

The day we've been waiting for is finally upon us. I roll over in bed and see that Aria is already up and moving around. Actually, she's nowhere to be found, but the bathroom door is shut and I can see the glow of the light underneath the door. We go on the ice earlier in the day today and I'm secretly glad. I hate having to wait until late in the evening or even into the night. I would much rather get it done and over with so I don't have to feel like I'm going to die from the anxiety.

I hear something on the other side of the door and it sounds like Aria is in there throwing up. Worry washes over me and I quickly get up from bed and go knock on the door. If she's sick, that could derail everything. As fucked up as it is, unless you're in the hospital on your death bed, you have no choice but to get your shit together and skate through illness in a situation like this. This is one of the most important competitions of the year for us. This is the one that is the final determination of who competes at Worlds.

"Are you okay?" I ask Aria, keeping my voice soft as I stand on the other side of the door.

I hear the toilet flush and her moving around inside there. "I'm good."

Deciding not to push her, I linger for a moment longer as I hear the water running in the sink, followed by the sound of the shower turning on. It's not my place to probe and dig to try and figure out if she's okay. Aria's a big girl, she's been through this countless times before. That thought doesn't stop me from ducking out into the hallway. I find myself walking to the vending machines as I press the buttons for a ginger ale and a pack of crackers. It's the least I can do to help and support her if she isn't feeling well.

She's still in the shower when I get back to the room, so I patiently wait, opting to make sure all my clothing is ready to go and everything we need to take is ready. I end up lying back in bed, scrolling on my phone as I wait for

Aria to come out. When she finally emerges from the bathroom, steam billows from the door and she steps out wearing nothing but a towel. Her hair is pulled back in a tight bun on the top of her head and her face is freshly washed and free of any makeup.

I slowly climb out of bed, grabbing the pack of crackers and soda as I walk over to her. I hold it out for her as she sets her makeup bag down on the vanity by the closet.

"What's this?" she asks me as she takes them from me, a quizzical look on her face as her eyes meet mine.

Suddenly, I feel fucking nervous under her gaze. *What the hell?* I shift my weight on my feet and shrug. "I got these in case you weren't feeling well. I thought maybe it would help?"

A slow, gentle smile creeps across her lips as she looks up at me. "Thanks, Leo. I really appreciate it," she tells me as she tears open the pack of crackers and pulls one out. "It's my anxiety. It happens most mornings of early competitions. These always help, though."

"You're welcome." I stand awkwardly in front of her for a second, like I've forgotten how to speak or move or do anything normal. I'm trying really fucking hard not to look at her wearing nothing but a towel while also trying to cover my stupid boner. "I'm going to go take a shower."

Aria laughs softly and I savor the sound against my eardrums as I step into the bathroom and shut the door behind me. I turn on the shower, setting the temperature of the water to as hot as it will go as I strip out of my clothes and discard them on the floor by the bathroom door. Pulling open the glass door, I step into the shower and directly into the burning spray. It's hot on my skin and rolls down my back as I close my eyes and inhale deeply. Steam still lingers in the room from Aria and it grows thicker from the heat pouring out of the showerhead.

I quickly wash my hair and body, scrubbing at my skin like I'm trying to wash away my thoughts of Aria in a towel. I've seen her naked, I've seen her in a robe, I've seen her fully clothed. It doesn't matter what she's wearing—she has my fucking attention regardless. I may never get to touch her again, but that doesn't mean I'm not going to imagine the things I would do to her if I could.

My cock is still as hard as a rock as I think about pulling down the top of her towel and watching it tumble to the ground, pooling around her feet before she takes a step toward me. Wrapping my hand around myself, I grip my length and slowly begin to stroke up and down. My eyelids fall shut and I picture her stepping into the shower with me instead. Her hair falls in waves down to the middle of her back. She steps closer, lifting her arms to wrap them around the back of my neck as she presses her body against mine.

The hot water falls down her taut body. My hand grips her waist as the other pulls her head back with a fistful of her hair. My lips find hers in a haste and I kiss her deeply before she pulls away from me. Her movements are deliberately slow and teasing as she makes her way down my torso until she's on her knees in front of me. She wraps her hand around the base of my cock and her lips around the tip. I groan, my hand gripping the back of her head as she inhales me. Her tongue feels like silk as it slides against the underside of my cock. She takes me deep in her mouth, gagging around my length as I hit the back of her throat.

She looks up at me, her eyes glistening, her lips plump and wet around the girth of my dick as she starts to bob her head. She pulls me in and out of her mouth, sucking as I begin to move my hips. She holds on to me as I begin to fuck her face, moving in tandem with her.

"Fuck, Aria," I moan, her name tumbling from my lips as I tilt my head back. Her mouth is warm and wet and I imagine this is exactly what heaven feels like.

I grip her hair even tighter as my hips buck. Warmth builds in the pit of my stomach. My balls constrict, drawing closer to my body as I get closer to coming. Aria continues to suck my cock, moving her head back and forth as she continues to stroke my length with her mouth. Her plump lips suction tighter around me and that's all it takes to send me soaring over the edge. The warmth begins to spread across my abdomen, spilling into my veins as it spreads through my body like wildfire.

Thrusting into her mouth again, my orgasm tears through me, lighting my body on fire. She keeps bobbing her head, swallowing every spurt of cum that I shoot into the back of her throat. I'm riding the ultimate high as I lift my head and open my eyes to look down at her.

Reality comes crashing down around me when I realize I'm standing in the shower alone. Aria isn't in front of me on her knees with my cock down her throat. It's my hand wrapped around my length, not her lips. Cum drips from the tip of my cock onto the tile floor and I see the rest of it across the shower wall instead of in her mouth.

I just jerked off to the thought of her while she's literally on the other side of the door. I just came, yet I feel more tension than I did before I started stroking myself.

Water streams down my face as I let out a frustrated sigh and let go of my cock.

I need to get her out of my head... and out of my bed.

CHAPTER FOURTEEN
ARIA

My stomach is in knots as Leo and I stand on the other side of the glass and watch the pair before us finishing up their routine. They were both decent skaters and they scored high on the technical side, but their routine comes nowhere close to how good ours is. All we need to do is make sure we execute every move perfectly and we should be taking home gold.

The palms of my hands are sweaty and I wipe them on the hand towel hanging from the pocket of my warm-up coat. Leo looks over at me, a touch of concern laced within his expression.

"Are you okay?" he asks me softly. His voice is like a warm embrace that I want to bury myself in. "Are you going to get sick again?"

I shake my head, half smiling at him. "That's just a one-and-done thing in the mornings of important competitions. It doesn't always happen." I pause and look back out at the ice as their routine ends. "I'm just ready to get out there."

The score for the pair ahead of us is announced as they come off the ice. My stomach rolls and anticipation builds inside me. There's a touch of anxiousness that mixes with the adrenaline in my veins, but I ignore it. My chest rises and falls as I suck in a deep breath and let it out.

Leo reaches out and takes my hand in his own before giving me a gentle, reassuring squeeze. "It's our time."

I look over at my partner, squeezing his hand in response before he lets go of me. He looks back out at the ice and I allow myself a moment to really look at him. My eyes start at his black skates, trailing up the length of his legs and his torso. He's wearing black pants with a black dress shirt tucked in. His sleeves are unbuttoned and rolled up, stopping just before his elbows. He looks good —really good.

Leo glances back at me as he brushes a lock of his hair away from his forehead. Hues of golden brown shine brightly in his eyes as he winks at me. I shrug out of my jacket and hand it to Alanna before falling in step with Leo. He walks over to the door and steps out of the way for me to get on the ice first. My gray chiffon skirt flows around the backs of my calves as I skate to the center of the arena and come to a stop.

As soon as I'm on the ice, the anxiety I was feeling completely dissipates. The lights cut out momentarily and Leo skates up behind me. I lean back, melting into him as he slides his arms under my armpits. Both of his hands find the sides of my head and he tilts my chin up to the ceiling so the crown of my head presses against his firm chest. My eyelids flutter shut as my heart pounds erratically against my rib cage. The soft sound of the music begins to play and I feel Leo's breath against my ear.

"As close to perfect," he murmurs the reminder as the lights flash on, illuminating our bodies and the ice around our feet. "I promise I won't let you fall."

We begin our performance, skating together flawlessly. We've been through this routine countless times, we know exactly what we need to do. Leo moves with me, both of us skating in rhythm together. It's harmonic and beautiful, even if every move has to be so precise and technical. We don't miss a single beat as we both spin in the air, our skates hitting the ice at the same time in our landings.

Confidence rolls off Leo, cloaking me as I begin to feel it too. My legs feel strong and stable. I'm centered and grounded. He helps to create that inside me. His hands grip my hips as we begin to skate backward together, my feet crossing over one another. He's calm and steady, strong and solid. I trust him with every part of me. I know he won't let me fall and he'll catch me before I hit the ice. With Leo, I feel completely safe. He will always protect me.

He bends his knees before springing upward, lifting me into the air before I launch higher up and out of his grip. I close my eyes, spinning in three rotations through the air before gravity begins to pull me back down to the ice. Leo catches me, his hands grabbing my hips again before he lowers me down onto the ice while he's still moving.

It all happens so fast that I don't feel like I even have time to process what's happening. It's complete muscle memory and from us practicing the movements repeatedly. Leo is completely effortless in the way he carefully helps me back to my feet while he's still moving around the rink.

We continue through the rest of our routine, going through another jump where he throws me into the air and instead of catching me, I land on the ice myself. There's a fluidity to the way we move together, yet there's a push and pull, a subtle tension that's stretching between us. It's like a rubber band. He pushes and I pull; I push and he pulls. In the end, we end up coming back together, melting into one another in the center of the rink as the music trails off and the light cuts off once more.

We're both completely breathless and Leo helps me stand upright. There's a pause before the lights flicker on. One passing moment, where he's standing in front of me, his breath fanning across my face as his hands reach up to cup my cheeks. My eyelids flutter closed as I anticipate the feeling of his lips caressing mine before the lights flash on, illuminating the entire arena. A loud applause erupts from the crowd, echoing throughout the entire building.

My stomach flips and my eyes quickly open as I find Leo still staring down at me. His nostrils flare, his throat bobbing as he swallows roughly before he pulls away from me. His hand drops down to mine and we face one side of the arena as he bows and I curtsey. We repeat the same action to all four sides of the stadium before we begin to skate to the exit together. Leo steps through the door first, his hand still in mine as he leads me out.

We head over to the bench where Coach Kincaid and Coach Davis are both waiting for us. The four of us sit down with Leo and I sandwiched in between them. His hand only leaves mine for a second as he drapes my coat over my shoulders and then slides his fingers through mine again.

"You two looked amazing," Eva says with so much excitement in her voice. "Seriously, such a beautiful performance."

Luca nods as he hands me a water bottle. "I had chills watching the two of you." He pauses for a moment and chuckles. I twist the lid of the bottle and put it to my lips to take a sip. "I was almost waiting for you two to kiss afterward."

I choke on my mouthful of water and Leo clears his throat as the tension grows thicker. I start to cough, drawing attention to myself as my eyes begin to water. *Way to play it cool, Aria.*

"Are you okay?" Eva asks me with a touch of concern in her voice.

I finally get my shit together and wipe the tears from my face. "I'm good," I tell her in a hoarse voice. Leo chuckles under his breath and I see him shaking his head in amusement from the corner of my eye. I resist the urge to drive my elbow into his ribs and focus my attention back on the ice.

The judges announce our score right before the next two skaters enter the rink. We're currently sitting in first place and have enough of a lead that it should be difficult for anyone else to have a better score than us. The four of us sit in silence as we watch the last four pairs go through their own performances before it's time for them to announce the winners from our group. The day is going to be filled with different skating events, but the pairs were scheduled first, so by the time the winners are announced, it's already close to lunchtime.

"You guys did it," Coach Kincaid says with a smile on his face as he claps his hand over Leo's shoulder. He and Eva both stand up, Leo and I following suit.

Leo squeezes my hand lightly and I look up at him as a soft smile touches his lips. My heart begins to pound harder in my chest. Based on the scores, we were sitting in first place for the gold medal, but I didn't let it fully sink in until it was announced. Not until after we were on the ice with our medals would I feel like we actually won.

The announcer works through bronze and silver before there's a pregnant pause over the speaker. Leo and I stand by the door, the coldness radiating from the ice as it slides up my legs. My heart pounds erratically and I hear the sound of it in my ears. I've never been more aware of my own heartbeat than I am at this moment. Leo's palm is warm and comforting against mine. I don't realize it, but my knuckles are turning white by how tightly I'm holding on to him.

"And our gold medal pair, Aria Reed and Leo Wells!"

I turn to look at Leo, the shock written across my expression even though there wasn't a chance we weren't going to win gold. "Oh my god, we did it."

"Yes, we did." He smiles at me, nodding. "I told you we would."

"Oh my god." I can't help myself as I let go of his arm and wrap my arms around the back of his neck. Leo's hands find my waist and he lifts me into the air as we embrace one another. I bury my face against the crook of his neck, inhaling the scent of him as I feel his skin against mine. He feels right, like this is where I belong. The world around us fades for a moment and the only thing that matters is the way it feels to be in his arms.

He holds on to me for a moment longer before he lowers me to my feet and presses his soft lips against my forehead. "Come on, tiny dancer," he says softly as his hand drops down to mine.

I let him lead me onto the ice and our feet move in sync as we skate to the center. A woman stands next to the announcer and she hands me a huge bouquet of flowers. I hold them in my arms, watching Leo as he ducks his head and she slides the medal down over his neck. I do the same, feeling the weight of it as it hangs down between my breasts. Leo's still holding my hand that isn't supporting the flowers and he looks down at me and smiles.

The crowd around us claps loudly, but the sounds and the sights around us don't exist in this moment. Time is suspended. All I can see are Leo's golden brown eyes as they shine down on me. I never want to step outside of this light. I want to live here forever, with his hand in mine, everyone going crazy around us.

We take our time, bowing and curtseying around the

arena before we exit once again. Our entire team is there when we get off the ice and Leo and I are pulled away. The girls all surround me, fawning over the flowers and the medal. The air is filled with nothing but congratulations and I can't help myself as happy tears spring to my eyes. Today's been filled with stress and emotion. When the relief finally hits and the weight is lifted, it's hard not to feel emotional. I wipe my tears away as Eva and Alanna both hug me.

Eva links her arm through mine and she starts to pull me in the direction of the locker rooms. "We need to go celebrate."

"Oooh, yes, champagne please," Alanna says from where she's walking ahead of us.

I glance over my shoulder once, catching Leo's gaze as he stands with Coach Kincaid and a few of the guys. A soft smile sits on his lips, but it isn't as wide and as bright as it was before. There's a longing dancing in his eyes, but he doesn't call out for me. He simply watches as I'm pulled in the opposite direction of him.

And fuck me for wanting to turn around and run back into his arms.

CHAPTER FIFTEEN
LEO

Sitting at the bar, I stare straight ahead, my eyes scanning the bottles lining the shelves. Luca is sitting beside me, but he's lost in conversation with Alanna. I haven't seen Aria since we got our medals earlier. When I finally made my way back to the hotel to shower and change, she had already been there and left before I arrived. That was hours ago now. I ended up getting dinner with a few of our teammates and then we wandered into a pub down the street. I have only had a total of two drinks all night and the one in my hand has watered down from the ice that melted in it about an hour ago.

Pulling my wallet from my pocket, I take out some cash and leave it on the bar as I begin to rise from my seat. I leave the glass with the watered-down liquor and turn to face Luca. He glances over at me, a little perplexed.

"I think I'm going to head back," I tell him as I fake a yawn. Our flight home isn't until early in the afternoon tomorrow, but I still haven't packed any of my things yet. My body was tired from the toll of the stress this morning. It's only nine o'clock at night and my mind is still running rampant. I don't want to drink the thoughts away. There's only one person I feel like entertaining, but she's not here.

And finding her isn't an option.

Luca nods and smiles at me. "Sounds good, man. See you tomorrow."

"Good night, Leo," Alanna says with a matching smile, her face relaxed from the alcohol in her system. I think everyone felt like they could finally breathe after the competition, but as soon as we get back home, we're going to be thrown right back into the cycle.

I leave the two of them in the pub and walk out onto the sidewalk. There's a steady stream of people trickling along the storefronts. I walk past couples and groups of people, tuning out their conversations as I focus on their faces instead. I can't help myself as I scan the crowd, my eyes searching every person's face, hoping that it ends up colliding with her gaze.

She's everywhere I look, yet she isn't here at all.

My chest feels heavy, like there's a vine snaking around my rib cage before it begins to constrict, wrapping tightly around me. In a way, it feels like I can't breathe, even though my body is having no trouble drawing oxygen from the air. The glass doors of the hotel slide open and I step inside. As I walk into the lobby, it's relatively empty, but there's a lot of noise coming from the bar tucked away in the left corner. I let my gaze drift over there as I begin to make my way in that direction.

There's a group of people crowded around the bar and a handful of other patrons throughout the small space, some occupying tables and some standing and talking. I look at the group by the bar and as soon as I see her black hair, I can't help but inhale deeply.

It feels like I can breathe.

Aria smiles brightly, laughter spilling from her lips. She doesn't see me, so I move closer but keep enough distance to not be noticed. She's wearing a pair of black flared leggings and a dark gray sweater that hangs off her left shoulder. Her midnight hair is pulled back in a high ponytail and the locks are wavy and long, hanging down her back. I stop by a high-top table and lean against it, finally looking at the entire group of people. And then I see who Aria is smiling at... and it's not one of the girls from our team that she disappeared with earlier. It's some guy that I've never seen before.

My blood instantly boils, but I don't intervene. Aria is allowed to make her own decisions. I didn't stake my claim. Hell, I don't even like her like that. I don't give a shit what she does or who she does it with. My jaw tightens as I watch him hand her a shot. She raises it in the air and taps it against his before she lifts it to her lips. As she tips her head, the ends of her hair dance across her back. Her throat moves in a delicate motion as she swallows the liquid.

Flames of irritation lick at my veins. Abandoning the table I'm standing at, I stride over to the bar, positioning myself a few seats away from Aria. She still doesn't notice me and I order a drink. I wasn't planning on getting drunk, but fuck. The bartender pours me a shot of bourbon and I down it in one gulp, not bothering to savor how the expensive liquor tastes. I can hear the sound of Aria's voice drifting past the two people separating us.

I hear her laughter as I down another shot. I hang on to the sound of it, analyzing it. She sounds happy, she looks happy, but there's something off in the way she's laughing. It's a little more high pitched than normal. It's something most people wouldn't notice. There's a hint of nervousness laced within the sound.

"Don't do that," she says to the guy in front of her, although I didn't see what he did or if he said anything to her first. I turn my head to the side, leaning back in my seat as I watch the interaction between the two of them. Aria's back is now to the bar and it looks like she's trying to step away from him as he closes in on her. "Stop. I already told you no."

Instantly I'm on my feet, closing the distance between us. Aria and her friend don't see me coming as I reach for him. My hands land on his shoulders and my fingers dig into his flesh as I haul him away from her. Aria's eyes are wide as they meet mine and her jaw falls open.

"What the fu—" the guy starts to say as I spin him around to face me. I cut him off before he can get the last word out as I move my hands to grip the front of his shirt.

I shake my head at him as my free hand curls into a fist. She told him no and he couldn't respect her. What if I wasn't here to stop him? This man is a total stranger. Who knows what he would have done with her or to her that she didn't consent to. "You should have listened to her when she told you to stop."

His mouth falls open to argue, but I silence him before he even gets the chance to speak a single word. I pull my arm back before driving my knuckles directly into the side of his jaw. His head whips to the right and the sound alone has everyone looking at us. Aria gasps loudly and the guy stumbles backward when I release the front of his shirt and shove him with my other hand.

His hands fly up to cover his face as blood begins to drip from his lips. His eyes are wild as he turns his head to the side and looks at me. My chest heaves, rising and falling with every shallow breath I take as my heart runs wild from the adrenaline. The guy drops his hands, forming his own fists before he comes charging at me. I try to duck out of the way, but he collides into me. I regain my footing, grabbing onto him just as his fist connects with my mouth. Pain erupts in my face and I instantly taste blood on my tongue.

"You should have minded your own fucking business," the guy barks at me as he tries to throw another punch but he isn't quick enough. I block him with my forearm before driving my other fist into the side of his ribs. The air leaves his lungs in a rush and he coughs as he goes to lean forward.

I'm not even thinking as I grab him, hauling him back up before punching him in the face again. "She *is* my fucking business."

He lifts his hands to shield his face and he still can't catch his breath after I knocked the wind from his lungs. I don't register her hands at first, but her voice is what breaks through the blind rage I'm in.

"Leo, stop."

I release the guy, giving him a shove for good measure as he stumbles back into the bar again. He falls forward, struggling to catch his breath. Ignoring him, since I know he can't do anything to me now, I turn around to face Aria. Worry is written across her facial expression and she stares up at me with her eyes damp. Her gaze falls down to my mouth and back to my eyes. My lip is cut open and blood is smeared across my chin. My breathing is erratic and my heart is thrumming away in my chest.

"We should probably go," she says quietly, not bothering to look at anyone around us as she pulls me toward her. Her hand finds mine and her fingers lace with my own as she leads me away. "Come with me."

She doesn't have to say anything more than that.

Her movements are quick as she pulls me out of the bar. No one follows after us and we walk in silence over to the elevator before getting inside. Aria scans her key card and pushes the button for our floor as the doors shut. I don't know if I'll end up getting in trouble for what happened, but hopefully not. Losing my shit on a stranger in a public place doesn't exactly look good for me. I stare straight ahead at the doors, still trying to calm myself down from the thought of that man doing something to Aria that she didn't want.

My mind barely registers when the elevator dings and the doors slide open. Aria's hand is soft against mine and she pulls me with her out into the hall. We're halfway to our room when I pull her to a stop. She spins around to face me, her eyes desperately searching mine.

"What's wrong?"

I swallow roughly, my fingers still laced with hers as I stare down into the depths of her gray eyes. My jaw tenses for a moment before I release the muscle. "Did he touch you?"

She pulls her lips between her teeth, wetting them. She blinks and shakes her head. "No. He was trying to, but you stopped him."

I close my eyes for three breaths. My nostrils flare as I inhale deeply and exhale. I'm relieved that he didn't do anything and I was able to stop him before he did. That still doesn't erase the thoughts of him already disrespecting her when she told him not to do it. The thought of someone hurting Aria has me seeing red. Blood red. That man's blood painted all over the wood floor of the bar.

"Come on," she says quietly as she pulls on my hand. I open my eyes and look down at her as my breathing slows to an even pace. She nods her head in the direction of the hotel room, her ponytail bobbing with the movement. I let her lead me down the hall and we pause for a second outside as she holds her card to the keypad. The light flickers green and it beeps as the door unlocks.

Aria turns the handle and I push open the door, my hand meeting the solid wood above her head. I hold it open for her, letting it fall shut behind me as I step inside after her. I watch her for a second as she disappears into the bathroom and I turn back to lock the door. I walk over to the bathroom, stopping just inside the doorway as I see her at the sink running a washcloth under the water.

She lifts her head, her gaze meeting mine in the mirror as I stand behind her. Her eyes don't leave mine as she finishes wetting the washcloth and turns off the water. Spinning on her heel, she turns to face me. "Come sit," she instructs, pointing to the edge of the bathtub.

I obey without any hesitation. I step into the bathroom and drop down onto the edge as she moves closer to me. She lowers herself down between my spread thighs until she's on her knees in front of me. I had imagined her like this before, except the circumstances were a little different. The way I imagined it she had my cock in her mouth instead of her cleaning blood from my face.

Her touch is gentle as she slides the washcloth against my skin. She wipes the blood from my chin and below my lip before she makes her way to where it is split open. Her eyes are on my mouth as she begins to blot it against my swollen lip. "You know, I never asked how your shower was this morning."

I resist the urge to tilt my head to the side as I raise an eyebrow. "It was good. Why do you ask?"

"I heard you in there."

My heart skips a beat in my chest as I replay my early morning shower. The same shower that I stroked my cock to the thought of her and came all over the wall. "What do you think it is that you heard?"

She stops for a second, a fire burning in her eyes as she looks at me. "I heard you moaning my name."

Fuck.

My cock is hard at the thought alone and the memory plays out in my mind again. Aria presses the washcloth against my lip again. I let her linger for a second before I reach for her. My fingers wrap around her wrist and I slowly pull her away from my mouth. "Did you like listening to me come?" I ask her softly as I take the washcloth from her hand and drop it onto the floor. Cupping her chin, I tilt her head back as I run my thumb over her perfect bottom lip. I simultaneously run my tongue along the cut in mine. "Did you like knowing I was fucking my hand thinking about you?"

Her breath hitches. "I did," she admits as her hands fall onto my lap. She spreads her fingers on my thighs, gripping them through my pants. "I want to hear it again, but this time, I want to be the one making you come."

Jesus fuck, the mouth on her.

"First, I want to fuck that pretty mouth of yours."

Aria rocks back onto the balls of her feet, the fire burning with intensity in her irises. "Be a good boy and stand up and take out your cock."

I waste no time as I rise to my feet and do what she says. I unbutton my pants and slide down the zipper as Aria lifts herself up on her knees. Her hands reach for me as soon as I push my pants and boxer briefs down. Her palm is warm and soft as she wraps it around the base of my cock before wrapping her lips around the tip. A groan rumbles in my chest and I instantly tip my head back as my hand grips the top of her head. She inhales me, taking as much of my length in her mouth as she can before it's too much.

She begins to move, pumping her hand as she bobs her head back and forth. She tightens her lips around my cock as she pulls me in and out, fucking me with her mouth. The real thing is so much better than what I imagined. Her mouth is warm and wet, her tongue soft like silk as it slides along the underside of my dick. I could die now and I would die the happiest man on the fucking planet. I lift my head to look at her, watching my cock slide in and out.

"Look at how fucking sexy you look with my cock shoved down your throat."

Aria smiles around me as she begins to move faster. She doesn't stop as she takes my cock in deeper every time until I'm hitting the back of her throat. She gags, but she quickly recovers and doesn't let it deter her. I can't help myself as my hips start to buck. I hold her head, guiding her as I meet her with my own thrusts. I'm fucking her face while she's fucking me. A warmth builds inside me before I combust without warning. It spills over into my veins, running rampant through my system, as my orgasm takes over my entire body.

"Fuck, Aria," I moan as I spill my cum into her mouth. My head falls back and my entire body is a blazing fire of pure ecstasy. "That's it, baby," I murmur as I look at her again, my orgasm still tearing through me. "Suck me until there's nothing left."

Her head bobs a few more times, milking me dry. My body's humming and my cock is tingling as she slowly pulls back, releasing me. I straighten my head and look at her as she rises to her feet. She grabs the hem of her sweater and pulls it up over her head before she drops it onto the floor. My gaze is locked on hers as she unhooks her bra and lets that fall to the ground. Her hands slide beneath the waistband of her pants and she pushes them down her thighs, dragging her panties with them until they're pooling around her feet.

My cock is instantly hard again.

Aria stands back upright and she turns away from me as she walks to the door of the bathroom. My eyes follow the curves of her body, watching the way her ass moves as she walks. She stops, looking back over her shoulder as her gaze meets mine with mischief dancing in her eyes.

"Now you owe me."

CHAPTER SIXTEEN
ARIA

As I walk over toward the bed, I hear the sound of Leo following behind me. A smile lifts my lips and my heart skips a beat as it begins to pump faster. Adrenaline floods me and I spin around to face him as I stop by the side of the bed. He's right there, entering my space as he pulls his shirt up over his head and tosses it onto the floor. My gaze drops down to his mouth and I watch his lips part, expecting him to say something, but he doesn't. He closes the small amount of space between us, his hand sliding through my hair as he grips the back of my head, claiming my mouth with his own.

His other hand drops down to my ass and he inches me closer to the bed. His lips don't leave mine and the backs of my legs press against the side of the mattress. He tastes like regret and I relish it. I know there will be the inevitable walk of shame afterward, but for a little while, I want to pretend like that doesn't exist. I want to pretend like being with him is where I'm supposed to be.

Leo's tongue is soft like silk as it tangles with mine. He's slowly devouring me, like a predator feasting on its prey. What Leo doesn't realize is we are one and the same. He's my prey while I'm simultaneously his. If he didn't want me, his mouth wouldn't be melting with mine and he wouldn't be pushing me down onto the mattress.

I'm completely naked, sprawled out on my back on the bed. Leo hovers over me for a second before he pushes off the mattress. I lift my head, watching him as he strips out of his boxers and pants and discards them on the floor. Now we're equal.

Leo moves back to me, his hands pushing my knees farther apart as he lowers himself onto the bed and settles between my legs. Moisture pools between my thighs. Leo pauses for a second, pulling away as he spits into his hand and strokes his cock three times to get it wet. He looks down at me, the tip of his dick pressing against my center.

"Is this what you want, pretty girl? Is this going to wash away my debts?"

I stare at him for a moment, absentmindedly reaching up and trailing my fingertips over the chiseled planes of his torso. "Only if this is what you want."

A deep groan rumbles in his chest. "I want nothing more than to sink deep inside you." His eyes are on mine, the flames burning brightly in his irises as he begins to push the head of his dick inside me. My body stretches around his length, accepting him. I lift my arms, sliding my fingers through his hair as I grip the back of his head. Applying a subtle pressure, I pull him closer to me.

He shifts his hips, sinking deeper inside me, filling me

completely. My lips part and a soft moan escapes me. Leo's mouth instantly crashes into mine and he swallows every sound that leaves me. He draws the oxygen from my lungs, breathing me in. Consuming me. Instinctively, I lift my legs to wrap them around his waist as I pull him as close as I can. He thrusts into me and our mouths melt together.

Shifting his hips, he pulls out slightly, just leaving the tip inside before he slams back into me again. We break apart, both of us coming up for air as pleasure ripples through my body. My hands drop down to his shoulders. My nails bite into his flesh as I cry out in unadulterated ecstasy.

"Jesus Christ, Aria," he murmurs against my lips before he slides his tongue along the seam. "I could fuck you forever."

His hands move away from my hips and slide down to my ass. He shifts onto his knees while simultaneously lifting me up. It creates an angle that gives him deeper access. Thrusting again, he fills me to the fucking brim. It's a tight fit, but he feels like he was made for me.

"I hate you, Leo," I moan, my back arching as his balls smack against me and he starts to fuck me harder. "I hate the way you make me feel. I hate *that* you make me feel."

"Yeah?" he murmurs, nipping at my bottom lip. He pulls his hips back and slams into me with such force it feels like he's inside my rib cage. "Don't stop there, baby. Tell me how you hate me." He chuckles softly, his hips moving in a rhythm that has me lifting my own to meet him. "It's a mutual feeling."

He shifts, his mouth dropping down to my breast, and he pulls my nipple into his mouth. I writhe underneath his touch. He thrusts once again, pounding into me, over and over. It feels like at any moment he's going to split me into two. With every movement, he pushes me closer to the edge. It won't be long until we're both falling into the inevitable abyss. I never want this to end.

His hand trails back down my body until both of his hands are gripping my ass again. Pain mixes with pleasure and we're both a mess of moans. My nails scrape his back. There will undoubtedly be marks all over his flesh in the morning. I don't care.

I want anyone who looks at him to know that he's mine.

Even though he really isn't...

Leo lifts his head, a smirk playing on his lips as he watches me. I can feel his balls constricting. Our surroundings are fading away and we're both losing ourselves in one another. But I'm not ready. I don't want him to come. I don't want it to be time for us to fall asleep, only to wake up in the morning like this never happened.

I want this to last as long as it can.

I still my body, blocking him with my hips as I plant my hands against his chest. Worry crosses his features and he abruptly stops. We're both breathless and it feels like a wasted attempt to try and catch my breath. Leo tilts his head to the side, his eyes searching mine with a hint of desperation.

"Are you okay? Did I hurt you?"

I shake my head at him. "No, I'm fine."

"Do you want me to stop?"

"Yes and no," I tell him, as I try to push him to the side. My efforts are useless. I can't move him at all. A frustrated sigh escapes me and Leo laughs softly. "Roll onto your back."

A smirk drifts across his lips and his hands grip my ass harder as he flips us over. His cock stays inside me and he rolls onto his back, pulling me on top of him at the same time. The mattress shifts under our weight and the bed frame groans as we shimmy back to the center of the bed. My legs are on either side of him as I straddle his hips. The roles are reversed and I'm in control now. At least, I feel like I am, but I know I'm really not.

Leo is still running the show here, even if he's letting me think he's not.

Leo's hands find my hips and he starts to lift me in an attempt to take over. My pussy clenches around him and I stare down at him, shaking my head as I try to pin him down with my hips. That movement is also a joke. Leo lays there because he wants to. If he wanted to be the one doing everything, I wouldn't be able to stop him.

"Stop trying to top me from the bottom," I grumble, my hands finding his wrists and pulling them away from my hips. I plant his hands against the mattress and hold him down. "I want to fuck you."

"Well," he drawls as a look of amusement mixes with the lust that is burning in his gaze. "That's all you had to say. Have your way with me, please."

His body relaxes against the bed and I begin to shift my hips, rocking up and down. Using my hips, I lift up before sinking back down his length. His cock fills me, stretching me in all the right places. Releasing his hands, I move my own to his chest and plant them against him as I start to move a little faster. Leo brings one of his hands back to my hip and the other settles between my legs.

His skilled fingers find my clit and he begins to circle them, driving me closer to the edge as I ride him. My movements become frantic, the warmth building deep within the pit of my stomach. My orgasm hits me without any other warning. I cry out as I clench around him, coming apart at the seams. I can't think straight. I can't move. I'm paralyzed by pleasure and entirely lost in Leo Wells.

I feel his hands move to my hips and he takes over as he fucks me from the bottom. It doesn't take long—only two thrusts—before he's losing himself inside me, filling me with his cum. I feel the warmth and he says my name into the darkness of the room as he continues to pump his hips.

"Fuck, you were made for me," he murmurs as he begins to slow. Leo stares up at me, both of us completely breathless, and he's transfixed. I collapse onto his chest and he links his arms around the small of my back. He pulls out of me and I feel the mattress shift as he gets off. "I'll be right back."

"Where are you going?" I ask him as I turn to look at him, but he's already in the bathroom.

I slowly sit up as I hear the water start running in the shower. Leo walks back into the room, still wearing nothing as he walks over to me. He leans forward, bending his knees as he slides his hands under my ass and lifts me into the air. I let out a gasp and instinctively wrap my arms and legs around him. Turning back around, he heads in the direction he came from, carrying me into the bathroom with him. The glass door to the shower is hanging open and he steps inside before lowering me to my feet. My hands are still on his shoulders, holding on to him as he pulls the door shut behind us.

Leo backs me into the hot water and I close my eyes as it pelts down on my skin. The heat soothes my muscles and my body grows even more relaxed. Releasing Leo's neck, I lift my hands and begin to smooth my hair under the stream. Leo moves closer to me, his body almost completely flush with mine. I feel his arms as he reaches past me and pumps some of the shampoo into his hands. He pulls me a step away from the showerhead so my hair isn't under the spray anymore. His hands push mine from my head and begin to lather, rubbing the soap against my scalp.

I can't help it as I moan and melt against him. The aftershocks of the orgasm he gave me, the feeling of the hot water and him massaging my scalp, has my knees feeling like they could buckle. His hands lightly push me back into the water. With my head tilted back, he rinses the shampoo from my hair. The water soaks it, the long strands stretching down the length of my spine. After he washes my hair with conditioner, we switch places. I take my time, working the shampoo into his scalp. He lets me push him back into the water as I make sure the soap is washed away. We take turns washing each other's bodies and I stand in front of Leo under the water, washing the soap from his skin.

Leo opens his eyes and slowly drinks me in, his gaze starting at my toes, trailing over the entirety of my body, before landing on my face again. His hands find my hips and he pulls me flush against him. The water beats down on the two of us. He lifts his hands to cup my face.

"You're so fucking perfect," he murmurs as his mouth drops down to mine. Our bodies are wet and slick from the water. Leo pushes his hand through my hair, gripping the back of my neck as he kisses me with an intensity. His tongue slides inside my mouth, dancing with mine as I clutch his shoulders, afraid I'm going to slip and fall.

I feel his cock pressing against my stomach. Reaching down, I wrap my fingers around his length and slowly begin to stroke him as he kisses me deeper. A moan escapes him and I swallow the sound as we take turns stealing the air from each other's lungs.

"I need to fuck you again," he groans, his teeth biting into my bottom lip. He releases my flesh and runs his tongue across the half-moon indents he left behind. His hands drop down to my hips. "Turn around for me, baby."

Spinning on my feet, I face the glass wall, turning my back and my ass to Leo. He pulls my ass back toward him and I lift up on my tiptoes to give him better access with our height difference. His cock presses against my center and then he's sinking inside me, not stopping until he's filling me completely.

A breathy moan falls from Leo's lips and he begins to shift his hips, pulling out before sliding back in again.

Every movement is calculated and fluid. He strokes my insides with skill, quickly pushing me closer to the edge of ecstasy. Planting my hands against the glass wall, I push back against him, taking every inch as he begins to pick up the pace, fucking me harder. His movements become frantic, driven by a need deep inside. One hand grips my hip as the other moves up to my neck. He slides his hand around the front of my throat, squeezing it lightly.

"I love how you look taking my cock," he groans, pumping his hips harder. My body rocks with the force of his thrusts and I brace myself harder as I take it all. His grip on my throat tightens, restricting my airway just enough that I can still breathe, but it also has me seeing stars.

Warmth builds in my stomach as my orgasm nears. It doesn't take long. A few more thrusts and I'm coming undone, losing myself around him. My pussy clenches around the length of his cock, squeezing him as he slides in and out. I cry out, my body shaking from the pleasure that explodes within me. Leo comes half a second after I do. He slams into me, my name leaving his lips as he fills me with his cum. He doesn't stop until there's nothing left, until the two of us are riding out the waves of euphoria.

Moving his hand from my throat, he slowly drags his fingertips from my spine before pulling out of me. I instantly feel his absence and my body feels thoroughly satiated and simultaneously exhausted. Dropping my heels to the floor, I straighten my spine and Leo turns me around to face him before he's pushing me back into the water.

His hands are gentle as he washes the cum from between my legs. I'm lost in a daze, lost in his touch. He washes himself off again and turns off the shower. My eyelids are heavy as he wraps a towel around me. I step out of the shower and he grabs another towel, crouching down as he begins to dry my legs. "Let's get you dried off and into bed."

"I can do it myself, you know."

He looks up at me as he begins to stand upright again.

"I know you can," he tells me as he begins to dry the rest of my body. "Which is exactly why I want to do it for you."

A lazy, sleepy smile pulls on my lips. "If you want to pamper me, I'm not going to argue with you."

"I may have to fuck you more often if it makes you this agreeable."

"You wish," I say playfully as I let him dry my hair. Leo's silent for a moment as he wraps a towel around me and begins to dry himself.

When he finishes, his hand finds mine and he threads our fingers together. He leads me out of the bathroom and back to the bed. The mattress dips under our weight and he pulls me down with him, wrapping his arms around me as he pulls me flush against his body. My eyelids flutter shut and I feel his warmth as he buries his face in the nape of my neck.

I'm drifting off to sleep when I finally hear him speak. His words are barely audible, but they don't get lost in the darkness of the night as he whispers them against my skin.

"If only wishes came true."

CHAPTER SEVENTEEN
LEO

"I think congratulations are in order."

I direct my gaze back to Austin as he takes a forkful of food and pushes it into his mouth. Aria and I got back to Idyll Cove two days ago and we still haven't talked about anything that happened while we were away. In a way, it's probably for the best. None of it meant anything. We were both swept away by the moment and the win. Since we returned home from Germany, we've settled back into our normal pattern of ignoring each other's existence except for when we have to skate together.

"I heard you and Ari won the gold."

"Yeah, we did," I tell him, confirming the fact he already knew. My fork pierces the piece of cauliflower on my plate and I hold it down as I slide my knife through it. "Our performance went really well."

Austin nods and takes a sip of his water. "I saw the

highlights on TV. You guys look like you have a lot of chemistry together."

"I suppose so." I take a bite of my food.

He cocks his head to the side. "Are you telling me after everything so far, you still don't like my sister?"

I finish chewing and let out a sigh as I set my knife and fork down on my plate. "It's not that I don't like her... it's just better if I don't."

He watches me for a moment, his gray eyes boring holes through mine. For a moment, I feel like I'm looking at her. Aria's eyes are the exact shade as her brother's except in her left eye, there's a small fleck of dark blue on the right side. Austin doesn't have that.

His face is free of any judgment, but his tone is a little terse. "So, you do like her, you just think you shouldn't?"

"I don't know," I admit with a shrug, wanting this entire conversation to evaporate. "It's complicated."

Austin raises an eyebrow. "Do you have a thing for my sister?"

"Absolutely not."

The words tumble from my lips in a haste. I do not have a thing for Aria Reed. I just like to fuck her occasionally.

"I don't know whether or not I believe you," Austin says with a raised eyebrow. "At the same time, you are both consenting adults, so what you do together is your own business." He pauses for a second, his eyebrow falling in line with the other as he fixes his gaze on mine. "My earlier warning of fucking you up if I have to still stands.

Not only in relation to you and her working together, but I guess now on a more personal level as well."

I stare at him for a moment. This is the exact conversation I don't want to have with him. He has no idea we slept together—multiple times now—nor do I ever plan on telling him. It's one of those secrets I plan to take to the grave with me. "You have nothing to worry about."

It's not a lie. There is nothing for him to ever worry about. Aria and I already have an understanding concerning what has happened and anything that happens in the future.

"I hope not," he tells me after a pregnant, awkward pause. "If anything changes, do tell me."

I bark out a laugh, shaking my head at him. There's no way in hell. "You'll be the first to know."

Austin gives me a smile, but it doesn't quite reach his eyes. There's something lingering in his gaze, but I'm not going to question him on it. Even though he's my best friend, I wouldn't blame him for making sure his sister is good. She deserves to have someone on her side like that. I can keep her safe on the ice, but I offer no layer of protection for her heart.

"What's been new with you? What's brought you back to Idyll Cove?"

Austin finally made the official move to NYC recently. He had been bouncing back and forth from Charleston and the Big Apple for the past few years after his business took off. He designed a refrigeration system for ice rinks that is more energy efficient and leaves less of a carbon footprint.

After he signed a contract with the biggest hockey league in the world, things really went wild for him. He had quite a few contracts and different things in the works.

The unreadable look that was in his eyes vanishes. "Well, you're looking at the new owner of Idyll Ice Rink."

A smile spreads across my lips and I grab my drink before leaning back in my seat. "No shit. I didn't know it was up for sale."

"Yep." He pops the P with his lips. "Mr. Belmont had been talking about selling for a few years but he wasn't ready to give it up. Things started to get tight for him financially and, as I'm sure you've noticed, he hasn't been able to keep up with all the maintenance for it. We put the new cooling system in for free and then he decided he was ready. We've been in negotiations for a little bit since there was a lot of sentimental value in the place for him, but I guess for the right price, anything can be bought."

I stare at him for a moment. "And what exactly are you going to do with an ice rink?"

Austin knows how to skate, but he doesn't do it often. Hell, I don't even know how long it's been since he was on the ice last. When we were kids, he used to come dick around at the rink when Aria was there. That was as far as his skating career went. He wasn't interested in hockey, and definitely not figure skating. Austin was only ever interested in building his own empire, even from a young age.

He shrugs with indifference, setting his utensils down on his plate before pushing it off to the side. He settles back in his seat, lifting his own glass from the table as he takes a drink. "I'm not really sure yet. I plan on talking to Ari about it. I'd like to see if she has any ideas."

"Have you thought of turning it into a training facility or anything like that?"

"I have. I've thought about quite a few different routes I could pursue." He tilts his head to the side. "Maybe you and Aria can talk about it and see what you two can come up with. I know you guys are relatively busy right now, but any input would be appreciated."

I nod. "I'll see her tomorrow morning at practice. I'll say something to her then."

"Thanks." Austin smiles with a hint of mischief dancing in his eyes.

I can't help but feel like he's setting both of us up in a way. He knows how much of a struggle it has been working with her and now he wants us to figure out what the hell to do with the ice rink he bought.

Our server shows back up at the table and Austin gives her his black card before she even bothers to bring the bill over. I give him a look of frustration, but he ignores it. It's not unusual for him to cover the check. I've learned it's not worth arguing with him over it because Austin Reed is always going to get his way.

"You don't have any other plans tonight, do you?"

I shake my head at him as my brow furrows for a fraction of a second. "No. I was just going home after this."

"I told Aria I'd meet her for a drink. Come with."

My stomach knots at the thought of her. "I don't want to impose."

"Nonsense. I'm inviting you and I'm sure she won't

care." He pulls his phone out and taps on the screen. "I just texted her to let her know we'd both be there. If she has an issue with it, she'll tell me."

I level my gaze on his. "Why are you doing this?"

A sly smile slides across his lips and he winks. "Because I can." He looks down at his phone and then turns it around to show me the screen. "See, look. She doesn't care."

I narrow my eyes on his. "You're almost as annoying as she is."

"How delightful." He claps as he rises to his feet and removes the white cloth napkin from his lap. He drops it on the table and pulls the keys to his Maserati from his pocket. "Let's go, Wells."

A sigh escapes me and I follow his lead, standing up before we begin to head out of the restaurant. "Don't you need to get back to New York or something?"

A chuckle escapes him and he slings his arm around my shoulders as we step out onto the sidewalk. "That's a tomorrow thing." We head in the direction of where our cars are parked as Austin removes his arm from my shoulders. "I'll meet you at The King's Inn."

I nod, bidding him goodbye before I get into my own car. He's an asshole for doing this. I didn't need to see Aria again. This doesn't align with my plan to avoid her. It goes against it completely. My heart races at the thought of seeing her off the ice right now.

I'm fucked.

***

Aria is already waiting at the bar when I get there. I see

her from across the room sitting at a high-top table by herself as she sips a glass of wine. Her midnight-colored hair is tucked behind her ears, hanging in soft curls that frame her heart-shaped face. I walk closer, heading directly toward her as she slowly lowers her glass away from her lips. Her gaze meets mine and the electrical current ripples through the air between us.

"Leo," she says quietly in greeting as I take the seat across from her. She stares at me for a moment before glancing behind me. "Where's my brother?"

"I'm not sure," I tell her honestly. "We left at the same time but I didn't pay attention to where he was while we were driving."

"Hmm," she hums without amusement as she reaches into her purse and pulls out her phone. It begins to vibrate instantly and she smiles at the screen. "Speak of the devil." She slides her finger across it and lifts it up to her ear as she looks at me again. "Hey."

I watch her, studying her expression as she talks to Austin. Her eyebrows pull together and she frowns.

"What do you mean you're not coming?"

Rolling my eyes, I shake my head as I cross my arms over my chest and lean forward. I rest my forearms against the top of the table as Aria finishes up her call. I knew he was trying to set us up in one way or another, I just didn't anticipate this.

"Yeah, okay. I'll talk to you tomorrow. Bye." Aria ends the call. A sigh slips from her lips as she lifts her eyes back to mine. "He's not coming."

"You don't say," I muse out loud as I reach across the

table and grab her glass of wine. I drain it, swallowing the fruity liquid. "He set us up."

Aria nods. "It appears so." She looks around before looking back at me. "We don't have to do this."

She piques my curiosity. "Do what?" I ask, cocking my head to the side.

"This," she says, waving a flustered hand between us. "We don't have to act all cordial and hang out just because Austin set us up. You've been ignoring me since we got home, Leo. I get it, okay?"

"It's for the best, Ari," I explain, my voice borderline pleading. I don't need her opening up this conversation between us. She'll never understand where I'm coming from. She'll never understand that if I let her in, I'll never let her out… and believe it or not, I don't want to hurt her. "What we did can never happen again."

"Thank God we can at least agree on one thing," she says, forcing out a laugh. "I hope you got whatever it was out of your system." Her jaw is set and there's a coldness that rolls off of her, filling the space between us. Abruptly, she gets up from her seat and grabs her purse. "I'm tired, I'm going home. Enjoy the rest of your night, Leo."

Guilt floods me. I can't let her walk away like this.

She has my mind completely fucked up.

"Aria, wait," I call out to her, unable to stop myself. There's an underlying plea in my tone.

She glances over her shoulder and there's a touch of sadness in her irises as she shakes her head. "I'll see you in the morning."

My lips part, but I don't say anything else. She turns

back around and continues moving in the opposite direction of me.

I let her walk away as I repeat my own words to myself in my head.

It's for the best.

CHAPTER EIGHTEEN
ARIA

Leo's hand grips mine, my muscles stretching and lengthening in my arm as he holds himself in place with the toe pick of his skate and continues to spin me in a circle around him. My body is so close to the ice, I'm parallel with the surface. Cold radiates from below, enveloping my body as my hair trails behind me.

Every move we do together requires an insane amount of trust. The death spiral doesn't require anything less. Leo has to be able to keep his body stable and in place as he leans back, creating torque to propel me around the rink. He has to have the ability to hold on to me and not let go as he spins me.

I have to keep my body stable, strong, and in the proper placement as I hold on to him with a fierce grip. I've never had someone let me go before. I don't think Leo will be the one to do it, but the thought alone scares the shit out of me. I get the same thoughts and feelings with jumps and the throw lifts.

The spin starts to slow down and Leo begins to straighten his body as he lifts his hand that is holding on to mine. I let him guide me, while also using my own strength to be back in an upright position. The music continues to play and we don't miss a beat as we move forward in our routine.

We go through the same moves we've been working on for weeks now. The same routine we did at our last competition. Even though we won gold there, we haven't gotten to the competition that secures our position on the Olympic team. The world championship. It's one of the biggest competitions that we work toward as figure skaters. I made it before and won with Preston, but this time it's different.

The odds are stacked against us. It's never been heard of for a pair to just start skating together this far into the competition season and then to go on and win Worlds and qualify for the Olympics. I want it even more than I did before because of that.

I want to be able to say that Leo and I did that.

We finish our routine before we both begin to skate separately around the arena to let our bodies begin to cool down. Leo glances over at me and it feels like the first time he's really paid attention to me since Austin tried to set us up last week. Since that night, we've fallen into a weird silent working partnership. I was still annoyed with both of them for that. Leo hasn't tried to talk to me unless it's something pertaining to our routine and even then, I keep it as brief as possible.

I'm not wasting my time with him any more than I have to.

Hell, I've already wasted enough time either with him or thinking about him.

"I want to ask you something."

I look over at Leo as we begin to slow down. I shouldn't entertain him, but I'm also curious to hear what it is he might need to ask me. "Okay."

He's silent for three heartbeats and it feels like the time stretches to an eternity. Tension fills the air and anticipation mixes in my bloodstream. I need him to spit the damn words out already. We reach the break in the boards where the door is hanging open from the other skaters who exited earlier.

"What are your thoughts about changing the routine up a bit?"

Leo's question isn't what I was anticipating. I don't know what I actually thought he was going to say, but I thought it would be a little more invasive than a question about our performance. A sigh leaves me and I'm flooded with relief. There's a touch of disappointment that lingers beneath it all.

"Do you think there's something wrong with it the way it is?"

Leo shrugs, motioning for me to walk ahead of him as we exit the rink. He walks behind me until we walk into the locker room. I sit down on the bench, smelling the stench of hockey with the smell of the cooling system. It doesn't smell as bad as it did before my brother's company replaced it. The chemicals must be ingrained in the fibers of this building now.

"Kincaid and Eva both pointed out last night that they think we need to increase the emotional pull."

I pull off my skates and clean the snow from the blades, making sure they're dry before I slide my microfiber protectors over the sharp edges. "What did you have in mind?"

Leo turns to face me on the bench as he straddles it. "I was hoping maybe you had an idea or two."

I put my skates into my bag and pull the zipper closed before I turn my attention back to Leo. Thinking back on our routine, I can see why Luca and Alanna would say that. There is just enough tension and emotion to keep you engaged in the performance, but there needs to be more.

Just as I'm about to answer him, my phone begins to ring. Leo raises an eyebrow at me as the annoying sound of my ringtone echoes inside the room. My nostrils flare in annoyance as I fumble with the side pocket of my bag. I pull out my phone and those feelings disappear as I see Griffin's name on the screen.

"Hold on," I tell Leo as I answer the call and hold my phone up to my ear. "Hey, Griffin," I say through the speaker, keeping my voice light, even though I'm weirdly nervous. Leo's eyes narrow slightly and the muscle in his jaw tightens.

It's not because Griffin called me.

It's because Leo is staring me down, unmoving like a statue as he sits facing me.

"Hey, Aria," Griffin says cheerfully through the phone. "Is now a bad time?"

I hold Leo's gaze, refusing to be the one who backs down. Leo will not win this. "Not at all. I just got off the ice."

"I'll keep this short. I wanted to see if you'd like to get dinner again."

I raise an eyebrow. "You're still in town?"

Leo doesn't even look like he's breathing.

"I extended my stay by a few weeks, so I leave next weekend." He pauses for a moment. "I was hoping to get a redo of our dinner before I head out."

"Absolutely," I tell him, a smile pulling across my lips. "I'll be out of town this weekend for a competition, but text me a day that would work for you for next week."

"That sounds perfect," Griffin says and I can hear the smile in his voice. "I'll text you in a little bit."

Leo's eyes are hard and colder than ice.

"Thanks for calling, Griffin. I'll talk to you soon."

Pulling my phone away from my ear, I end the call and lock my screen before tucking it back into the pocket of my bag. Leo's back is stick straight and his knuckles are white as he holds on to the sides of the bench. "Sorry about that," I apologize, giving him a small smile. Pushing off the bench, I rise to my feet and grab my things. "Let me think about some different things we could add to our performance and I'll let you know what I come up with tomorrow morning."

"What did he want?"

My eyebrows pull together momentarily before I

recover from his question. I level my gaze with his. There's a part of me that's now addicted to this push-and-pull thing we have going on. He's hot and he's cold. He lets me in and he shuts me out. I'm no better than him because I do the same exact thing. I may trust Leo Wells on the ice, but I don't know that I will ever be able to trust him with my heart.

"That's none of your business," I answer, not bothering to hide the irritation in my tone.

Leo rises, stepping directly in front of me. He's standing so close, I can feel the heat radiating from his body. I have to tilt my head back to meet his gaze. "It is now."

"No, it's not." There's a hardness in my tone and I hate it. I hate this tension between us. I want nothing more than to let him sweep me off my feet and to never put me down. That's a fucking pipe dream and I need to take Brynn's advice. Nothing less than queen treatment. I already messed up by letting him fuck me in Germany. "You don't get to act like you care, Leo. We both know you don't. You don't want anyone else to have me, but you don't even want me for yourself."

"What did he want?" he questions me, the words coming out with a bite in his tone. He doesn't bother commenting on a single thing I said. It's like he didn't even hear the words I spoke. "He wants to take you out again, doesn't he?" He rolls his eyes and mumbles something under his breath. "So fucking predictable," it sounds like, but I can't quite make out every word.

Hurt washes over me. I try my hardest to not have a

reaction to his word. It's impossible. My efforts are futile and feeble. Any ounce of self-control over my emotions is thrown out the window.

"Is it so wrong that someone wants to take me out to dinner?" I can't help myself as my voice jumps an octave higher and I'm speaking loudly. I throw my arms out in defeat, dropping my bag to the floor. "Is it that hard to believe that someone might be interested in me?"

Emotion washes over Leo's face, filling his honey brown eyes as he closes the distance between us. He reaches out, cupping the side of my face. His palm warms my skin and he gently brushes the pad of his thumb against my cheek. "Your heart is an unattainable dream, Aria Reed."

My lips part, but words fail me. I can't pull my eyes away from his. A fire burns deep within his irises, but it's different from what I've seen before. Instead of lust and need, there's a deep-seated longing mixing with twinges of sadness.

"No one on this planet is deserving of it."

Leo drops his hand away from my face. He bends down to pick up my bag and his eyes meet mine again as he stands back up. He lifts the strap over my shoulder and positions it perfectly. "Don't go out with him."

"Why not?" I ask him, my voice is barely above a whisper. I don't fully trust my voice and the words feel unsteady on my tongue.

Leo hears the words I speak for him. He takes a step back and it feels like miles are thrust between us. He's so far away even though I could easily reach out and touch him. All it would take is just one touch…

"He doesn't deserve you."

He grabs his own bag, turning on his heel as he strides across the room to the door. Just as he pulls it open, I find my voice again. It's a challenge more than anything. A way of testing the murky waters between us. "Do you think you do?"

Leo looks at me as he pauses in the doorway. He smiles a heartbreaking smile and shakes his head. "I never said that."

He disappears through the door without another word and I'm left alone with my thoughts and the realization of Leo's actual problem.

He doesn't think he's deserving of love.

And he's determined to push away anyone who threatens that belief.

CHAPTER NINETEEN
LEO

My chest rises and falls with every shallow breath that escapes me. We're nearing the end of our routine and Aria spins through the air before landing again on her skates. Her movements are calculated. She doesn't miss a beat as the blade of her skate meets the ice and she begins to skate with me. Her eyes meet mine, her face tinted pink from the blood pumping through her veins. The adrenaline is incomparable. I reach for her and she slides her hand into mine as we move toward the center of the rink.

The music is beginning to slow as the song comes to an end. Pulling Aria toward me, her hand leaves mine and she breaks out in a spin until she's sliding into my arms. I grab her biceps, holding on to her as she reaches for my waist. We melt into one another, my face inching toward hers as the music stops and the lights cut out.

Her breath is warm, smelling faintly of mint as it

dances across my face. Her lips are almost on mine. My heart pounds erratically in my chest, threatening to break through my rib cage. I hold my breath while she's in my arms. Time is momentarily suspended. My eyes bounce back and forth between her steel orbs before the lights flash back on. Everyone in the crowd is clapping and Aria and I are abruptly ripped back to reality.

I release her, and we break apart like the other is on fire.

We are the last pair to skate today and we head off the ice, only to wait a few minutes for them to announce us as the winners. The tension between Aria and I is so thick, you could pluck it out of the air. She looks at me after we get our medals and we're skating back toward the door.

"Good job today," she says softly with a small smile.

Really? That's what she decides to say to me?

I nod, feeling the tension in my jaw. "We got the job done."

Aria's lips part like she wants to say something else, but she simply stares at me for a moment. She half shakes her head at herself and walks through the door. Her strides are long and I pause for a moment, watching as she ducks to the right and disappears into the women's locker room.

I head into the men's locker room and change into a pair of dark jeans and a t-shirt, then trade in my skates for a pair of sneakers. When I come back out into the hall, I don't see Aria anywhere, but I see my sister Charlie and her group of friends she brought with her.

Her boyfriend Wes is a professional hockey player and

one night when I was in Orchid City to visit them, he wanted to make a bet. He bet me that he could get a few other hockey players to come watch the competition and they would like it.

Charlie smiles brightly and she meets me as I walk toward them. She wraps her arms around my neck, pulling me in for a hug. "You guys were amazing, Leo," she says with a sense of pride in her tone.

"Thanks, Charles," I tell her, smiling back at her as we break apart.

Wes looks at me with his hands out. "What did I tell you?" He points to Nico and Mac, two players from his team. "Look at who came to show their support."

I look past him to the two other guys. "How much did he have to pay you?"

Nico chuckles as he wraps his arm around his fiancée's shoulders. He shakes his head and Wes rolls his eyes as he cracks a smile.

"We wouldn't have missed it," Mac chimes in as a woman steps up beside him and Charlie.

Charlie motions to her. "Leo, this is Juliette. Juliette, this is my brother, Leo."

I hold my hand out to her, offering her a warm smile as she shakes it. "Thank you for coming out," I say with a nod. "We really appreciate all the support."

Her face lights up. "It was a beautiful performance. It left such a lasting emotional feeling." She pauses and looks past me as we release our hands. "Where is your partner, Aria?"

The question pricks my skin, but I don't let it show. I

don't tell her that I have been wondering the same thing. Instead, I shrug. "No idea. I suppose she probably went back to the hotel."

"They're not together," Charlotte informs her as she steps up beside me. "They just skate together as a pair."

Juliette looks a bit surprised. "Really?" She tilts her head to the side as her forehead creases and she looks back to me. "But there was so much chemistry between the two of you."

Forcing out a laugh, I shake my head at her. "Oh, God no. I hate her. We both just ended up without partners and weren't given much of a choice."

The words leave a bitter taste in my mouth, leaving me feeling conflicted.

"So, you hate her, but you're still able to skate together like that?"

"She doesn't particularly care for me either." I chuckle to continue with the charade and shrug. "It's complicated. Like you said, we have chemistry. We skate well together and complement one another. When we're on the ice, the way we really feel about each other doesn't matter."

"Talk about a mindfuck," Charlotte mumbles and shakes her head. "Okay, Leo. You ready to go celebrate?"

Mac steps up beside Juliette and gives her a long look. "I think we're actually going to head out for the night."

"I bet you are," Nico chirps as Wes beams at the two of them. She wasn't introduced as Mac's girlfriend, but I can't help but wonder if there's something going on between the two of them.

Everyone says goodbye to Mac and Juliette before they head in the direction of the exit. Nico and his fiancée follow suit and say their goodbyes before leaving. I turn back to my sister and Wes. I'm about to ask them where we're going, when I see Charlie look past me and her face lights up.

"Oh look, there's Aria!" Charlie looks excited as her eyes meet mine. Her face falls momentarily with a touch of sadness lingering. "I know you don't like her, but should we invite her to dinner?"

I stare at her for a moment as I weigh the option in my mind and feel the guilt eating at me. I know Aria. If she doesn't come to dinner with us, she's probably going to lock herself away in her hotel room and either order takeout or eat from a vending machine. As much as I want to keep my distance from her, I can't ignore the fact that I don't want her anywhere other than with me.

"Sure," I tell my sister with a sigh. I don't miss Wes's curious gaze as he assesses me. I can see the questions in his eyes. Entertaining his curiosity isn't what I really want to do.

Charlie stares at me for a moment before she gives me a gentle nudge. "Go ask her."

"Right. Okay." I give her and Wes a tense smile before turning around in the direction where Charlie was looking at Aria. I see her standing by the wall with her skating bag on the floor beside her. She has a duffle bag slung over her shoulder and her wavy hair hangs in her face as she scrolls on her phone. She took the braids out from how she had her hair styled. My eyes scan her body, starting with her bright white sneakers before trailing up the black leggings that hug the lean muscles on her legs. Her oversized t-shirt reaches the center of her thighs and hangs off her shoulder. "Hey," I say softly as I stop in front of her.

Aria lifts her head, her long black hair falling down her back as she brushes it away from her face. "Hey, Leo."

I shift my weight on my feet with an unwanted nervousness sliding through my veins. She does this to me and I'm not sure I like it. "Do you have any plans for dinner?"

Her gray eyes meet mine and she shakes her head. "I was going to order DoorDash from somewhere. Do you have any recommendations since you've been here plenty of times before?"

Something about the way she says it has my heart clenching. "Come to dinner with us."

"Who? Your sister and her boyfriend?" she asks me while glancing behind me. Aria gives me a small smile, but she shakes her head at me. "I don't want to impose, but thank you for asking."

"I'm not asking."

Aria tilts her head to the side as she narrows her eyes with a coldness settling inside her irises. "I'm sorry... I must have missed the part where you became someone who is in a position to tell me what to do."

"Ari," I breathe her name with frustration as I close my eyelids. My heart thrums away in my chest. My nostrils flare as I inhale deeply and open my eyes again to look at her. "Please don't be difficult."

"Please don't be an asshole," she counters as she raises her eyebrows at me.

I work the muscle in my jaw. "I am not an asshole," I grind out the words through my clenched teeth.

Aria doesn't look convinced and we both know it's a lie. "You can be."

"You know what," I tell her, throwing my hands up in defeat. She is under my skin like a fucking splinter and I can't get her out. "Fuck it. Eat your DoorDash."

"Right there. That's an asshole thing to say."

I lift my hands and run them down my face. "Jesus Christ, you are infuriating." I pause and square my shoulders as I let the irritation roll off me. "Will you please come to dinner with us?"

She stares at me for two heartbeats before she shrugs and pushes away from the wall. "Sure, that sounds like fun. Let me cancel this Uber."

I watch her with an incredulous look on my face as she grabs her skating bag and begins to wheel it behind her. We turn back to where Charlie and Wes are and I see them standing over by the door. Turning my head, I look over at Aria as she falls into step beside me. Instinctively, I reach out and take her duffle bag from her shoulder and carry it myself. "I never know what to expect with you," I muse out loud as I study the side of her face.

She looks over at me. "And you give me whiplash. I think that makes us even."

My lungs deflate. Everything between us is becoming a mindfuck anymore these days. It's a struggle, trying to mind the invisible line drawn between us. We've crossed it too many times that it's difficult to distinguish it anymore. "I suppose so."

We reach my sister and Wes. "This is Aria. Aria, this is my sister Charlie and her boyfriend Wes."

"Hi!" She smiles brightly at the two of them as she shakes their hands. "It's nice to meet you both."

My sister smiles at her as she releases her hand. Wes wraps his arm around Charlie's shoulders and pulls her flush against his side. "I've heard a lot about you."

I cut my eyes at my sister and Aria raises an eyebrow at me. I can't read her expression but it sounds like there's a touch of curiosity in her tone. "Oh really?"

I don't know why the hell Charlie said that. Sure, I've expressed my frustrations about working with Aria. I've also denied any personal involvement with her. My sister doesn't know what has happened between us, but she does have her assumptions.

"I've only told her about the unfortunate circumstances about how we've come to skate together."

Aria nods and gives me a knowing look as everyone turns in the direction of the door. "Yes, it's such a shame, isn't it? I never imagined I would end up stuck skating with someone like you."

My jaw falls open and my eyes widen slightly. Her words weren't necessarily mean, but there was a hint of contempt lingering in her tone. I can't blame her. She was right. I can be an asshole and I haven't been the nicest to her.

"Oof, okay," Wes chimes in as the four of us walk

toward the exit. He glances at my sister with mischief dancing across his features. "I think I like her."

Charlie looks back at me with a smirk. "Me too."

Well, this is just what I need.

My sister's approval of the woman who is slowly prying my rib cage open and making a home inside my chest…

CHAPTER TWENTY
ARIA

My feet leave the ice and my face is set in determination as I begin to spin through the air. Time is momentarily suspended and my arms are drawn across my chest and my ankles are crossed as my body whips around three times. Releasing my arms as gravity begins to pull me down, I get into position for my landing. At the last moment, my foot shifts and I miss by a fraction of a second. My skates abruptly slide out from underneath me and I land on the side of my thigh before sliding a foot or two across the frigid surface.

What the fuck.

I've been landing this jump for years without any issues. Every once in a while, there's always a random fall, but that's to be expected. It is ice, after all, and we are moving around on the thinnest blades of steel. This is the first time I have fallen three times in a row in years. Probably since I was first learning this jump.

Leo skates over to me, sliding to a stop as he points the toes of his skates toward one another. "Are you okay?"

"I'm fine," I assure him in a clipped tone. Avoiding his gaze, I plant my hands against the ice and push up onto my skates before brushing the snow off my pants. Saying I'm embarrassed is an understatement. It's one thing to have this happen when I'm alone, but not when I'm in the middle of working through a routine with my partner.

Leo closes the space between us just as I go to move in the opposite direction. He catches me off guard as he grabs my wrist and turns me back to him. "I don't mean about your fall," he says softly as his eyes search mine with a tenderness I'm not used to seeing in him. "What's going on?"

I pull my wrist free from his grip. I stare at him, ignoring the magnetic pull he has on me. "I'm just having a bad day, okay? It's nothing."

It has nothing to do with you fucking with my head.

"Hey," he says quietly as he tilts his head to the side. "Why don't we call it a day and we can just start fresh tomorrow?"

I raise my eyebrows at him as confusion washes over me. I can't help but feel like this is some kind of a joke or something. "Who are you and what have you done with Leo Wells?"

A chuckle rumbles in his chest as the sound encapsulates me. "Don't worry, I'm still me." His lips slowly curl upward into a smile that causes my heart to skip a beat. "You're having a bad day. I might be an asshole sometimes, but I don't want to make your day any worse than it already is."

"Does this mean you're going to be less of an asshole now?"

"Probably not," he tells me as he winks. "Might as well enjoy it while it lasts."

I can't stop the smile that dances across my own lips. "I like you like this," I tell him with honesty as the words fall from my lips before I get the chance to swallow them back.

"Like what?"

Under his gaze, a blush creeps up my neck and spreads across my face. He's looking at me like there's no one else around us. "You just seem lighter…"

"Lighter," he muses out loud with a thoughtful look on his face as he nods his head. "I've just realized I haven't treated you the best and if we're going to be a pair, I want you to feel respected. I want you to feel like you matter because you do. You are a vital part of this team and if we can't have some kind of cohesiveness, it's never going to work."

I'm floored by his response. There was a time where I didn't think I would see the day that Leo didn't hate me. I never imagined he would want things to work. This has always felt like a temporary solution. Almost as if I were replaceable. The moment he found a new partner, he wouldn't want to skate with me anymore.

"I've been thinking about what you said about changing the routine," he says, breaking through my thoughts. We're still on the ice, standing in front of one another. "I think we should do it."

What the hell is going on today? I feel like I've stepped into the twilight zone.

"Really?" I ask him, trying to keep the surprise and excitement from my voice. There isn't a part of me that is jealous of Leo and Delaney, but I want our performance to be ours. I don't want it to be theirs.

Leo nods. "We can go over it tomorrow and work through it, if that's okay with you?"

"I would really like that," I admit, feeling the warmth of happiness seeping through my veins. Today didn't start out the best, but Leo's kindness has really turned it around. "They were just some minor things I thought we could change or add."

He stares at me for a moment, his expression becoming unreadable. "We can change the whole damn thing if that's what you want."

My eyebrows pull together as the sincerity of his words settles inside my bones. I'm confused. I don't know where this is coming from or why he suddenly cares. It's a stark contrast to the coldness he usually shows me. I'm used to the whiplash and the hot and cold behavior from him. Perhaps this is just another degree to the varying temperatures of Leo Wells. My lips part and a breath leaves me, but I don't speak a single word.

"I'll see you tomorrow, Ari," he says with another smile and a nod before he exits the rink.

I'm left speechless with my skates cemented to the ice as I stare after him. Leo disappears into the locker room and I break free from my stupor. Another skater moves past me, dodging to the side so she doesn't hit me. I give her an apologetic look, even though she doesn't see it. Glancing around once more, I head off the ice and into the locker room to take the rest of the day off like Leo suggested.

He's different today and it has me questioning everything, but I like it.

Today, I like him... We'll see about tomorrow.

***

Brynn gives me a look as she sets her martini glass down on the bar in front of us.

"Girl, what did I tell you about sleeping with him?"

A soft laugh spills from my lips and I shake my head at her, holding my hands up in defense. "We were in a different country sharing a bedroom. You can't tell me you wouldn't do the same thing?"

Her face remains set in stone before she cracks. A smile erupts across her lips and she laughs with me. "Okay, you're right. I suppose what happens in Germany stays in Germany, right?"

"My thoughts exactly," I tell her, nodding in agreement. I take a sip of my own mixed drink before setting it down. "Since we've been home I've been keeping my distance and things are back to normal... for the most part."

Her brow furrows. "What do you mean for the most part?"

"He was weirdly nice today. Don't get me wrong, Leo can be nice, but this was different. He was kind of sweet."

Brynn's eyes widen and she presses her palm against her chest, showing off her manicured nails. "Not Leo Wells."

"Yes Leo Wells," I tell her, half laughing. "I know, it sounds like I'm crazy or something."

"Or maybe you're finally breaking through that cold exterior," she says with a slow smile and she raises an eyebrow. "Perhaps he has a sweet spot for you, Ari."

"Okay, now that is a little far-fetched," I argue as I glance around the bar. I wasn't planning on going out tonight but when Brynn asked me to get dinner and drinks after work, I couldn't turn her down. My day did a complete one-eighty after skating practice. I've been trying to ignore the gnawing feeling inside me that is focused solely on that damn jump. What if I can't do it again? What if something happened inside my body and my mind that I cannot physically do it anymore?

"Aria," Brynn says louder as she snaps her fingers in front of my face. "Are you in there?"

Snapping my head, I blink twice and focus on her face. "Sorry, I was just thinking about this bullshit from practice today."

"Did something happen?"

I chew on the thoughts before pushing them all from my mind. "No, I was just having trouble with this jump, but it will be fine."

"Tomorrow is another day. I'm sure you'll get it sorted out when you're back on the ice."

I force a smile on my lips, although I'm not sure who I'm trying to convince. "You're right." The bartender sets two shots in front of the two of us. I give him a quizzical look.

He smiles and shrugs. "Some guy ordered them, but I don't see him now."

Brynn and I look at each other and after a moment of hesitation, we both lift the small glasses up and tap them against each other's. "To random men buying beautiful women drinks."

"Well, if it isn't two of my favorite people."

A real smile lifts my lips as I hear my brother's voice and turn around to look at him as he steps up behind Brynn and I. I'm surprised to see he isn't wearing dress clothes for once. He has a simple black t-shirt on, revealing the artwork on his arm and a pair of dark-washed jeans. Brynn mumbles something under her breath before she downs her shot. "Hey, Austin," she says slowly as she turns around.

"Hello, Brynn," he responds with a soft smile before looking between the two of us.

"What are you doing here?" I ask my brother, a bit confused by seeing him.

"I had to fly in for a few days to check out some things with the cooling system at the rink." He pauses and points to our glasses. "I see you got the shots I ordered for you."

"Ah, shit," Brynn sighs and looks momentarily disappointed. "We thought it was going to be some random rich man who would want to make us sister wives."

"Sorry to disappoint," he retorts as he steps beside her and sits down. "I guess you won't let me buy you another drink then?"

I roll my eyes. Thank God Brynn has known him long enough that she's immune to his charms. If anything, she plays along with it and gives him shit back, almost as if it's a running joke between the two of them. The banter and the stolen glances... I'm not an idiot, even if they both claim to just be friends.

"If you're buying, we will always be drinking," Brynn tells him as she pulls her hair back into a ponytail. "Whip out that black card, baby. We're drinking top-shelf tonight."

"As if you'd really drink anything else." Austin gives both of us a knowing look. "Neither of you like cheap liquor."

"I still have flashbacks from drinking in college." Brynn laughs and makes a look of disgust as she shakes her head. She looks directly at me. "You know exactly what I'm talking about."

"Oh god, our twenty-first birthday," I groan at the memory. That was one hell of a night. "You were glued to the toilet all night long."

Austin props his elbow on the bar and rests his chin on his hand as he watches us take a trip down memory lane. He wasn't there that night because he was out of the country on business. The next day, he took the first flight he could get home and insisted he take me out to celebrate, even though I had the hangover from hell.

"I'm so glad I was a night late for all that," Austin chimes in with a chuckle.

"Thank God for that," Brynn agrees as she laughs with him. "Talk about embarrassing."

Her words bring my mind back to earlier today and a frown pulls on my lips as I stare down at my drink for a moment. My movements are slow as I reach for it, wrapping my fingers around the cool, damp glass.

"I'm going to run to the restroom quickly," Brynn tells me before she disappears from the bar. I nod as I take a sip of my drink and set it down.

"What's wrong, Ari?" Austin asks me as he slides over into Brynn's seat. He stares at me head-on and I can't do anything other than sigh. I know my brother and he knows me. He knows something is wrong and he isn't going to let it go until I tell him.

"Leo and I were practicing today and every fucking time I tried to do an Axel, I fell." I close my eyes and rest my hand against my forehead. "I couldn't land it. It's a jump I've done thousands of times with no issues." I pause and turn my head to look at my brother. "What if I can't do it again?"

A sympathetic look washes over his face and he tilts his head to the side. "Why wouldn't you be able to do it again? Are you hurt?"

I shake my head as feelings of frustration mix with the anxiety inside. "What if this is just the end of my career? Maybe my body and mind forgot how to land it and this is just the end for me." I drop my hands to my lap in defeat.

"Ari, no," he says as he grabs my shoulder and gives it a squeeze. "This is not the end and everything will be fine. It was just a bad day."

"I can't afford bad skating days, Austin," I tell him with no humor in my tone. The anxiety is a beast inside me, running rampant.

"I get that. You've been stressed out and working your

ass off," he reminds me. "You're letting self-doubt turn into self-sabotage right now. Just try and relax. Try not to think about it or focus on it too much."

"And do what?" I demand in a defeated tone. Not thinking about it and not focusing on it is easier said than done.

Austin gives me a smile that's filled with warmth, and there's a tenderness in his eyes as he beams at me. "Just trust yourself, Ari."

My brother's right. There's a reason why I've always looked up to him and valued his advice. This reminder is exactly what I needed and coming from him, it means so much more to me. I've never had an issue trusting myself before, but today I definitely let myself get in my head about it.

I need to trust myself on the ice…

Just like I trust Leo.

He would never let me fall.

CHAPTER TWENTY-ONE
LEO

As I walk outside of the building, I see Aria getting into her car. She was in a better mood today. All of her issues with landing a triple Axel seem to have vanished. She skated well today—flawlessly, really. It feels like I'm always in awe of her. I'm completely captivated by her beauty on and off the ice. I've never witnessed someone quite as graceful as she is. I'm simply caught in Aria Reed's orbit.

After she told me her thoughts on our performance, we made some adjustments and worked through the kinks. I don't know how many times we went through the routine today until it felt like we had it right. It's absolutely perfect. We removed a few things Delaney and I had decided on together. Not much changed, but there are some very noticeable differences and some grand features we've added in.

It isn't completely different, but it's ours.

The performance and the routine belongs to no one

other than Aria and I. I know it brings her peace of mind, but I like it. There's something about it never being done by anyone but the two of us that makes me feel something deep inside. It's an unfamiliar feeling. It's comforting and simultaneously exhilarating. Her in my arms as we move around the rink just feels… right.

She makes me feel more alive than I ever thought was possible.

I stop by the trunk of my car and load my things into it as I watch her pull out of her parking space. She didn't see me when she came out of the locker room with some of the other girls. I caught the tail end of her conversation, but it was all I needed to hear.

She has plans to go get dinner with Griffin.

My lungs deflate in defeat. I ruined their last date, so she's giving him another chance. I have no one to blame but myself. I've been such an asshole to her, I shouldn't blame her for wanting to spend time with someone who isn't me. I don't want a relationship or a commitment. I shouldn't even care.

I want her to feel secure and safe with me. I don't want to come off as a threat to her anymore. We've crossed so many lines, everything is so goddamn blurry, but I don't want any of that to come between us or our partnership.

Keeping her at arm's length feels wrong, but I know I can't let her get close. My resolve has broken completely. If I let her in, I won't ever let her out. She's forever etched into my memories already. The sounds of her moans, the feeling of her skin. Aria Reed is under my skin and I've given up trying to figure out how to get her out. As much as I hate to admit it, I'm terrified of her. I'm terrified of the things she makes me feel. She has me questioning everything in life. She has me fucked up and I'm struggling to conceal it anymore.

She's the one who has always been a threat... I just didn't realize it until now.

She's out for my heart.

And I just might give it to her.

None of that really matters right now. Not when she's going out with another man. As much as I want to follow her and tell her she's making a mistake, I know I can't. I have to show her I'm not the asshole I've pretended to be. The things in the past—they don't matter anymore. I can let bygones be bygones and move on. There's no reason to hate her. We've both grown as people. We've grown up and have started to grow together.

I want to be a part of that. I don't want to sit on the sidelines and watch her anymore.

It's not right for me to interfere in her life, and I'm here for her whenever she needs me. There will never be strings attached. My feelings for her are no longer conditional. If Aria decides she wants nothing to do with me, I will never fault her for that. I might not like it, but that's her choice. I have no control over that. All I can do is treat her better, make her feel respected, and let her know that I care about her. Being cold to her wasn't beneficial to anyone. If anything, it was causing more of a strain between us. It was being harmful more than it was being helpful.

Griffin doesn't deserve her. I don't deserve her. If I think about it, I don't know that there is anyone who truly does. I hope she will one day see that he isn't the man she thinks he is. She doesn't know the measures he took to try to sabotage me when we were younger. Thankfully the allegations he made were never brought to light. No one that we skated with ever knew what was going on behind closed doors. When we were in high school, I beat him in a competition. He was livid and decided to retaliate. He went to the judges and claimed I was doing drugs. They launched an investigation and I wasn't allowed to skate until they cleared things.

It was all a lie, and they knew as soon as I took the drug test that came back clean. That only pissed Griffin off even more. He was at the rink the one night Aria and I skated together. We thought no one else was there, but when we were getting off the ice, I saw Griffin sneaking out of the building. The next Monday at school, he made a comment about how we looked together.

It wasn't long after that when I saw him walking around the school with Aria on his arm.

Griffin knew exactly what he was doing then and he knows what he's doing now. I warned her about him, and I don't know what else I can do without it feeling like I'm crossing a boundary. It's up to Aria to decide what happens now. I know if I see him again with her, it's not going to end well, so it's better if I keep my distance...

For now.

My drive home is extremely uneventful and I pull into my garage before shutting the door behind me. I slip inside the house and it's as quiet as it always is. Though it's far too big for one person, the location is amazing. I walk through the house until I'm stepping through the glass French doors that lead to the back deck. It's right along the coast with a private beach at the end of the yard.

I walk over to the railing and rest my hands against it as I look out at the waves rolling in. The smell of salt and sun drifts across the sand as the breeze blows past me. It's a cooler evening, but I don't mind it. I look up at the sky and it's completely clear. Being out here is the perfect place to stargaze.

There are no streetlights that obscure the view. My property is tucked along the cliffs, so it's not far from town, but it's just far enough that you don't have any of that traffic or the lights. Millions of stars pepper the sky above and the moon hangs heavily in the darkness of the night. It's a full moon tonight and you can see the craters in the surface of it with the naked eye.

It truly is peaceful here, but sometimes it's too quiet. A scratching sound at the door draws my attention from the ocean and I turn back to look at the door. Both of my cats are sitting there, staring at me through the glass. I was quick when I walked through the house, they didn't have a chance to find me until now. A smile pulls on my lips and I walk back inside to see them.

"Well, hello there, Penny," I say as I crouch down and scratch behind the calico's ears. The other one pushes his sister out of the way and rubs against my leg. "Yes, you need attention too, don't you, Max."

When I first moved in, I realized how empty the house seemed. I thought about getting a dog, but with how much I have to travel for competitions, it didn't seem fair to get a dog. Charlie was the one who suggested cats. At first I didn't love the idea, but when she showed me these two one-eyed kittens that needed to be adopted, I couldn't resist.

My sister and I went and picked them up and they have been more like dogs than any cat I've ever met before. Charlie was taking care of them for me until she moved to Orchid City. Now, I have Coach Davis's teenage daughter stop by to take care of them.

Standing back upright, I walk over to the laundry room where their food is and fill their dishes before heading back into the kitchen. I look around for a moment, unsure of what to do with myself. Today is no different than most days, yet I feel like there are a ton of bricks weighing on my chest.

After rifling through my fridge and cabinets, I find enough ingredients to season the fresh fish in my fridge and make a pasta dish to go with it. Cooking isn't necessarily my favorite thing to do, but I know how to do it if I need to.

I quickly head upstairs into my bedroom and change into a pair of sweats and no shirt before heading back down. Just as I walk into the kitchen, I see my phone screen is lit up and it's vibrating away on the counter. My heart begins to race and I lengthen my stride as I move over to it. A frown pulls on my lips when I see the wrong Reed name on my screen.

"Hello?" I say solemnly as I answer the call. The disappointment is heavy in my tone. I don't know why I was hoping his sister would have been the one calling when she's out with Griffin right now. She has absolutely no reason to call me—yet I was hoping it was her instead of anyone else.

Austin sucks his teeth. "Hello, Leo."

"What's up?" I ask him as I balance my phone between my ear and shoulder as I begin to get my stuff ready to prepare dinner.

"Are you in a prickly mood today?" Austin asks instead of answering me. It's loud wherever he is and sounds like he's half shouting over the sounds in the background.

Taking the fish out of the paper packaging, I set it on a plate and begin to season it. "No. I'm just making dinner."

"What are you making?"

"Fish and pasta that has mixed vegetables with it." My eyebrows pull together. "Did you just call me because you're bored?"

"I'm actually on a date right now."

I pause for a beat, truly confused by this whole interaction. "So, why are you calling me?"

"I need an exit strategy," he explains as the sounds get a little quieter. "I met her through a mutual friend and asked her to dinner, not realizing she's potentially the most conceited person I've ever met. This woman is in love with herself, I swear. She should have taken herself out."

Laughter rumbles in my chest as I wash my hands. "Where is she now?"

"She's in the bathroom. I tried to part ways after dinner, but she dragged me to this damn club in New

York." He lets out an exasperated sigh. "I was hoping if I called you, we could make it seem like there's some kind of emergency so I can bail on this nightmare of a date."

"Sure, whatever you need."

I'm a damn sucker for both Reeds, apparently.

"Okay, hold on, I see her coming back," he says as the sounds in the background get louder again. "Wait, no. What do you mean it is leaking everywhere?"

Pulling my phone away from my ear, I put it on speaker phone and set it down on the counter. Austin doesn't need me to speak. This is his show now and he's the main character. He starts rambling on, truly playing the part like there's an emergency he needs to deal with. I listen to him as I move about the kitchen and start cooking.

"Macy, I'm so sorry to cut this short," he says to her before his voice comes back through the speaker. "Yeah, hold on, give me a second and I'll be on my way." He turns his attention back to his date. All of his sentences are broken up, most likely from him pausing while she responds. "There's been an emergency at one of the rinks, so I need to get it sorted out. Yeah, I'll call you. No, we can reschedule. Of course. I really am sorry. I didn't anticipate this happening. Yes, you're right. Okay, have a good night."

I'm laughing to myself, sautéing vegetables with water boiling in another pot and the fish in the oven, when Austin finally comes back onto the phone.

"Good Lord, she did not want me to go." Austin lets out a sigh and it sounds like he has left the club as his background sounds much quieter now. "Thanks for doing that."

"That's what I'm here for," I tell him. Austin and I have been friends for long enough for him to know that if he ever needs anything, I will do whatever I can to help him.

"What are you doing tonight?" he asks me as I hear the beeping sound of his car. "Are you making dinner for yourself or do you have someone there? I probably should have asked that earlier."

I chuckle. "Just me and my cats. I'm not cooking dinner for them, though."

"I don't get it. You have enough money, let someone else cook the food for you," Austin tells me like it's a simple math equation.

"I'm perfectly capable of cooking for myself. Plus, sometimes I like to do it. It occupies my time."

"You need to find a person to occupy your time," he counters. "At least find someone you can cook for instead. I picture you sitting at a table that seats, like, eight people all by yourself with a candle in front of your plate. And your cats are sitting on the floor by your feet."

He paints the scene in my head and I don't know if I'm offended or find it hilarious. "Jesus, you make it sound like I'm this reclusive monk living alone."

"I mean, am I that far off?"

I think about it for a second. "I don't have a dining room table that seats eight people."

"All right, sorry. I meant six." He pauses and laughs as I hear his car engine revving in the background. "You know what I'm saying, though. When was the last time you went out with someone who wasn't me or your sister?"

Okay, he really is making me sound like I have absolutely no one.

"I've gone out with your sister."

Austin is silent for a second. "Is that so?"

Shit. I need to backtrack or something. I didn't mean to admit that I've gone out with her. But then again, it was only ever just as friends. There's still a way to save myself here.

"Not like that," I explain half assed. I don't know what else to say. Might as well throw her and Griffin both under the bus. "She's out with Griffin Carr right now, anyways."

Austin makes a disgusted sound. "That fucking tool? I thought he was living over in England."

"He is. He's back in Idyll Cove visiting right now." I leave out the part that she's already been out with him before and I crashed their date.

His sigh is loud and exaggerated. He's not happy, that much is clear. Aria is an adult and she's free to make her own decisions. Plus, it's not like her older brother can scare guys away like he used to.

"I can't believe I'm saying this, but I would have rather heard she was out with you or at your house instead of out on a date with him."

My sigh matches his, but I don't admit the words out loud to him.

Me fucking too.

CHAPTER TWENTY-TWO
ARIA

Griffin waits for me outside of the restaurant as I walk toward him, straightening my dress that hugs my curves. After skating with Leo, I went home and showered and changed before heading here. Griffin picked a small Italian restaurant in the heart of Idyll Cove.

While Leo and I were in Orchid City for our last competition, Griffin asked me if he could get another chance at dinner with me. He was leaving to go back overseas soon, so I thought it would be the right thing for me to do. Even though we had a relationship many years ago, he was just a friend. There was no reason why I couldn't meet him for dinner.

I'm not sure what any of Griffin's intentions are. I thought I made myself clear when we last made plans to go out. He isn't someone I'm interested in romantically, but I can't help but feel like maybe he doesn't feel the same way I do. Griffin seemed all too eager to get dinner again after Leo interrupted the last time. I would be lying if I said I wasn't glad Leo chased Griffin away that night.

As much as I don't want to admit it, when it comes down to it, I will always choose Leo. Until someone comes along and completely sweeps me off my feet, my partner will always have to come first. After all, my livelihood rests on how cohesive our partnership is. What kind of partner would I be if he couldn't trust me to be there when he needs me?

Griffin's face lights up as I make my way closer to him. I shift my weight on my feet as his eyes scan the length of my body before landing on my face. "You look amazing, Ari," he says with a soft smile. He pulls me in for a hug and I wrap my arms around him before trying to take a step away. His arms linger for a little longer than I'm comfortable with before he releases me. "I think I might have the best-looking woman in the restaurant sitting across from me."

A part of me feels like I should be flattered by his kind words, but the other side of me resists the urge to cringe. I don't need him to say nice things to me. I also don't need him to say cringey things like that. It's a bit boastful and comes off as arrogant rather than flattering.

"Have you been here before?" I ask Griffin as I avoid responding to his comments.

Griffin shakes his head with his eyebrows momentarily drawn together. "No, I don't remember this place ever being here before."

I nod my head as I remember he hasn't been back in quite some time. The restaurant has been here for a few years now, but it's new compared to when he was last home. A lot has changed since Griffin moved away.

"Well, they usually have great specials on Thursday evenings," I tell him with a smile as I motion toward the building. "Shall we?"

He nods, walking ahead of me before he pulls the door open for me. I catch a whiff of his cologne and the scent is pungent. It's so strong, I can almost taste it. I'm not a fan of the smell of patchouli and I smell hints of it. I step to the side as Griffin walks in and heads to the hostess to give her his name. For the sake of my nose, I keep a healthy distance.

She finds Griffin's name, grabs two menus, and motions for us to follow her to a table. She seats us at a booth on the far side of the restaurant. I slide into my seat, sitting across from Griffin. The hostess disappears with the promise that our server will be with us soon.

"This place is nice," Griffin comments as he glances around the room before picking up his menu. "It seems like they have a lot of options for food too."

I nod. "It's not always easy to find vegetarian options."

Griffin raises an eyebrow. "I didn't realize you were a vegetarian."

I stare at him for a moment as he directs his attention back to the menu. I've been a vegetarian since middle school. Given the fact that we aren't strangers, he should remember this. Disappointment settles deep inside my bones. He begins to ramble on about the different food options and I'm still flabbergasted at the fact that he really forgot something like that.

Leo remembered.

Our server appears at the table and I smile at her, trying to push the uncomfortable feelings away as she tells us about the different specials. Griffin and I both order a drink and he orders an appetizer, but I don't hear what he orders.

"So, how was the competition in Orchid City?" Griffin asks me after our server disappears. He looks up from his menu as if he's momentarily interested.

"It went really well. Leo and I came in first."

Griffin's nostrils flare and he half grunts. He's acting differently than he has before. Typically, he was pleasant and easygoing. The mere mention of Leo has Griffin bristling.

"You deserve an award just for the fact that you can tolerate spending that much time with him."

His words almost feel like a slap in the face. I tilt my head to the side, feeling the uncomfortableness spreading through my body. Irritation pricks my skin and I feel offended.

Our server returns with our drinks. I smile and thank her, just as Griffin does. He takes a sip of his and I don't touch mine. I look at him again as she leaves us once more.

"What does that mean?"

Griffin's eyebrows pull together as he swallows the liquid and sets his glass down. His face relaxes and he waves his hand dismissively. "Look at how abrasive he was when he interrupted our last date. He acted like he was entitled to your time. Like him talking to you was more important than us spending time together."

A date?

I don't bother correcting him.

"Yes, it was rude of him, but it was also something we did need to talk about," I argue, struggling to keep the bite from my tone.

Griffin laughs and rolls his eyes. "Come on, Ari. He's an asshole and you know it."

I don't like the way he's talking about Leo. He's not wrong. Leo can be an asshole and has a cold exterior. That doesn't mean Griffin gets to sit here and talk badly about him to me. Leo is my partner, he's someone I care about, someone I will protect. My lips are set in a straight line and the anger radiates from my body in waves as I glare at Griffin.

"What?" he questions me, his eyebrows pulling together. "You don't think he's an asshole after the way he acted that night?"

Our server shows back up with a plate of food. It looks like bruschetta, but there's something that resembles pieces of bacon on the top. The server tells us that she'll be right back to get our order for our food. Griffin picks up one of the small pieces of bread and takes a bite before leveling his gaze back on mine.

"You don't know Leo," I tell Griffin, half feeling defeated and tired, but also extremely angry at the audacity of this man.

"I don't need to know him to be able to see how he is," he counters before pointing at the plate. "Aren't you going to eat any of these?"

I tilt my head to the side. "Is that bacon?"

His face transforms as realization sets in. His eyes widen slightly, his mouth forming an O. "Shit, I didn't even think about it." He drops his gaze down to the plate.

He didn't even think about it. He didn't fucking think I wouldn't want any of it because it has meat in it when I literally reminded him that I don't eat meat two seconds before he ordered.

"I think I'm going to go."

His head snaps up. "What?"

I shake my head at him as I pull my napkin from my lap and set it down on the table. "This was never a date, Griffin. Your first mistake was assuming that. I was never interested in you as more than a friend." I pause. "Your second mistake was forgetting I don't eat meat and then ordering meat for me to share with you." I rise to my feet and stare down at him where he is sitting. "Your third and final mistake was saying anything about Leo. You don't get to speak about him. Hell, you don't even get to think about him."

A slow, sinister smirk pulls on Griffin's lips. "Holy shit. You're in love with him."

Something flutters in my stomach, but I ignore it.

"I'm not and even if I were, it wouldn't be any of your business." I shake my head at him in disappointment. I really thought Griffin was a better person than this version he showed me tonight. "Please don't call me if you're in town again."

"Aria, wait," he says as he climbs to his feet. "I'm sorry. Just sit back down and we can still have a nice dinner."

"I'm good, thanks," I tell him as I take a step away.

Without waiting for a response from him, I spin on my heel and stride out of the restaurant. I don't take a full breath until I'm out on the sidewalk, far enough away from him that I know he won't be catching up with me. I should have listened to Leo when he told me Griffin wasn't a good guy. I never wanted to be anything more than friends with him, but after hearing the things he said tonight, a friendship isn't even an option.

He should have never said anything about Leo.

No one gets to speak badly about that man and think I'll ever be okay with it.

Just because we don't always see eye to eye or get along, doesn't mean I won't protect him. He could tell me he never wanted to skate with me or see me again and it would still stand. Leo may have a cold exterior but deep inside, that man has a heart of gold.

And I trust him more than I trust anyone else.

As I walk out to my car, I pull my phone from my purse and unlock the screen before opening my messages. Tapping on the screen, I start a new one and type in his name. I wait until I'm sitting in my vehicle with the doors locked before I finally type something out to him. I know I shouldn't be doing it. I don't know if he will even respond.

ARIA

> Hey. So, I know this is completely out of nowhere and I don't know if you're busy or not. Tonight has been a really weird night. I didn't know if you would want to go out or anything.

I don't bother diving into the details about my short

evening with Griffin. I already feel stupid enough for the message I just sent. I cringe to myself as I read over the words three times before locking my phone screen. There's no way to take them back now. There's a sixty-second window where you can unsend a message after you hit send, but that time has passed.

My lungs deflate in defeat and my stomach turns at the realization that I'm going to have to face Leo tomorrow at practice. He's going to read that stupid message and I'm going to look like a vulnerable idiot who has her head in the clouds about a guy who doesn't even like her. Pressing my foot on the brake pedal, I push the ignition button on the dash and the engine of my car starts just as my phone vibrates in my lap.

My stomach drops. My heart kicks into overdrive, pounding erratically against my rib cage as I lift my phone up and see Leo's name on the screen. A ragged breath slips from my lips. I will my heart to slow down in my chest before it ends up exploding. I didn't expect him to respond and now that he did, there's an unwanted anxiousness quickly filling me. Closing my eyes, I count to four as I inhale, hold my breath and do the same as I exhale. I repeat it five times, feeling no different throughout my body as I look at my phone again.

Taking my chances, I unlock the screen and Leo's response is right there on the screen.

LEO
I'm home. Come here.

My heart crawls into my throat. It wasn't what I was

expecting from him. I lock my phone and drop it onto my lap before pulling my car out onto the street.

Leo Wells always keeps me guessing. He keeps me on my toes.

And I am hooked.

CHAPTER TWENTY-THREE
LEO

Lights illuminate the front of my house and it casts their beams through the windows, dancing across the floor. My breath catches in my throat and I pull two wine glasses from my cabinet before setting them down on the island. The light disappears and I hear the sound of her car door shutting a few moments later. The sound of my heart pounding drowns it out, filling the silence that surrounds me. There's a soft knock on my front door and I slowly turn on my heel, willing my heart to get itself under control as I walk to let her in.

My heart stops and my footsteps momentarily falter when I see her through the glass panes in the door. The front porch light shines down upon her and I drink her in as I take my time walking to her. Her midnight-colored hair falls in soft waves that frame her heart-shaped face. A black dress hugs the curves of her body and the hem falls just above her knees.

She's absolutely breathtaking.

She's fucking perfection.

My feet carry me closer to the door and I'm about five feet away when Aria's eyes meet mine through the glass. She shifts her weight on her heels and wraps her arms around her body, most likely in an effort to shield her bare arms from the cool ocean breeze. Where the hell is her damn coat? Her lips lift upward into a soft smile when she sees I'm here to let her in. Reaching for the door handle, I push down on it.

I step out of the way and motion for her to come in. "Hey."

"Hey," she says around a shiver as she steps into my house. My chest brushes against her arm and I inhale the scent of her as I close the door. "I didn't know it was supposed to get cold tonight."

I lift an eyebrow, my eyes raking down the length of her body before resting on her gaze again. She went out with Griffin in that dress. Irritation and jealousy mixes with lust. I want to take it off of her. "It's usually a few degrees colder here because of the water."

Aria nods and slips her feet out of her heels. Her toes are painted a soft pink. A sigh slips from her lips and she doesn't look as uncomfortable as she did when she first walked in. "I hate those things," she mutters, shaking her head.

"Come with me," I tell her as I begin to walk deeper into the house. Aria follows behind me, her bare feet padding against the hardwood floors. She follows me into the kitchen and leans against the counter of the island. Her eyes dance under the soft lighting above. Leaving her standing there, I walk into the living room and grab a blanket from the couch. Aria turns around, watching me as I walk back over to her.

Opening the blanket up, I step into her space and drape it around the back of her body, wrapping it around her shoulders. "I wasn't sure you were going to come."

She tilts her head to the side, her long hair falling down her back as I hold the blanket in front of her chest. "Should I not have?"

I shake my head, my tongue darting out to wet my lips as my gaze drops down to her mouth. "I'm glad you did."

"Me too."

My hands are still holding the ends of the blanket together by her chest. I look into her eyes and find her looking at my lips before her gaze collides with mine. Every molecule of oxygen is sucked from the room. My lungs burn, screaming for air, but my throat constricts. Aria Reed has a vise grip around my goddamn chest and all I can think is I want her to squeeze harder. Slowly lowering my face to hers, I feel her breath across my lips. My eyelids close and my lips are just about to touch hers, when there's a loud crashing sound behind her.

Lifting my head, I see Penny falling off the counter, knocking over the surviving wineglass with her. "Shit! Penny! What the hell!"

Aria spins around to see what is going on as she grabs ahold of the blanket when I let go of it. Penny runs away with the hairs on her back raised, like she's not the one who just did this. "Oh my," Aria breathes as she walks over to me and sees all the glass on the floor.

Shit. My hand darts out to stop her from walking any closer. I whip my head to the side to look at her before making up my mind. Aria lets out an audible gasp as I lift her into the air and set her down on the counter. "What are you doing?"

"Your feet," I tell her as I take a step back. "I don't want you to step on any glass."

Aria laughs quietly as she shakes her head. "I can sit on a chair like a normal person."

"Don't you dare move," I warn her as I narrow my eyes at her. "I will be right back."

Aria's laughter follows me as I walk over to the closet and pull out a broom. She surprises me as she obeys me and stays seated on the counter. As she sits on the island, she studies me as I begin to sweep all the pieces of glass into a pile. She's quiet as I clean it all up and throw it away. "Can I get down now?"

"If you must," I tell her with a smirk as I reach into the cabinet and pull out two champagne flutes since the other wine glasses are in the dishwasher. I look for a bottle of wine, but all I have is sparkling and champagne left. I pull out a bottle of bubbles and pop the top off before pouring the clear liquid into the glasses. I hand one to her move to stand across from her as I lean back against the counter.

She takes a sip and gives me a small smile. Hesitation dances across her features before she speaks again. "Thanks for letting me come over."

Something in her tone has my heart clenching. I want to reach out for her and pull her flush against my body as I wrap my arms around her.

I take a sip of my own champagne. "You're always welcome here."

Holding the blanket with one hand, she holds the stem of her glass with the other. "I went out to dinner with Griffin." She pauses and lets out a breath. "I never should have agreed to it."

My spine straightens and my body is suddenly on alert. *If he did something to her…*

"Did something happen?"

Aria frowns and looks at her glass for a moment. "You were right about him. He's not a good guy."

I swear to God, I will kill this man if he did anything to her.

I don't bother trying to stop myself as I close the distance between us. My feet are right by hers. There isn't much space left between us. My hand slides under her chin and I tilt her head back. Her gaze instantly finds mine.

"Did he touch you?"

She stares at me for a moment before shaking her head. "Thank God, no. He was under the assumption we were on a date and then he said some things I didn't like."

Relief washes over me as I realize I won't have to remove his hands from his body. However, he said something to her that has her feeling unsettled. I don't like it at all. My blood boils at the mere thought of someone making her feel uncomfortable.

"What did he say?"

"It was nothing, I promise. I left before we even got our food."

The muscle in my jaw tenses. "Aria, what did Griffin say to you?"

"Please, Leo. It's not a big deal."

"You have three seconds to tell me what he said or he can tell me himself."

She narrows her eyes on me. "A threat isn't going to get you your way, Leo."

A smirk pulls on my lips and I take the champagne flute from her hand and set it down on the counter behind her. "It's not a threat, baby. I'll be paying him a visit either way."

"He said some things about you that I didn't appreciate."

My head cocks to the side and my stomach flutters. "Did he say anything about you?"

"No," she admits as she drops the blanket. It falls away from her body and pools on the floor around her feet. "It was just about you."

Relief settles the rage that threatened to bubble over inside me. I still don't like that he made her upset, but I'm glad to hear he didn't say anything directly about her.

Wrapping my arm around her lower back, I pull her body flush against mine. "I don't give a fuck what he says about me, as long as he doesn't say anything about you."

"I care what he says about you," she argues as she lifts her hands up to link her wrists behind my neck. Her words warm my heart. She shouldn't care, but I love that she does. I set my glass down beside hers as my face dips down to hers, capturing her lips with mine. I run my tongue along the seam of her mouth, urging her to open them. She parts them, letting me in, and I want to drink from her until she runs dry. She tastes like champagne and sunshine. Our tongues dance together and I press her against the island with my hips.

Her hands drop down to my waist and she tries to push my pants down before I grab her wrists to stop her. I take a step back as I slide my hand down to hers. "Not here," I murmur as I pull her toward me. "Do you trust me?"

Aria nods. "I do." She pauses, pulling her bottom lip in between her teeth before she releases it. "And not just on the ice."

She lets me lead her through the dark house. With the full moon outside, I left the window treatments open, so it casts its light across the floor, illuminating the way for us. The skylight above the stairs lets the light in and the hall is dimly lit, but I lead Aria to my bedroom. She follows me into the room and I step around her, pushing the door shut behind us. Aria steps farther into the room, looking around.

She walks over to the built-in bookcase along the right side of the room. It's the largest room in the house. The far wall is made up entirely of glass and leads out to a balcony that overlooks the ocean. I watch her as she walks along the bookcase, dragging her fingers along the spines of the books. She stops and pulls one out, flipping through it as I walk over to her. Turning her head to look at me, I reach for the book and pull it from her hands before I slide it back into its place.

Aria turns to face me. "I didn't know you liked to read."

Sliding my hand along her throat, I wrap my hand around the back of her neck as my other arm goes around her torso. "There's a lot you don't know about me."

"What if I told you I want to know everything?" she asks me as she lifts her hands to hold on to my shoulders.

I slowly begin to back her across the room until the side of my mattress hits the backs of her thighs. My lips find hers in the darkness of the night as I silence her. There isn't a single thing I want to keep from Aria Reed, not even my heart. Whatever she wants, she can have. I don't want it. It never was mine to begin with.

Abruptly, I pull away from her and trail my fingers along her collarbone, slowly making my way down her sides. "I like this dress on you," I tell her as I reach for her shoulders and begin to push the straps down her arms. "But I think I like it better on my floor."

She hums in approval as I begin to strip her clothing from her body until every shred of fabric is on the floor. Aria's completely naked, fully exposed under my gaze. She doesn't shield herself from me. Instead, she takes a step closer, her hands reaching for me as she begins to remove my clothes. I don't protest and I don't fight her. Instead, I let her have her way, stripping me bare, literally and figuratively.

I take a step back, allowing myself the opportunity to fully consume her. "You take my fucking breath away, Aria." I inch closer to her, gently pushing her down onto the bed. I stare down at her and I'm obsessed with how she looks right now. Spread out on my bed, ready for me to devour her.

Her breath catches in her throat. "Leo," she murmurs, my name sounding like a plea falling from her lips. I crawl onto the bed with her, settling between her legs as my cock throbs against her damp pussy. Dipping my face down to hers, I steal the air from her lungs as I kiss her deeply.

Pulling away again, I shift my weight as I'm about to begin my descent down her body, when her arms dart out and wrap around the back of my neck. She lifts her legs and hooks them around my waist, pushing me back toward her.

I cock my head to the side and lift an eyebrow. "What are you doing?"

"I need you, Leo," she breathes, applying as much pressure as she can with her legs. The tip of my cock presses against her center and I revel in her warmth.

"What if I told you I wanted to taste your pussy first?"

She shakes her head at me, biting down on her bottom lip as her fingernails scratch against my flesh. "I want you now. I want to feel you deep inside me."

My face dips back down to hers and I pull her bottom lip between my teeth. Aria lets out a sharp exhale as I dig into her flesh, leaving half-moon marks along her lip. My tongue slips out and I run it across them, soothing the small wounds as I sink deep inside her. Aria lets out a moan as she takes every fucking inch. This is what she wants and I'm never going to be the one to deny her that.

Her wish will always be my command.

I begin to slowly pump my hips, easing my cock in and out of her. "God, you were made for me," I tell her as I plant my hands beside her head. "So fucking perfect. You take my cock so well, baby."

She stares up at me, her lips parted slightly as I continue to pound into her. I love the way she looks right now. Her pussy clenches around me, gripping my cock as I stroke her insides. We stay in this position for a little bit before I pull out of her and rock back onto my knees. Aria watches me, a slow smile curving her lips as I grab her ankles. Straightening her legs against my torso and chest, I pull her feet up until they're on either side of my head as I sink into her once more.

Aria hooks her ankles around the back of my neck and I reach down to hold her ass as she lifts it off the bed. I slam into her again, watching the way she's coming apart as I fuck her slowly. "You're so good," I groan as my balls begin to constrict, drawing closer to my body as the warmth begins to blossom across my lower abdomen.

"Oh my god, Leo," she moans as I reach down between her legs and my fingers dance across her clit. I press down on it, rolling my thumb over the bundle of nerves. Her eyes practically roll back in her head. I watch her back as it begins to arch from the pleasure that ripples through her body. Goddamn, she's the most beautiful thing I have ever seen.

This isn't the first time I've been inside her or seen her naked, but fuck... this is the first time I've seen her like this.

"That's it, baby," I murmur as I pound into her, filling her to the brim with my length. "Take every fucking inch like you were made for my cock and no one else's."

Her hips buck involuntarily. "Don't stop, Leo," she moans, completely breathless. "I'm so close."

"Let go," I urge her, thrusting into her harder and faster as I work my fingers over her clit. "Come for me, Aria."

As I thrust into her once more, she inhales sharply before crying out. She loses herself around me as her orgasm tears through her body. Her pussy tightens around my cock like a vise grip as she drives me past the point of no return. I'm right there with her, falling over the edge as I breathe her name. We're free falling together, plunging deep into the abyss of ecstasy. I'm not sure I ever want to resurface from this. I want to be lost in her for the rest of eternity.

My name falls from her lips like a breathless chant, like she's praying for my soul.

If only she knew, she's the one who now possesses it.

CHAPTER TWENTY-FOUR
ARIA

Lying on my side, I stare at Leo as he peacefully snores. His face is relaxed and there is a youthful innocence in his features. Lifting my hand, I reach for him, running my fingertips across his forehead, over his eyebrows, and down his straight nose. He wrinkles the tip of it as I tickle him and he stirs awake.

I don't know what time it is, but I imagine it's in the early hours of the morning, as the sun hasn't begun to crest the horizon. Leo made sure I was thoroughly satiated before I drifted into an ecstasy-induced coma. Spending the night wasn't part of my plan, but I found myself wrapped up in him, reveling in his warmth as we danced through my dreams.

There's no way any of this is real.

We're going to wake up in the morning and this is all going to go away. He's like sand running through my fingers. He's tangible, but I know he's not something I can ever hold on to.

A smile curves Leo's lips, but he doesn't open his eyes. "Why aren't you sleeping?"

I shrug, even though he can't see it. "I don't know." I chew on the inside of my lip for a second as Leo's eyes open and they slowly search mine. Letting my guard down, I show him a vulnerable card. "I was afraid if I went back to sleep, I'd wake up and this would all be a dream."

Something unreadable passes through his expression and his eyes soften as he reaches for me. He pulls me across the mattress, until I'm flush against his naked body. His legs slip between mine and I wrap my arm around his waist as I hold him tightly.

"Sleep, Ari. I promise when you wake up, all of this will still be real."

Nestling against him, I breathe in his scent and allow my eyes to close as I feel him holding me. With him, I'll always be safe. I don't know if that insurance policy includes my heart, but I'm willing to roll the dice just to find out.

I drift back asleep with thoughts of Leo dancing through my mind. Whether I'm awake or asleep, I can never escape him. Leo Wells is everywhere I go and he's the only thing I see.

And I know he'll never feel the same way.

***

Leo's in the bathroom when I wake up again. This time, the sun is shining brightly through the windows as it hangs in the clear blue sky. I slowly climb out of bed, wrapping the sheet around my body as I pad across the room and stand along the wall of glass. The door is in the center and I press the handle down before pulling it open. I step out onto the deck, feeling the wood beneath my feet. The door shuts softly behind me.

Wrapping the sheet tighter around my naked body, I walk over to the edge and lean against the railing as I stare out at the ocean. The waves break and roll against the shore in a rhythmic melody. It's calm and peaceful. Closing my eyes, I tilt my head back and soak in the warmth of the sun against my skin. Leo has his own slice of heaven here, undisturbed by the rest of the world.

If I were him, I don't think I'd ever leave here.

I'm lost in my thoughts, watching the ocean as she dances across the sand, when I hear the sound of the door opening behind me. Leo walks across the deck, stepping up behind me as he cages me in with his arms. His chest and stomach press against my back as he gently leans against me, planting his hands on the railing beside my elbows.

"There you are," he murmurs against my ear before pressing his lips against my neck. "I was wondering where you disappeared to."

I laugh softly as I rest the back of my head against his shoulder. "Where did you think I would have gone?"

"I don't know," he says quietly, with a hint of reservation in his tone. "Anywhere but here."

The way he says the words, his tone laced with sadness, has me feeling a little unsettled. My mind begins to run wild and anxiety begins to build in my veins as I question everything that has happened between us in the past twelve hours.

"Should I have left?"

Leo drags his nose against the shell of my ear. "I wouldn't be mad if you did."

What?

My body is on high alert and dread floods me as I push away from the railing, moving him with me. Straightening my spine, I stand up straight, clutching the sheet in my hands as I spin around to face him. "What do you mean?"

Leo stares at me for a moment, tucking his hands into the front pockets of his jogger pants. My eyes betray me, traveling over the dips and curves of his chiseled torso and toned arms before reaching his eyes again. Damn him for looking the way he does. I can't decide if I'd rather kiss him or go slash his tires.

"I mean, I would get it if you left. I don't know what I'm doing here, Ari." He shrugs with simplicity, although there's a hint of pain woven in the golden flecks of his irises. "Things like this—they don't last."

I'm floored by his response—and not in a good way. Every syllable is like a dagger to my already bleeding heart.

"I see," I say softly, attempting to conceal the torment that threatens to wreak havoc. "This is the last time any of this happens between us, Leo. I'm done riding this roller coaster with you until you know exactly what it is that you want."

"What?" He tilts his head to the side, the color draining from his face as he sets his lips in a firm line. "I never said I don't want you." He lets out a frustrated breath as confusion mixes in his expression. "We're not on a roller coaster."

"Yes, we are," I argue, feeling the tears prick the corners of my eyes. "You give me whiplash, Leo. One moment, you're keeping me at arm's length and you hate me. The next, you're pulling me into your orbit." I pause, shaking my head as I can feel my facade cracking. "I won't do it. I won't just be a toy for you to break."

"I don't want to break you."

I level my gaze on his, feeling the defeat in my shoulders. "I don't think you know what you want."

"I know what I want," he retorts, the muscle in his jaw tightening. "You're no saint, Aria Reed. You've been playing the same fucking games, giving me the same mixed signals."

"I know," I let out a shaky breath. "I've tried to hate you, but I can't anymore. When I'm around you, nothing else matters. When I'm not around you, you're the only person I want to be around. I fucking hate it." My lungs deflate. "I want more than this with you, Leo."

His eyes widen and shock settles in them. "Wait, what?"

I've already said too much. I've shown my cards and I have nothing left to play. All there is are my truths hanging heavily in the salty air between us. Turning on my heel, I walk back to the door and push it open before I look back at him one last time.

"Aria," he says softly, my name a plea as his eyes search mine. Pain is etched in his features, and I know this is what I have to do. If I respect myself in the slightest bit, I have to let him go. I can't keep falling into bed with him and act like it can be something casual.

I'm not a casual person.

I need more than a hookup.

"I need to go," I tell him, instantly feeling regret, but I can't let that fuel my decision. "I'll see you at the rink."

"Please, don't go," he says with panic in his tone. I hate the way his face looks right now. Like he's begging me to stay while his chest is cracking wide open. "Not like this."

I shake my head at him. I can't keep giving in to him. "I need space."

"You mean space from me," he says with hurt lacing through his words. His face momentarily falters and I don't miss the coldness as it settles in his expression.

I nod, blinking back my tears. "I can't think straight when I'm around you."

A harsh scoff escapes him. "You say it like you're the only one who's fucked up right now."

"How are you fucked up?"

A dark shadow dances across his face and Leo stalks across the deck to me. He doesn't stop until he's less than a foot away. He reaches and grabs the threshold, holding on to the doorframe as his eyes probe mine. "You drive me fucking insane, Aria. You consume my thoughts, you command my feelings. Every goddamn thought I have always circles back to you." He lets out a pained laugh. "I've tried to get rid of you and yet you're so deep under my skin, I can't get you out."

"You want more?" He pauses, his face softening. "I'll give you everything. You want the stars? I'll find a spaceship and a way to bring them down to you on Earth."

His words are everything I want to hear. The way my

heart instantly swells, only to have my anxiety poke it with a pin. It deflates just as quickly as it inflated. The anxious voice in my head begins to question every word he says. He doesn't mean it. It's all a ploy. He'll only hurt me in the end.

"All we do is argue," I remind him, my voice coming out like a whisper. What the hell am I saying? My anxiety slides into the driver's seat and I'm merely a passenger as I begin to self-destruct. "How could there really be more when we fight more than we actually get along?"

He drops his hand from the doorway and takes a step back as if I slapped him. Rejection flashes in his eyes. "And you say *I'm* the one who doesn't know what they want?" He throws his hands up in defeat. "You know, I never thought I deserved you... But I don't deserve this either," he says with a shake of his head as he spins on his heel.

Leo leaves me standing in the doorway as he exits the deck, taking the steps down to the first floor. A war wages inside me. I should go after him and tell him the truth. He does deserve me. If there's anyone who does, it's him. I just royally fucked up and my anxiety has me running in the opposite direction of him. I rush into the house and quickly put my clothing on before I leave.

He's nowhere to be seen.

The tears don't fall until I'm in my car driving away.

Until his house is disappearing in my rearview mirror.

Until I'm far enough away from him so he won't see me fracturing into a million pieces.

I never thought I would be crying over the one person I hated. Life's funny like that, and I guess I'm the one who is really the fool for ever thinking I hated Leo Wells. We may have never gotten along in the past, but I don't truly believe I ever felt that way about him. He showed me softer sides that he never showed to anyone else, but I always felt hurt when he would flip the script and play the part of my enemy. Around other people, I never existed to him. He was always cold and indifferent. Until recently.

Leo never felt like he was deserving of me, for whatever reason, but something inside him must have changed. This entire time, I thought he was just being nicer because he felt compelled to, when in reality there was a myriad of things going on beneath the surface with him.

While he was breaking through my walls, he was letting his own guard down. He was showing me the vulnerable sides of himself, slowly letting me in. I didn't realize it until I saw the hurt written across his face.

And here I am, running away from him like a goddamn coward.

CHAPTER TWENTY-FIVE
LEO

Picking up a seashell along the sand, I chuck it out into the water. There's a small splash followed by another wave rolling in. I watch as it crashes against the shore and white bubbles float across the surface of the ocean. The sun is warm on my skin and I close my eyes as I tilt my head back and relish the feeling of it.

I hear the sound of a car door shutting and I keep my eyes plastered shut. Her car starts and I listen as she quickly pulls out of my driveway and leaves.

This is all so fucked up.

I don't know how we went from last night to now. I didn't expect to hear from her after her date with Griffin. When she asked to come over, I didn't give myself the chance to even think. There wasn't a doubt or question about it. She wanted to see me and I would never turn her away.

Since we've known each other, she has always been a

mindfuck for me. She was my best friend's little sister. I couldn't date her when we were younger. And then she dated my rival—which was a whole different issue. After that, she became the enemy. We were in constant competition with each other, until we were forced to compete together.

Aria was always beautiful and I've always had perfect vision. When we started crossing these damn lines together, that's when it got worse. I tried to keep her at arm's length. I tried to keep her out. I failed—horribly on both accounts—and now I was completely fucked.

Because I want her.

I want every fucking piece of her, and I want her all for myself.

I rake a frustrated hand through my hair as I slowly turn back to face the house. I shouldn't have let her leave. I shouldn't have walked away, but I did. My mind was reeling, while still trying to process what the hell really happened.

There is a part of me that knows I don't deserve her. I never will. My first mistake today was telling her I wouldn't be mad if she left. Instead of being filled with joy because she was still here, I was questioning it. It all came out wrong. I never meant for it to get to this point after I brought it up.

I shouldn't have told her that things like this don't last, because I don't know if I fully believe that shit. That was all my own personal self-doubt and I projected it onto her, which made her question me instead. What started out as her questioning me on what I wanted, turned into her acting like she's the one who doesn't know what the hell she wants.

I know what I want, and it's her. I was an idiot for ever thinking it wouldn't be her. Hating her feels like such a distant memory.

Now that I know what it feels like to love her.

My hand curls into a fist and I press it against my lips as I stare at the back of my house. Butterflies flutter in my stomach as my heart rate quickens. Those thoughts have been drifting around in my mind, but this is the first time I've really paid them any attention.

Goddammit.

I'm in love with Aria Reed.

My footsteps feel heavy as I walk up onto the back deck. Since admitting it to myself, it feels like there's been a weight lifted from my chest, yet I don't know what I'm supposed to do with this information. Do I tell her? Do I give her the space she thinks she needs? I pushed her away when I should have washed away her worries.

As I reach the French doors that lead into the first floor of my house, my phone starts to vibrate in the pocket of my sweatpants. Reaching inside, I pull it out and sigh when I see Austin's name on the screen. I weigh my options carefully. It can't be a coincidence that he's calling me after Aria just ran off. If I ignore his call, he's going to rip me a new asshole. But if I answer his call, he's probably going to do the same.

It's really a lose-lose situation.

"That was fast," I say into the speaker as I answer the phone and hold it against the side of my face. I wander across the deck and drop down onto the outdoor sectional that looks out at the ocean.

Austin is silent for a beat. "What?"

Oh, shit. Maybe he doesn't know.

"Nothing, I thought you were someone else," I lie in an attempt to cover it up. I really need to start thinking before I speak. "What's up?"

"Who did you think I was?" Austin questions me with a touch of curiosity in his voice. "Actually, tell me later. I was calling to tell you I'll be in town for a few days. Did you want to grab drinks or something tonight?"

I shake my head even though he can't see me. "I think I'm just going to stay in tonight."

"Then I'll come by your place. I can grab food from somewhere."

Austin fucking Reed. He never could take a hint or read the room. The last thing I want is for him to come hang out while I'm dealing with this shit with his sister. "By staying in, I mean I don't want any company."

"What's going on?" he questions me without hesitation. Austin has always been very in touch with his feelings and if someone else isn't feeling the best, he wants to talk it out. He's emotionally regulated and mentally healthy. I'm not saying I'm not, but somehow he has a way of always looking at things objectively and from an outsider's perspective. If I need sound advice from anyone, Austin is always my go-to person... except for right now, when it has to do with his little sister.

I don't know what to tell him. "It's nothing."

"Bullshit," he argues, not willing to let it go. "I can tell when something is going on. If you don't want to talk about it, I won't push you to, but you know I'm here if you need a sounding board."

I'm silent for a moment. I trust Austin more than any of my other friends or family. He's my best friend and I don't want to fuck that up. I don't want to lose him while I'm already in the process of losing his sister. "It's not something I can talk to you about."

There's a pregnant pause. He doesn't speak a word for the longest time and I find myself glancing at my phone screen to make sure our call is still connected. "It's about Ari, isn't it?"

"Yes."

"Fuck," he mumbles into the speaker. I hear some commotion in the background but don't bother asking where he is. "My flight lands a little after four. I have to get my car and then I can pick up food and stop by."

Staring out at the ocean, I close my eyes, my nostrils flaring as I inhale deeply, feeling my lungs expanding as I take in a massive breath. There's no sense arguing with him, especially since he knows something happened with Aria. "I'll see you then."

"Yep," he says in a clipped tone before abruptly ending the call. I sigh as I lock my phone screen and resist the urge to throw it over the side of the deck. He didn't speak a single word about it on the phone, so I have no way of knowing how this is going to go. It can go one of two ways: really well or poorly. He's either going to be understanding or put his fist through my face.

I probably deserve the latter at this point.

***

It's later in the evening and I just spent the entire day doing nothing productive. It was our one day off from skating, so there wasn't anywhere I needed to be. There were at least a dozen times throughout the day that I picked up my phone, opened my messages, and stared at the thread between Aria and I. I wanted to text her so badly, but I couldn't do it. Not after the way she left. What was I supposed to do? Beg her to come back? Go find her?

I wasted the day being stuck in my head instead.

My doorbell rings and I slowly get up from where I've been vegging out on the couch. I flip on the light in the foyer and pause inside the door that leads into the kitchen. I see Austin standing on the other side, holding a bag of takeout as he peers through the glass window. His gaze catches mine and I motion for him to open the door and come in. He usually doesn't wait for me to answer the door if it's unlocked.

This feels like a bad sign.

Austin begins to let himself in, so I walk into the kitchen to wait. I reach into a cabinet and pull out two glasses and set them down on the massive island that occupies the space in the center of the room. Austin walks in just as I'm grabbing a bottle of whiskey and I set it down next to the cups.

He raises an eyebrow at me as he lifts his arm and puts the bag on the counter. "Well, the whiskey tells me everything I need to know," he says with a frown as he reaches into the bag and pulls out two Styrofoam containers. He pops them open, revealing rice and empanadas. Austin walks past me, grabs two forks from the drawer, and moves around to the other side of the island. I watch him, tilting my head to the side as he sits down on one of the stools and slides a container of food in front of himself.

"What is that?"

He pushes his fork into the rice and lifts his head to look at me. His eyes are a mirror of Aria's, except he's missing the freckles. "That it isn't good."

I let out a sigh and grab one of the stools, carrying it over to the side I'm standing at before I sit down. Austin pushes the other container across the island for me and hands me a fork. We sit across from each other the awkward silence wrapping itself around us as one of us waits for the other to speak. I don't know where the hell to begin, but I'm going to have to start somewhere. I just need to rip off the Band-Aid and get it over with.

After swallowing a mouthful of food, I grab the two glasses and pour the whiskey into them before handing one to Austin. I take a slow sip and set my glass back down. "I fucked things up with your sister."

Austin pauses mid-chew before beginning again. "Professionally or personally?"

"Personally," I admit as I push some of my rice around in the Styrofoam container. "Things are going really well with skating, so there's no concern there."

"Okay," he nods as he lifts his own glass to his lips and swallows some of the burning liquid. "What happened then?"

Rolling my lips between my teeth, I pause. Now is when I need to think before I speak. I don't know how much to tell him because I don't want to piss him off or anything like that.

Austin interrupts my thoughts and it's as if he can read my mind. "Pretend she's not my sister."

"That's easier said than done," I tell him with a nervous laugh as I adjust in my seat. "I don't know where to start."

"At the beginning, maybe?" he offers, although it comes out more like a question.

I want to be honest with him. I want to tell him everything because I've been sitting on all of these feelings by myself for so fucking long.

"Promise you won't punch me in the face if I do that?"

Austin chuckles and shakes his head. "No dice."

I shrug. It was worth a try. Tilting my head back, I take a deep breath before I straighten my spine and look back at my best friend. "I had a crush on her in high school, but after she started dating Griffin, it transformed into hate."

Austin raises his eyebrows at me but then his face goes back to a neutral expression as he waits for me to continue. He doesn't know about that night we skated together. He knew I didn't like her back then, mainly because of Griffin, but he never knew there was more to it. He doesn't need to know the specifics.

"It started after we started skating together," I tell him, leaving out the part where we almost had sex a few months prior to that. "I struggled for a long time with my attraction to her while also trying to convince myself and everyone around me that I didn't like her. It was easier to hate her because those feelings are easier for me to deal with. All of this confusion is much worse."

He stares at me for a moment, his expression revealing nothing. He has an excellent poker face and I'm slightly envious of it. His fork is resting in his container of food and he takes another sip of his drink. "I don't think anyone likes feelings when they are uncomfortable."

I shake my head, agreeing with him. "I'm sure you can imagine that we've gotten closer given the nature of our working relationship. It's hard to not have the tension and emotion bleed into regular life. The first time we skated together, we were both so caught up in the moment that I almost kissed her. After that, I tried to keep her at arm's length and failed miserably."

"Did you sleep with her?"

Fuck. There is the question I was hoping he wasn't going to ask.

"Yes."

The muscle in his jaw twitches and he nods. "So, what happened that has you all fucked up right now?"

"She came over last night, and then this morning it all went to shit. I went to the bathroom and thought she had left, but I found her out on my deck. I went out to her and stupidly told her I wouldn't blame her if she left because I don't know what I'm doing right now." I pause and shake my head, feeling the defeat in my muscles. "I told her that things like this don't last."

Austin's face is still blank and he tilts his head to the side as he assesses me. "Do you actually believe that?"

"I did," I say quietly as I mull over his question, letting it sink into my bones. "I don't know now. I want to believe that good things do last."

"They do," he assures me before he drains the rest of the liquor from his glass. He reaches across the counter and grabs the bottle of whiskey and refills it. "If it's the right person and the right time, I truly believe they do."

"Well, she fucking bolted after I said all that to her." I let out a frustrated, contradicting laugh. "She told me she wanted more, assumed I didn't want the same, and then told me she needs space. I told her I know what I want and that it's her, and then she shut down."

Austin purses his lips. "So, you both spent all morning sending each other mixed signals and pushing one another away." A smile lifts the corners of his mouth as he rolls his eyes. "You two really are made for each other."

"Fuck you, Reed." I chuckle as I give him the middle finger and throw a grain of rice at him. Our laughter trails off and the silence returns again. I hate it. "I don't know what to do, man."

"You stop being a fucking idiot and you go get her."

My eyes widen and I pull my shoulders back as I stare at him. "She wants space from me."

"Fuck her space," he says as he picks up his fork again. "I know my sister. She doesn't want space, it's just what she does when her anxiety causes her to second-guess things. She withdraws and retreats when she really needs someone to be there. When you told her about good things not lasting, you solidified the doubts that were already circulating in her mind."

"I told her that I do want her," I explain to him, feeling a small spark of hope inside my chest as I play his words over in my head. There's a small twinge of guilt for me because I didn't try harder to get her to understand what I was saying.

"You have to understand that Aria moves in survival mode when she gets stressed out. She specializes in self-preservation. If she has feelings for you, you are now a threat because you have the ability to hurt her." He runs a hand through his hair. "Are you in love with her?"

My throat clenches and I swallow roughly over the lump lodged there. "Yes."

"Did you tell her that?"

"No," I admit as I prop my elbows on the island and drop my head into my hands.

"Good," Austin says and I can hear the smile in his voice.

I lift my head at the sound and cock an eyebrow. "How is that good? Shouldn't I have told her how I feel about her?"

He laughs softly and shrugs. "I mean, yeah, probably, but this gives you something to work with when you go see her. It's something you didn't already tell her, so you're not trying to convince her that you meant those words. She hasn't heard them yet. If there's anything that can get someone's attention, it's admitting your feelings for them *to* them."

A part of me feels like this is a joke. "Are you being serious about this?"

"Yes," he assures me with a warm smile. "If there's anyone who I trust enough to be with my sister, it's you." He takes a breath and narrows his eyes on me. "If you break her heart, I will rip yours from your chest and feed it to you."

"That's extremely graphic," I tell him as I try not to imagine what that experience might be like.

He shrugs with indifference, as if the threat was completely normal. "You should know what you're getting yourself into."

"You have nothing to worry about. I have no intention of ever breaking her heart."

Austin Reed smiles at me, revealing his bright white teeth. "Then I think it's time to start planning."

"Planning what?"

"How you're going to get her back."

"She was never actually mine," I remind him with a sigh.

Austin laughs and shakes his head. "Trust me... she was. And I think she still is."

CHAPTER TWENTY-SIX
ARIA

Lying on the couch, I flip through the TV channels before settling on some home improvement show. My nose tickles and I reach for the box of tissues that is on my coffee table just before I sneeze. I don't know where this head cold came from, but I blame it on the stress I've been enduring. And of course this happens right before we have our most important competition coming up.

I should be on the ice practicing, but I feel like complete ass. I know I'll be a worthless partner to Leo and, if I'm being completely honest, I could use a day away from him right now.

My phone vibrates from where it's laying on the couch and I pick it up to look at the message that came through. It's Leo. I texted him a little while ago to tell him I wouldn't be there this morning. There was disappointment when he didn't respond at first.

LEO

Are you okay?

I roll onto my back, pulling the plush quilt up to my chin before I type out a response to him.

ARIA

I think it's just a cold. I need the day and will hopefully feel better tomorrow.

I only owe him an explanation because of our partnership. Other than that, he doesn't need to know what is going on with me. He doesn't need to know that I spent all day in this same exact spot after I left his house. He doesn't need to know that I struggled against the urge to run back to him all fucking day yesterday.

There's a lot he doesn't need to know... but at the same time, there are things I want him to know.

LEO

I hope you start feeling better soon.

I frown as I read over his message again and then lock my screen and toss it onto the other end of the couch. Fuck Leo and his mundane response. I don't know what I was expecting, but for some reason, it wasn't that. I had hoped maybe he would care a little bit—that he would care about me.

I was right all along.

Leo only cares about winning and he's just using me to get what he wants. There was a point yesterday where I started to convince myself that maybe he meant what he said, that maybe he wouldn't hurt me and I could trust him with my heart.

What an idiot...

I don't doubt that he wants me. I know he does. I have felt it and I have seen it. But there is a difference between wanting someone sexually and wanting all of them. It's very easy for someone to say one thing when they mean another. How am I supposed to know that Leo is actually being truthful when I haven't extended the same to him? What I told him yesterday just barely touched my feelings for him.

I need him to show me he means what he says. I don't just want his words, I want the actions to support it—to make me believe. I should have told him that yesterday and now I'm unsure of where to even begin. Do I reach out to him and ask him to talk? That feels far too formal compared to what has transpired between us.

An exasperated sigh escapes me and I drop my head back down on my pillow, feeling the ache within my temples. This is exhausting and I'm tired.

I know what I need to do. We need to talk. I need to be clear with him about what I want and what I don't want. Life is too short to leave things unsaid... I just need to figure out a way to tell him.

I need a moment to breathe, a moment for my anxiety to slide back into the back seat so I can be honest with Leo and myself.

He was right, he doesn't deserve this. He deserves the truth.

And the truth is I'm in love with him.

After spending most of the day drifting in and out of sleep, wasting away on the couch, I'm beginning to feel a little bit better. I don't feel one hundred percent. I'm still congested and sneezing, but my headache has started to dissipate, so that's a positive.

Hopefully sleeping all day isn't going to mess up my sleep schedule. I need all the rest I can get because I can't afford to take off tomorrow. Leo needs me on the ice with him. We have to be prepared for our next competition and this isn't helpful for anyone.

Plus... I think I'm finally going to pull on my big girl panties and come clean with him about how I feel. The thought alone is terrifying, but it has to be done. That's one thing I at least figured out while I spent the day sick on the couch.

I finally pull myself from my comfy spot and see it's almost three thirty. My hair feels disgusting, so I drag myself to the shower and turn the water on as hot as it will go. After stripping out of my clothes, I step into the steaming stream and feel it helping to ease away the remnants of my headache. The heat helps with the congestion and by the time I finally get out of the shower, my skin is bright red from the temperature, but I feel like a brand-new woman.

There's no doubt in my mind that I won't be able to get back on the ice tomorrow. We really need to make sure we have this new routine down. We can't afford to mess it up, not after all the work we put in to get this far. It's the world championship. We've both won it separately, but never together.

It has easily become my number one goal. Ultimately, all of this will help us to qualify for the Olympics, but that's a goal for next year. This year, I want nothing more than to win Worlds with Leo Wells by my side.

After getting dried off and dressed, I'm standing in front of the mirror, running a wide-toothed comb through my long hair when I hear the sound of my doorbell ringing through the house. My body freezes and a chill slides down my spine. My stomach quickens with anxiety. I'm not expecting anyone, so I have no idea who it could possibly be.

My brother Austin is in town for a few days while he gets some quotes for work he wants to do at the rink, but I haven't talked to him other than through text messages. I didn't tell him I was sick and we didn't talk about anything of importance. Hell, I didn't even tell him about Leo.

We didn't talk about getting together, but I can't think of who it would be other than him or Brynn. I talked to her this morning and she knew I wasn't feeling well, but she's working until five today.

Leaving the bathroom a mess, I glance down at the Christmas pajamas I put on, even though it's not even winter right now, and shrug as I leave the room. My footsteps are light and hesitant as I make my way to the front door. Lifting on my toes, I look out of the small pane of glass and my heart leaves my fucking chest.

It's Leo.

He's standing on the other side, one hand holding a paper bag and the other is tucked in the front pocket of his black joggers as he stares down at his sneakers. Dropping down onto my heels, I hold my hand over my chest as I give myself a moment or two to catch my breath and get myself together. He's the last person I was expecting to show up here. My hand is tentative as I unlock the deadbolt and reach for the doorknob.

Slowly turning it, I open the door and move into the doorway as my eyes find Leo's. "Hey," I say softly, my voice hoarse and thick with sleep. "What are you doing here?"

Leo gives me a small apologetic smile and lifts the brown paper bag into the air. "I thought some soup might help you feel a little better."

Shifting my weight on my feet, I return his smile, although the apology in mine is a bit different. Silence momentarily hangs heavily between us before I step out of the way, making room for him to step inside my home. "I don't know if what I have is contagious, so I'm not sure if you want to come in or not."

"Nothing could keep me away from you," he says softly as he stares at me for two prolonged heartbeats. Leo steps through the doorway, kicking his shoes off in the foyer. "I'll take my chances with getting sick."

My plush socks slide across the floor as I close the door and lock it behind us. Leo follows me through the foyer and into the kitchen, but he holds his arm out to stop me as I go to reach for a drawer. "Go get comfortable on the couch and I'll bring you everything."

"I can't ask you to do that for me, Leo."

"You're not asking," he says with a sly grin and

mischief dancing across his expression. "Let me take care of you, Aria."

I'm torn between not wanting him to feel obligated and wanting to let him. The last thing I want him to do is think I'm taking advantage of his kindness, especially after what happened yesterday morning. I'm not even sure I deserve his kindness at this point.

"Okay," I reply softly before padding across the floor, back over to where my spot is on the couch. Sitting down, I tuck my legs in and pull the quilt back over my body. My back rests against the cushion and I have the perfect view of my kitchen as I watch Leo move around the room like it's where he belongs.

He pulls a container from the brown paper bag and sets it on the counter. Confusion washes over my face as I watch him pull out multiple containers, all filled with various vegetables.

"I thought you said you brought soup?" I ask him as he lays everything out.

His gaze lifts to mine, his eyes shimmering under the lights as he stares at me from across the room. "I did," he says with a shrug. "Well, I brought everything to make soup."

My heart skips a beat in my chest and I'm at a loss for words. He goes back to busying himself in my kitchen and I stare at him in awe. As if bringing me soup wasn't enough, he brought everything to make it. I don't know the last time I've had home-cooked soup when I was sick. I roll through the memories in my brain and realize the answer is never.

Leo isn't familiar with anything in my kitchen and a slow smile pulls across my lips as I watch him opening various cabinet doors, looking for pots and bowls. He isn't struggling, but he's opening all the wrong doors. My lips part, a soft laugh escaping me before I finally interject to assist him.

"They're over in the—" I start to say but he lifts his hand to silence me.

"Let me find it myself," he tells me with a wink. "I'm trying to memorize where you keep everything."

I tilt my head to the side with curiosity lingering in my voice. "For what?"

"So I know where to find things next time."

Good Lord.

The air leaves my lungs in a rush as my heart drums harder against my rib cage, threatening to break through. I'm left speechless again, unsure of what this life is that I'm living. I tried to push him away in an effort to protect myself and here he is, knocking down every wall possible. He refuses to be shut out and I would be lying if I said I wasn't happy about it.

I always knew Leo didn't like to lose, but I didn't know the same concept would apply to me as well.

He looks like this is exactly where he belongs as he stands by my stove, stirring all the ingredients as he makes me soup.

He looks like he's at home… and maybe he is.

Maybe this is exactly where he belongs.

With me.

CHAPTER TWENTY-SEVEN
LEO

Spooning out a generous helping, I fill Aria's bowl with the homemade vegetable soup and set the ladle on the paper towel on the counter. I grab a spoon and slide it through the steaming liquid before walking across her kitchen and into the living room.

Aria's sitting on the couch, not bothering to watch the TV—opting to watch me instead. There's a little hop in my step, the excitement dancing in my veins as I see a smile lifting her lips as I reach her.

"For you," I say softly, handing it to her. I fight the urge to toss the soup onto the floor and pull her to me.

"Thank you," she practically whispers as she shifts on the couch, motioning for me to sit with her as she takes the bowl in her hands. Her eyelids flutter closed and she looks content as she inhales the steam drifting from the soup. "It smells amazing."

I shrug, suddenly feeling nervous under her watchful gaze. "It's nothing. It was my grandmother's recipe."

"Is there anything you can't do?"

"The jury is still out on that," I tell her as she lifts the spoon and blows on the liquid.

Her eyebrows pull together. "Why is that?"

My eyes drop to her mouth as she parts her lips and slides the spoon between them. My cock twitches in my pants as she sucks the liquid from the piece of metal, her throat bobbing as she swallows. Now is not the time, but apparently my dick didn't get the memo.

I do love the way she looks when she's swallowing...

"I haven't made you mine, so that might be something I can't do."

Aria's head snaps up to look at me, her body momentarily turning rigid as the tension hangs heavily in the air between us. She needs to know the truth. I was coming here to talk to her whether she was sick or not—it just so happened to work out that I had an excuse to show up.

"I didn't come here just to make you soup."

She inhales sharply. Her eyes are glued to mine and I don't miss the way they widen the slightest bit. Her pupils grow, like her vision is trying to soak me in. "Okay," she says quietly before pausing to chew on the inside of her cheek. She sets her spoon back in her bowl, not taking her gaze from mine. "I feel really stupid for reading this all wrong," she admits with a quiet, awkward laugh.

My eyebrows pull together. "What did you read wrong?"

A sigh escapes her, followed by a small cough as she turns her head and covers it with the inside of her elbow. "It doesn't even matter." A sad smile lifts the corners of her lips. "Were you planning on finishing the rest of this season together or did you want a clean break now?"

Her question throws me off completely and I can't help myself as I'm the one laughing nervously now. "I'm sorry, I'm failing to understand what you're saying right now."

"You came here to end our skating partnership," she says matter-of-factly, like I should know what she's talking about when we are clearly on two different fucking pages. "The soup was like a consolation prize. Like a 'thanks for playing, try again.'" She pauses and shakes her head . "I'm sorry if I'm the reason this didn't work out. I tried not to let my feelings get involved and obviously, I failed."

My jaw is literally on the ground. She is coming from left field with a claim that she has little to no support for. I don't even know where any of this is coming from, but I plan on getting to the bottom of it… right after I tell her what I really came here for.

"You're right," I tell her, nodding in the most convincing way possible. "You failed miserably." I pause, watching her eyes drop from mine as she directs her gaze to the bowl of soup in her hands. "And so did I."

Aria's eyes snap back to mine again. "What?"

"I'm in love with you, Aria Reed. Addicted and infatuated. Hopelessly and irrevocably in love."

Her lips art, her nostrils flaring with emotion as she blinks twice. I watch her throat bob as she swallows roughly. "Don't you dare say things you don't mean, Leo Wells."

"You are so goddamn difficult, you know that, right?" A soft laugh leaves me as I shake my head at her. "You want more, I tell you I'll give you everything. I tell you I'm in love with you, and you're still questioning me." I pause, reaching for her soup and set it down on the coffee table before taking her face in my hands. "What do *you* want?"

Aria's eyelids close, her dark lashes resting against her lightly tanned skin. The silence is deafening as it stretches between us. Slowly, her eyes open once more and I count the freckles in her irises. The same ones I've had memorized for years.

"You," she whispers as her tongue darts out to wet her plump lips. "I want you, Leo, and I'm sorry for making you think otherwise yesterday." She pauses, a smile breaking out across her face as tears shimmer in her eyes. "You terrify me."

My thumb catches one of her tears before brushing it away from her perfect face. "Why?"

"Because I know I won't survive a heartbreak from you. I'm teetering on the edge of giving you every piece of me and I know if I do, I'm not sure what will be left of me if you decide you no longer want me."

"You silly, silly girl," I whisper as I bite back my grin. Shaking my head, I chuckle softly. "You don't get it, do you? You're it for me. I promise there will never be a day in my life that I don't want you. Believe me when I tell you, I will never hurt you."

She gives me a playful smile as she reaches up and wraps her hands around my wrists. "My brother threatened you, didn't he?"

"He did," I admit, feeling the butterflies fluttering away in my stomach. "But that doesn't change anything."

I pause, pressing my lips to her forehead before I press my forehead against hers. "My heart is yours, Aria. To have, to hold, to throw in the trash. It's yours now and even if you decide you don't want me, I don't want it back."

"What if I told you I wanted to keep it forever?"

Her words warm my soul and I can feel myself falling even harder for her in this moment. When I look at my future, I can't imagine it without Aria anymore. I didn't realize what was happening until it was too late—until she had already situated herself inside my heart.

She took that black hollow organ in my chest and nourished it back to life before making it her home.

"Can I tell you something?"

Pulling my forehead away from hers, I stare down into her molten steel eyes. "Always."

"I'm glad you interrupted my date with Griffin that one night." She pauses for a moment, rolling her lips between her teeth before releasing them. "You gave me everything I needed that night and I don't feel like I properly thanked you for it."

"I can think of a few ways you can thank me," I tell her with a wink as she swats her hand at me. "When you're feeling better." Releasing her face, I reach back for the soup and hand it to her. "Eat this before it gets cold."

"Yes, sir," she says with a nod as she takes it from me. Those two little words send a rush of blood to my cock but I ignore it again. I really need to get myself under control here. I don't know what the hell has become of me. Anytime I'm near her, I'm like a teenage boy again, about to come in my damn pants just from her touching my hand or looking at me a certain way.

"This soup is seriously so good," Aria says as she takes another bite. There's a small droplet of broth on her bottom lip. Lifting my hand, I brush it away with my thumb before popping the digit in my mouth to lick it off. "Aren't you going to eat any?"

I shake my head at her as I settle back on the couch and look at the home improvement show she's watching. "I might later. I just wanted to make sure that you eat something. We need to make sure you stay hydrated. Have you been taking any medicine to help?"

She rolls her eyes at me. "Yes, daddy." Fuck, there's that rush of blood between my legs again. "I've been doing everything I need to do and I think this soup was the last thing I needed to really start feeling better."

"I missed you on the ice today." I pause for a moment, letting those feelings sink back in again, and the feeling of dread fills me. "When you didn't show up, at first I thought maybe something bad happened. Then you texted me and I wasn't sure if you were actually sick. Not that I didn't believe you—but after yesterday, I wasn't sure you were going to want to skate with me again."

Aria leans forward to set her empty bowl of soup on the table. "Well, I already exposed myself with that fear. At first, I thought you came here because you wanted to see me and then I thought it was because you were leaving me."

Kicking off my shoes, I rise to my feet and Aria moves over as I climb onto the couch with her. She pulls the quilt up over my body, our legs tangling together as I lay on my back. She scoots close until her body is plastered to my side with her arm around my torso and her head resting against my rib cage.

"I shouldn't have let you leave yesterday," I say softly as I stroke her soft wavy hair with my hand. "I should have made you stay and listen to me. I should have ran after you when you did leave." A disappointed sigh leaves me. "I should have done something, *anything*."

Aria trails her hand down to the hem of my shirt and slides her hand underneath the cotton material until her palm is pressed against my bare skin. I revel in her touch, in her warmth. "I never should have left. I let those stupid negative thoughts get the better of me. After they entered my mind, I couldn't see past them and I should have taken a step back and let myself breathe before reacting."

"We both have a lot of should-haves from yesterday," I murmur against her head before pressing a gentle kiss against her hair. "There's nothing we can do to change that now. All we can do is change the way we communicate moving forward." I roll slightly onto my side as I pull her closer to the front of my body and wrap my arms tightly around her. "I need to start thinking before I speak. I know sometimes the way I word things may come off cold and abrasive, so that's something I'm trying to work on."

"And I need to give myself time to think and process before I respond. Sometimes my anxiety takes a hold of me and I react based on emotion rather than thinking things through first.

I run my fingers through her silky locks. "That's the

beauty of being human, Ari. We're all constantly a work in progress. We're fluid like water, changing shapes and forms. We're always evolving and growing."

"No one is perfect," she murmurs, and I'm not sure whether she's telling me or telling herself.

Having to be perfect is something Aria struggles with, but she's been doing a lot better considering the stress we've been under. I've already seen the growth within her, just from the minor hiccups we've had while learning to skate together.

"No, they're not," I agree, pressing my lips to her forehead again. "But you're the closest to perfect as someone is going to get."

"That's your infatuation talking." She laughs quietly as she nestles her body against mine.

"No, love," I tell her, my voice dropping lower as I whisper the words against her skin. "That's just my heart."

***

Aria's cold thankfully only lasted a few days, but after the first day, she was feeling better and able to get back to practice. I made sure she took it easy and didn't overdo it. The last thing we needed was for either of us to be exhausted or overworked. That is never a good combination when you're trying to win an extremely important competition.

"Are you okay to get on the plane?" Aria asks me as we stand at the terminal and they've begun boarding passengers. I'm standing by the glass, staring out at the other planes as they land and take off.

I nod, feeling the anxiety washing over me. I absolutely

hate flying and I know it's completely irrational. It's not like I know anyone who has been in a plane crash or that I've experienced anything traumatizing like that myself. I blame it on the *Final Destination* movie I watched when I was a teenager.

"I'll be right here with you," she says softly as she bumps her shoulder against mine. It's the most minimal contact and I revel in the way it feels. Things haven't been weird between us, but trying to balance working together and sleeping together when no one knows the specifics of our relationship has been a little different. No one knows we've been spending every night together for the past two weeks.

There have been many times I've caught myself about to kiss her or pull her into my arms in front of people and I have to stop myself. I don't know what she expects or wants from me in terms of that. Hell, I told her I'm in love with her and didn't even accomplish what I set out for. We don't need a label to define what we are, but I've been finding myself craving one. Almost as if I need that reassurance of having a title for her—something tangible that I can shout from the rooftops to the rest of the world.

I want things to be official between us. I don't want it to be our little secret.

I want everyone to know that Aria Reed is mine and I'm hers.

"That brings me even less comfort," I tell her as they call our group and she begins to walk toward the line at the gate. I fall in line behind her. "I don't need the plane going down while you're on it too."

Aria looks over her shoulder and gives me a sideways glance. "The plane is not going to go down. We are safe, Leo. I won't let anything happen to you."

I raise an eyebrow at her as I blow air out of my nose. "Have you been hiding that you're a pilot from me too?"

The line shifts and Aria doesn't bother responding to me as we step up to the counter and have to show our boarding passes. I adjust the straps of my backpack on my shoulders and follow behind her as we walk down the loading bridge to board the plane. My phone vibrates in my pocket and I pull it out, seeing a message from Austin.

He knew about Aria and I, mainly because he wouldn't leave me alone after I went to her house when she was sick. I told him everything and he has been nothing less than supportive. He even eased my worry when I confessed that Ari didn't tell me she loved me back. He assured me she would in time, and I will give this woman as much time as she needs.

AUSTIN

Stop staring at my sister's ass.

My eyebrows pull together and I glance behind me, catching Austin's gaze as he walks about eight people behind us. "What the hell?"

Austin gives me a huge wave. "There's my favorite guy!"

Aria turns around with the same confused expression on her face. I nod back to where Austin is, grinning like a fool. "Looks like your brother is flying to Vancouver too."

Another hand rises beside Austin's head and I move mine to the side to see who it is. "Hi, Ari! Hi, Leo!"

"Brynn?" Aria questions me as a smile lifts the corners of her lips. "What are they doing here?"

The couple behind us looks unhappy and the man grumbles something under his breath as the woman clears her throat. I turn back to look at the line and see that we're holding everyone up right now.

"I'm not sure what they're doing," I tell Ari as I grab her hand and pull her along with me. "Come on, we're holding up the line and I think these people want to get on the plane." I pause and let her walk past me. "Even if I don't want to."

Aria laughs quietly and shakes her head at me. She leads the way and I follow.

We had forgotten to select seats for this flight until last week. It was a miracle that there were two seats available that were right next to one another. The world championship is being held in Vancouver, so it's not a short flight. You would think I would be used to having to travel like this, but it doesn't get any easier. It does bring me a sense of comfort having Aria with me, but at the same time, it only makes me even more nervous.

It's one thing if the plane were to explode or crash with me on it. I can't have anything happening to Aria too. I know they say you're supposed to put your own oxygen mask on first, but that will never happen. Aria will always get hers on before I even consider touching mine.

We walk down the aisle through first class until we find our seats. Aria was hoping they would have beds, but they're just oversized seats with only two in a row. Thankfully we don't have to share the space with anyone else. Neither of us brought a carry-on, so Aria slides in first and sits down before she tucks her bag under the seat. I do the same with my backpack and try to get comfortable.

Suddenly Austin is there, leaning against the back of the seat in front of me. "Hey, bud," he says with a lopsided grin. "Hey, sis," he lifts his chin at Ari.

Brynn slides up next to him. "Hey, guys!"

"What are you guys doing?" Aria asks her brother and her best friend. Excitement dances in her voice and I love the way it sounds. It's enough to momentarily take my mind off the fact that we're about to be tens of thousands of feet in the air in fifteen minutes.

"I ran into Brynn last night and we decided to take an impromptu trip to Vancouver to watch the two of you compete."

"I didn't even know you were in town," I tell Austin. He never said anything to me or Aria.

He shrugs. "I was only supposed to be here for a day but was able to clear my schedule for the next week."

"You were able to get off work?" Aria asks Brynn. She manages an art gallery, but doesn't own it. That has always been a dream of hers.

She nods and smiles sheepishly. "I kind of quit."

Aria's eyes widen, Austin laughs, and I tilt my head to the side. "What?"

"Yep. I was tired of working for Jean. You know I wasn't happy there and honestly, it was time."

Aria joins in the laughter and shakes her head at her

friend before pinning her gaze on her brother. "Did you encourage this? You're known for your impulsive behavior."

Austin holds his hands up innocently. "I had nothing to do with this." He looks at me and winks. "I may have told her I could get her a job in New York," he tells me in a hushed voice so his sister doesn't hear.

Oh, hell no. I will not be keeping his secrets from Aria.

"Austin set up an interview for me with someone he knows in New York who owns a gallery." She pauses and smiles sheepishly. "He is also interested in checking out some of my art too."

"Okay, but this is amazing!" Aria says excitedly, clearly choosing to ignore the way her brother only has eyes for her best friend. He's never acted on anything, though–they've only ever just been friends. "I know how badly you've wanted to move to the city. This is big. This is something we need to celebrate as soon as we get to Vancouver."

A flight attendant steps behind Brynn and Austin. "Excuse me, but the two of you need to find your seats. We need to prepare for takeoff."

"Oh yes, I am so sorry," Austin says, giving her the sweetest smile. "Buzzkill," he mumbles under his breath as he walks a few rows ahead and finds his seat.

"See you guys in Vancouver," Brynn tells us with a smile and a small wave before she heads to her seat beside Austin.

"So bizarre," I mumble as I look at Aria. "I hope they know our actual competition isn't until later in the week."

Aria shrugs and smiles. "Who knows what they're up to. It will be fun to have them along, though."

"Oh yeah, I'm sure." I laugh, rolling my eyes as the sarcasm drips from my voice. "Your brother who is a fucking menace and your best friend who is right there with him."

"They really do complement one another," she tells me with a wink as the flight attendant's voice comes through the speaker. She begins her speech, going through the different safety reminders in case of an emergency. It brings me back to reality and I buckle my belt and tilt my head back. Closing my eyes, my chest expands as I inhale as much oxygen as possible.

Have I mentioned I hate flying?

I can feel Aria's gaze on me and I slowly turn my head to the side, opening my eyes as I meet her gaze. "What?"

"You know, you can hold my hand," she says with a smirk. "I promise I won't tell anyone."

My mind drifts back to the first time we flew together, when we ended up stuck sitting next to one another. At that point, I was still convincing myself I hated her, while Aria was also doing the same. I impulsively grabbed her hand during takeoff and told her if she told anyone, I'd deny it. Neither of us ever brought it up until this very moment.

Reaching for her, I side my palm against hers and thread our fingers together. I'll never get tired of the way her soft skin feels against mine.

"Tell everyone."

CHAPTER TWENTY-EIGHT
ARIA

This is it.

This is the moment we have spent months working toward.

Leo looks over at me, his golden brown eyes flashing to mine as he gives my hand a gentle squeeze. "Are you ready?"

Pulling my bottom lip between my teeth, I nod. "I am. I'm ready to do this with you."

There's no one else I would rather be here with right now. No one else I would rather be sharing this moment with. The way we skate together feels like it was always meant to be. It was always meant to be us.

Leo smiles that goddamn smile that makes my body feel like it's melting before he releases my hand as they call our names over the speakers. He walks over to the break in the boards that surrounds the rink and steps out of the way, waiting for me to go first. My blades hit the ice and all the fears and anxieties cease to exist. It's like they were never even a real thought before.

Side by side, we slowly skate to the center of the rink, taking our positions beside one another. We've practiced this routine so many times, I could do it in my sleep. Leo and I have spent countless hours preparing for this. We can do this. We got this.

Leo stands behind me, his hands holding my cheeks as he presses his body against mine. His lips dip down to my ear just as the lights cut out.

"As close to perfect as possible," he murmurs before gently pressing his lips to my temple. The music begins to play, the soft melody echoing throughout the arena as Leo lifts his head away from mine. My heart pounds to its own beat inside my chest—steady and strong.

And then the lights flash on, focusing solely on Leo and I as we begin.

Our surroundings fade away and the music becomes a distant sound. I listen to the way our skates cut through the ice as we match one another, skating in perfect harmony. We find our familiar rhythm, moving effortlessly and fluid like water. Each movement is calculated and planned. We're in sync with not even a fraction of a second separating his moves from mine.

We're better than close to perfect.

We are perfect.

Leo flashes a smile at me, revealing his straight white teeth as we move around the rink together. We go through the motions, breaking out in various types of spins, skating forward and backward together. It's an act of push and pull, like there's an invisible thread tethering us together. He moves one way, I move with him. I shift the other direction and he's right there following.

Until we come together.

Leo grabs both of my hands, crossing his feet as he digs one toe pick into the ice while he begins to spin me around him. My body straightens out and I'm parallel with the cool surface, almost lying against it as he spins me around over and over. I trust him completely. He uses his strength to hold me, to support me, and, most importantly, to make sure he doesn't let go of me.

This was one of the movements we added to our routine after we talked about changing things up. One thing he and his old partner Delaney didn't have. One thing we have together.

We spin for four rotations before standing upright again. Breaking apart, we begin to skate side by side again, falling into a series of other moves. Spinning to skate backward, we move together around the bend before we both begin to soar into the air. The blades of our skates leave the ice at the same time and Leo and I spin in synchrony for three rotations before we land. It all happens within seconds and neither of us miss a beat as we land on the same skate at the same moment in time.

It's a flawless performance.

Leo and I continue to move, not breaking up our routine at all as we transition from one move to the next, the exact way we practiced and anticipated for the competition. I skate backward with him and Leo's hands find my hips. "I love you," he breathes softly, his voice barely audible, but just loud enough so I can hear him.

A smile lifts the corners of my lips, just as we both begin to squat. Leo's hands grip my hips and he lifts me into the air before he straightens his own body and tosses me upward. Keeping my legs straight, my ankles are crossed and I tuck my arms against my chest as I begin to twirl. My body begins its descent toward the ice and I land the jump perfectly as I meet with Leo and we skate together again.

We go through the rest of our routine, moving with the melody of the music. Our final move is a throw triple Axel. Leo's hands find my hips once again as we skate backward. This time, he lifts me into the air, throwing me upward as my body starts to spin. I'm in perfect form moving above him as he skates to stay with me. Gravity pulls me back to the ground and the air leaves my lungs in a rush as I fall into Leo's arms.

He catches me, just like he has every other time. It's effortless. Exactly how it should be.

His smile is breathtaking as he sets me down on the ice while we continue moving. I don't miss a beat, falling back into rhythm with him again as our movements and the music begin to slow. The emotion hangs heavily in the air between us, our bodies moving together in exaggerated, sweeping motions.

We circle each other around the center of the ice. Then the music slows to a stop as he reaches for me, pulling me to him. He starts to fold into me, both of us collapsing into one another as the music fades and the lights cut out.

Except, he doesn't let me melt into him. Leo holds me upright as both of his hands cup my cheeks.

"Leo," I breathe his name softly, as my eyes adjust to the dark. It's just light enough that I can make out his facial features and expression.

"Aria," he murmurs, his voice just as breathless as mine. His fingers stroke my temples.

The people filling the stands begin to clap, but it's all background noise. Everything around us has faded and all I see is him. All I've really ever seen was him... I was just too ignorant and blind to see it until now. The lights flicker on and I'm still holding on to his arms while he holds my face.

I'm inevitably lost in him and he's the only one who can ever find me.

His mouth captures mine, his lips sweeping across my own in a rush as he steals the air from my lungs. My fingers dig into his arms as I cling to him, and I part my lips as his tongue traces the seam. We're caught up in each other, his tongue dancing with mine as he kisses me deeply.

Things had been a little weird the past few weeks. It felt like we were sneaking around, like he was keeping me a secret and no one was supposed to know about us. I wanted to ask him about it, but every time I started to say anything, it just felt wrong. I didn't want him to think I was questioning his intentions, because I didn't truly believe he wanted this to stay hidden.

I didn't have to ask.

He chases my fears away with his lips on mine in front

of everyone in the stands. Everyone watching the competition on national television. Everyone in the world…

Leo slowly pulls away from me, leaving me breathless as I hold on to him for support. My knees feel like they could buckle and he drops his hands down to my hips. The sound of someone clapping slowly has my lips pulling upward. My brother is the type of asshole who would do something like that. And the rest of the crowd blindly follows him as they all start to clap again.

"What was that for?" I ask him, my voice quiet as he stares down at me with his soft eyes. Heat blossoms across my cheeks.

"I figured it was time that everyone knows."

I tilt my head to the side. "That everyone knows what?"

"That you're mine," he says with simplicity. There's nothing but admiration and love pouring from his gaze. "I don't want this to just be a fling. I don't want this to just be what we do. I want you to feel appreciated and valued. I want you to know your worth and know I will pay the price—whatever it is—just to be graced by your presence. You are exactly who and what I want and I never want you to question that, Aria."

His words penetrate my soul, sending a burst of warmth billowing through my body. "I'm in love with you, Leo. So stupidly fucking gone for you."

"I know, love," he says as his smile lights up his entire face and a soft laugh escapes him. "I've known it for a while. I was just waiting for you to realize it too." He pauses, his eyes searching mine. "Tell me your mine, Aria."

"I'm yours, Leo. I've always been yours," I assure him

as I momentarily get lost in his eyes. The clapping around us eventually tapers off and I remember that we're still standing in the middle of the rink. I pull away from Leo and duck my head. "Come on," I whisper-yell at him as I grab his hand. "We have to get off the ice."

A chuckle rumbles in his chest and we turn to face each side of the arena, Leo bowing and me curtseying before we finally take our leave from the rink. We are the last pair for the day and we lingered out here a lot longer than we were supposed to.

"Well, that was quite the performance," my brother muses as he and Brynn stand with the rest of the team waiting for us. He looks at Leo and lets out a soft laugh as he shakes his head. It's the only comment anyone makes about our kiss, but I'm sure it won't be the end of hearing about it from my brother. There's no way he's going to let us live down this moment.

"You guys were absolutely amazing," Brynn exclaims as she pulls me away from Leo and wraps her arms around me. "I need you to tell me *everything*," she whispers in my ear for only me to hear. She releases me and Leo and I are pulled in opposite directions as everyone from our team takes turns congratulating us.

The judges don't take long with the results. They start with the bronze metal, announcing the pair that wins third place. After they skate out to get their medals, they move on to silver. I stand next to my brother and Brynn, shifting my feet nervously as we wait. Time is suspended. I look over at Leo to find he's already watching me.

His face transforms before my eyes as the announcers

call out our names, stating to the world that we have won the world championship. It's no surprise that we won the gold medal, but tears still spring to my eyes as relief floods my body. We worked so hard for this, but suddenly winning is the furthest thing from my mind.

I look over at Leo and he winks as he waits for me by the ice.

I've already won.

EPILOGUE
LEO

Standing along the boards, I watch Aria as she effortlessly moves across the ice. Her feet move with perfect precision. Her knees bend slightly as she slows a bit, getting into position. I watch in awe as her skates lift from the slick surface beneath her feet. Her body rotates in the air and time feels like it's suspended for three heartbeats before she touches the ice again.

She lands the jump perfectly, her leg extended behind her body with her arms in front of her abdomen. Her leg lowers and both of her skates move across the frozen surface as she heads in my direction. A smile breaks out across her lips and she lets out a ragged breath as she comes to a halt in front of me.

"I have the most beautiful girlfriend in all the land," I tell her, reaching for her hand as I pull her closer. "I don't think I'll ever grow tired of watching you skate."

A playful grin dances across her face as she pulls her

hand from mine and skates in a circle around me, like a shark circling its prey. "There was a time you didn't," she reminds me with a wink.

"That's not true," I argue as I begin to circle around her, both of us staring the other down as we carve lines in the ice. "I grew addicted to watching you, until I was able to skate with you. Now I have the best of both worlds."

Her steps falter for a moment and her toe pick gets caught in the ice. She lets out a gasp as she trips and loses her balance. My hands dart out and I grab her waist, catching her before she hits her knees.

Aria laughs out loud, the sound of her voice lighting my heart on fire as her hands grab my forearms. "Whatever would I do without you?"

"You'll never have to find out."

Her face softens and her smile reaches her eyes as she holds on to me. "I love you."

I love this woman with my entire soul. The way we fell was like two atoms colliding. It wasn't slow and sweet. There was nothing graceful about it. It was fast. It was brutal, leaving scars on our hearts. It was inevitable. Neither of us realized we were falling until we were colliding into one another with severed brake lines.

I fall in love with her more every single day and I plan on loving Aria Reed for the rest of my days.

"Move in with me."

Aria's eyes widen slightly and her lips part as her breathing momentarily pauses. It's evident that I've caught her by surprise, but fuck it. I'm tired of waiting. "Like move in, move in?"

Chuckling, I pull her flush against my body. It's something we've been dancing around for months. My house already looks like she lives there. She has a few drawers in my bedroom that have her things in it, along with some outfits hanging in the closet. Not to mention the way my bathroom has become hers. "Yes. When is the last time we actually spent a night apart?"

She chews on the inside of her cheek for a second as she lifts her hands and links them around my nape. "Honestly, I don't remember."

"Exactly. So, why the hell are we technically living in two separate houses?" I ask her as I lift one hand and slide it along the side of her neck. She tilts her head back farther to look up at me.

"I've been wondering the same thing," she admits as a fire begins to burn deep in her irises. "Are you sure that's what you want?"

I tilt my head to the side, my nose crinkling as my eyebrows pull together. "I wouldn't have said it if it wasn't what I wanted." My hand slides to the back of her neck and I have her pinned against me. "You're what I want, Aria. You're all I'm ever going to want. Do I need to take you to the courthouse and marry you right now?"

She curls her lip in distaste and raises an eyebrow at me. "I'd rather you didn't do that."

"You don't want to marry me, pretty girl?" I question her as my mouth drops down to hers. I slowly move my lips across hers, just barely kissing her. Her fingers dig into my flesh and I smile against her at her reaction.

"Quite the opposite," she breathes, nipping at my lips.

"I want to marry you, but not in a courthouse wearing the clothes I'm skating in."

Spinning her around, her back is to the boards. My legs push against hers and I slide her across the ice until the small of her back is pressed against them. The benches are in front of me, so there's no glass behind her. Sliding my hands down to her thighs, I lift her into the air and set her down on the edge. "So, you've already been planning our wedding day inside your head."

Aria's hands plunge into the hair on the back of my head and she gives a small tug as I tip my head back to look at her. "Possibly," she says with an innocent smile as she wraps her legs around my waist. I'm standing between her legs with my hands holding her hips and blood rushing to my cock.

"Tell me about it," I say as I slide my hands under the bottom of her shirt, feeling her skin beneath my palms. It's late at night and the rink is empty. Austin has it closed for maintenance, but he has Aria and I overseeing things while he's in New York.

Aria's eyes are glassy and her smile is soft. Her lips are inviting. My gaze drops down to them before looking back into her eyes. "It's around the time the sun begins to crest the horizon. The clouds are wispy and the sky looks like cotton candy. We're standing in a vineyard in a valley with all of our friends and family surrounding us."

She paints the picture of our wedding day and I store it in my memory for future use. I need something to reference so I can make sure she has the wedding of her fucking dreams. I want pictures from that day plastered all through the halls of our home. I want her to look back on that day and never wish it was something more.

"You're wearing a black tux and your hair has that soft curl it does when you're freshly showered." Her smile grows wider. "I'm not going to tell you what my dress looks like because it could be bad luck."

"Hmm," I hum as I lift one hand to pull her face down to mine. "What can I do to convince you to tell me?"

"Nothing," she laughs softly as her lips brush against my own. She tightens her grip on my hair. "You're going to have to wait until our wedding day to find out."

"What if I can't wait that long?" I ask her as I begin to trail my other hand farther up her back beneath her shirt. My fingers brush against the strap of her bra and I unclasp it in one fluid movement.

"It will be worth the wait," she assures me. Her lips capture mine in one breath. My cock is already fucking hard, pressing against her as her tongue slides into my mouth. I breathe her in, drawing the oxygen from her lungs as our tongues tangle together.

Releasing the back of her neck, both of my hands reach for the hem of her shirt, pushing it up her body. "What are you doing?" she asks me breathlessly as we break apart. She doesn't stop me as I lift her shirt up over her head and toss it onto the bench behind her. "Anyone could walk in and see us."

My fingers hook the straps of her bra and I slide them down her arms before throwing it over where her shirt is.

Her nipples instantly grow hard from the cold air. I shake my head as I begin to move my mouth closer to her chest. "I locked the door before we got on the ice."

Her body involuntarily shivers as I draw her nipple between my teeth and suck. I roll my tongue around her pebbled flesh as I knead her other breast in my hand. Goosebumps break out over her skin and I feel her body shiver again.

Abruptly pulling away from her, my lips leave her nipple with a pop. Her legs are still wrapped around me and my hands land beneath her thighs as I lift her into the air once again. She's still topless, clinging to me as I carry her off the ice and walk toward the warm room. I kick open the door, feeling the warmth as we step inside. The heat isn't blasting, but it's definitely warmer than the rest of the rink.

There's a couch along the far wall and I don't stop walking until I reach it. I gently lower her onto the couch and she stares up at me, watching as I reach for her feet. My fingers work quickly to untie her skates before I toss them onto the floor, not giving a shit about the blades hitting anything. They can be resharpened or I'll buy her new blades or skates if I need to.

She wastes no time removing her pants and underwear as I take off my own skates. Aria's completely naked, lying on the couch waiting for me, as I rise to my feet. My eyes only leave her for a second while I remove my own shirt, followed by my pants and boxer briefs.

Words will never come close to describing how I feel about her. I spent so much time convincing myself and everyone around me that I hated her. And in a way I did. I think I secretly hated her because she wasn't mine. I always viewed her as someone I wouldn't have a chance with. I would have spent the rest of my life wondering what could have been with her. Wondering if the stars could have aligned properly, would we have ended up together? But those questions no longer matter. The universe heard my silent prayers and the stars *have* aligned.

The organ beating in my chest no longer belongs to me. Hell, after that night in high school, I'm not sure it was ever truly in my possession. That moment was the start of my heart falling for her.

Emotion wells in my throat as I push open her knees and lower myself down onto the couch with her. "Can you be like this forever?"

"Like what?" she asks as she wraps her legs around me, pulling me closer. Her hands feel like silk as they slide around the back of my neck. A quiet laugh falls from her lips. "Naked?"

I shake my head as I shift my hips and slowly sink into her. "Mine."

"Always," she breathes as she stares up at me with those breathtaking gray orbs. "I'm yours forever, Leo."

A groan escapes me and my face drops down to hers as I capture her mouth with mine, sinking deeper into her. Her nails dig into my flesh, holding on to me like her life depends on it as I begin to shift my hips and slowly thrust into her.

This is where I want to stay forever. Right here, with her, irrevocably lost in one another.

My soul has reached its final destination.

And it's her.

It's always been her.

EXTENDED EPILOGUE
LEO

I feel like I've been waiting my entire life for this day.

The day when I get to finally call her my wife.

And yet, nothing has been going right.

"You look like you're going to throw up," Austin points out to me, as if I don't already know that. "Are you okay?"

Rolling my lips between my teeth, I bite down and nod. "I feel like I'm failing at making today perfect for her. I just need one thing to go right today."

So far, it's been pouring all morning and we may have to move the wedding indoors. The catering company got the times wrong, so they're scrambling to get someone to the venue. The florist mixed up our wedding with another, so none of the colors of the flowers work. And somewhere along the shuffle, I misplaced my tie, so now I'm wearing one that is not what I had planned for my outfit.

I haven't seen Aria since yesterday. She stayed in a separate room at the vineyard with Charlie, Brynn, and her other bridesmaids. Not seeing her has literally been killing me. I just want to hold her in my arms and feel her close. Usually it's Aria who wants everything flawless and me reminding her that not everything is perfect. How the tables have turned today...

"You know, it's supposed to be good luck when it rains on your wedding day."

My lips form a flat line. "Aria had a very specific picture of how she wanted to get married and it was supposed to be outside."

"Well, that's why you guys have a backup plan to have it indoors, just in case." Leo reaches for me, straightening my tie before he checks his watch. "We should probably get out there. You have a bride to marry."

He gives me a once-over and smiles his brightest smile before patting my chest with his palm. I look him in the eye, silently thanking him for never judging me for falling in love with his sister, before I head out of the room. Austin leaves me to go find Brynn and I start walking down the hall toward where we're supposed to be getting married now.

It's still beautiful; it's just not what Aria had planned. With the help of a wedding planner, we were able to have everything set up perfectly. I glance out the window, noticing the rain has ceased and the sun is poking through the wispy clouds along the horizon.

I see Jenny, our wedding planner, standing by the door of where I'm supposed to go to wait for Aria. She looks up from her clipboard, pushing her glasses closer to her face as I reach her.

"You look handsome," she says with a smile and a nod.

"Guests have already started to take their seats. We're just waiting for you so we can start."

"Have everyone move outside to where we originally planned."

She frowns, her eyebrows pulling together. "None of the chairs are out there. Everything was moved inside."

"Then they can stand. Or they can wait until the reception." I level my gaze on hers as I cross my arms over my chest. I will be giving Aria the wedding she asked for—even if it makes me seem like I'm the groom-zilla. "I'm marrying her outside under the cotton candy skies as the sun sets, just like she envisioned."

Jenny lets out a sigh, her shoulders falling for a moment before she pushes them back. A smile drifts across her lips and she nods. "Okay. We can make it work. We're a little pressed for time, but we can do this."

Considering the amount of money we're paying her, agreeing with what I want is the least she can do.

"Thank you."

I don't know where she got all the manpower, but in less than fifteen minutes, they had everything moved back outside to the valley where the sun was setting behind us. I shift my weight on my feet, glancing at Austin from the corner of my eye as we both stare down the grass aisle. There are hedges that line the farther side of it, blocking any view of Aria as she makes her way to us.

All of our friends and family are gathered, everyone

sitting in the seats or standing by the vine-covered archway. The music shifts, the sound of the violins echoing throughout the valley as they begin to play the melody Aria picked to walk down the aisle to. It's the first song we skated to, but it's played only by string instruments.

My heart crawls into my throat as everyone rises to their feet and Aria steps out from behind the hedges and walks the aisle with her arm linked in her father's. She steals every molecule of oxygen from my lungs. Her long dark hair is loosely curled, with half of it pulled back. The dress she wears fits her body perfectly. It's sleeveless and made of lace, hugging her curves before it begins to flare around her knees.

She's more beautiful than anyone or anything in the entire universe.

Tears prick the corners of my eyes and Aria's gaze is locked on mine as she slowly makes her way down the aisle, her feet moving in harmony with the music. As they approach, I meet her and her father. He pulls her in for a hug with tears in his own eyes before handing her to me.

"Hey you," she says softly, her perfect lips spreading as she smiles brightly at me. She slides her hand into mine, but we stand facing each other instead of walking up to the officiant. "Fancy seeing you here."

"You're the only person I want to see here."

She laughs softly as she reaches up to cup the side of my face. "I heard you threw a little bit of a temper tantrum so we could get married out here instead."

My eyebrows pull together. "No, I didn't," I retort,

shaking my head. "I know how you were picturing things and I just wanted it to be perfect for you."

"It's more than perfect," she assures me, her voice soft and warm as it wraps itself around me. "I don't really care about any of this. As long as you're here with me, that's all that matters."

I take a step closer, both of my hands moving to cup her cheeks. "I'll always be wherever you are."

My face begins to dip closer to hers and I watch her eyelids flutter shut as she lifts her chin. My lips are just about to graze hers when Austin clears his throat so fucking loudly. I whip my head to the side to look at him and he makes a face and nods his head toward the archway.

"You're not supposed to kiss her yet."

Aria laughs softly, her hands reaching up to grab my wrists as she pulls my hands away from her face. She slides her palm against mine, her fingers threading through my own, and she winks. "Let's go get married, Mr. Wells."

"I'm ready to make you Mrs. Wells."

"Prove it," she challenges me as she turns and pulls me to the archway with her. The officiant starts to speak, but I don't hear a single word he says. I'm too busy getting lost in Aria's beautiful gray eyes. In front of our friends and our family, under the cotton candy skies, we say our vows and seal them with a kiss. Everyone rises to their feet, clapping, but the people and the sounds fade into the background.

There's only one person who matters here and she's standing right in front of me.

"My wife," I murmur as I brush a stray hair away from her face.

"I love the way that sounds." She looks up at me and smiles. God, I cannot wait to spend the rest of my life loving her. She's all I see. "Say it again."

A chuckle rumbles in my chest and I drop my face closer to hers, my lips brushing against the shell of her ear.

"*My* wife."

A LOOK INSIDE THE NEXT BOOK

Keep reading for a look inside Cali's next release, The Art of Breathing, a brand-new emotional new adult romance!

CHAPTER ONE
NOT TODAY, UNIVERSE

"We aren't sure what her life expectancy is."

Imagine your life if those were the words the doctors spoke after months of testing led them to your definitive diagnosis. Imagine living your life with a diagnosis so rare that every single provider was left scratching their heads while trying to figure out how to treat you.

On the outside, I looked normal. On the inside, my body was struggling to function properly. I was diagnosed with a rare genetic mutation when I was a few months old. My mother left the hospital with what she thought was a newborn with some mild breathing issues.

Our small town hospital never should have sent me home. They didn't have the capabilities to provide complex medical care. It wasn't until I started turning a dusky gray when my mother would try to feed me that they realized something was seriously wrong.

I was rushed to a nearby city that had one of the best children's hospitals in the country. It was a massive research center

CHAPTER ONE

and it was the place that I spent almost the entire first year of my life.

A majority of the smooth muscles in my body were affected by the rare genetic mutation. It severely impacted my lungs and intestines more than any of my other organs. The heart also tends to be affected with my diagnosis, but only as the disease process progresses.

Unfortunately, the handful of children who had a similar diagnosis to mine had all passed away from cardiac issues before reaching adulthood. That seemed to be the last leg of the disease. After the heart was involved, it was essentially game over.

I was fortunate enough to not have any major cardiac involvement… yet.

"Luna!" My mother called from downstairs, her voice floating up into my bedroom. Tank, my Italian Mastiff, lifted his head off my lap and looked to the door. "It's almost time to leave for school!"

A sigh slipped from my lips as I closed the pastel purple notebook in front of me, tucking my pen into the spiral binding. Since I spent the last few months of my senior year of high school in and out of the hospital with respiratory infections, I had been doing a majority of my school work virtually. I wasn't really looking forward to going back in person for the last three weeks. I was always known as one of the sick kids, the ones that everyone constantly looked at with some hint of pity in their eyes.

All I had ever wanted was to be treated normally.

Rising from the chair at the small wooden desk in my bedroom, I walked over to my closet to get dressed. I had awoken early this morning and ran through my mental

CHAPTER ONE

checklist. My mother had taught me over the years to manage my own home medical care at home and for that I was grateful. I spent the earlier years of my life with a home nurse and it felt like my privacy was always being invaded. My alarm on my phone chimed, alerting me with one of the numerous notifications I had set.

I no longer had a need for the central line in my chest, but they kept it there in case of an emergency. There was always talk of one day hopefully being able to remove that tube, along with my tracheostomy tube, but no one knew if I would ever see that day.

I have had a tracheostomy tube since I was a month old. It was one of the first surgeries that I had as a baby, when they realized that my airway was completely collapsing on itself. It was one of the main things that had kept me alive this long and continued to do so every day of my life.

Grabbing a syringe, I twisted it into the small balloon that is attached to the trach tube and deflated it before securing a small speaking valve onto the end of my trach. I was able to talk without the one way valve on, but my doctor preferred that I use it as it doesn't allow for air to pass through the tube, so I was forced to breathe normally.

Even though I was born with the lungs of a 90 year old person with a severe case of COPD, some of my lung tissue had regenerated from the years of advanced medical care. I only had to use the ventilator now while I was sleeping or if I was sick. It was a tad annoying, but by the end of every day, my body tended to reach a point of exhaustion.

CHAPTER ONE

After running through my list, I rechecked my outfit for the day in the mirror. My dark brown hair was as straight as a board, but I pulled it back in a French braid, leaving a few pieces framing my face. My porcelain colored skin stood out in contrast to my dark hair and my deep blue eyes looked like the darkest depths of the ocean.

Today was a good day and there was actually a pink tint to my cheeks. Instead of looking deathly, I only looked mildly sickly. Tilting my head back, I looked up at the ceiling and raised my middle finger in the air. *Nice try, Universe. You can take me another day.*

Readjusting the bottom hems of my shorts, I stared at the way my clothes hung on my thin frame. There was a little more definition to my body than there once was. Two years ago, I was fortunate enough to receive an intestinal transplant at the best children's hospital in the country after being in intestinal failure for many years.

No one knew the shelf life of my new intestinal tract, but I wasn't about to take it for granted. For the first time in my life, I was actually holding a steady weight and gaining normal pounds instead of constantly losing them. After giving myself another glance, I abandoned my bedroom and made my way down to the kitchen where my mother was waiting. Tank followed along after me, as he was always attached to my hip.

"Good morning, sunshine," my mother smiled at me over her cup of coffee. "Good morning, Tank," she greeted my dog as he walked in beside me. Her dark blue eyes looked tired, but they always have. I don't know that I've ever seen my mother looking refreshed

CHAPTER ONE

and not overstressed. "Sit down and eat. I made your favorite."

I glanced down at the table, noting a pile of French toast sitting in the center on a plate. Memories instantly washed over my mind from my seventh birthday. The doctor's approved that I could start trying solid foods right before my birthday. That morning my mother asked me what I wanted to have for breakfast and I randomly asked for French toast—something that I never had the pleasure of trying before, but always watched everyone else thoroughly enjoy.

That morning, she took me out, just the two of us and got me exactly what I asked for. After drowning the pieces of toast in maple syrup, I took two of the smallest bites possible. My mother cried tears of happiness that day, you would think that I won an Olympic gold medal. It was a memory that had stuck with me since then and my mother always made me French toast when she thought I might need a pick me up.

A sad smile crept onto my face. She made enough to feed an army, but sadly, it was just the two of us who were home most of the time. Both of my brother's were in college, so I was the last kid left. And my father—bless his soul—worked his ass off as a diesel mechanic to pay for whatever medical bills insurance wouldn't cover.

Unfortunately, for my mother and I, that meant he spent long hours in the shop and was rarely ever home. We made things work, though. My mother was my rock and the constant in my life. She was the glue that held all of us together and I would literally be dead without her.

CHAPTER ONE

Taking my seat at the table, I speared a piece of toast with my fork and slapped it onto my plate. After putting on some butter, I poured some syrup onto it before cutting it into pieces. My mother watched me carefully as I took a small bite and chewed it slowly. Even though I had been eating for a few years now, I was always careful with the way I consumed my meals.

The last thing that I needed was to choke on a piece of food.

"Are you ready for your first day back?" My mother questioned me with hesitation. She had been the one excited for me to attend in person the last three weeks. Me on the other hand—I was content just finishing the year at home.

Shrugging, I swallowed my piece of French toast before meeting her gaze. "Not really. It's not like my friends haven't visited me while I was home. It's kind of pointless for me to go back now."

"Nonsense," my mother waved her hand dismissively. "If you really don't want to go, I won't push you to, but I think it would be good for you. You'll be graduating in three weeks. You have prom next weekend. This is the last few times you'll be seeing a lot of these people."

An exasperated sigh slipped from my lips. "I'm alright with that. My real friends are the only ones that I care to see."

Melanie and Salem were my two closest girlfriends. They checked in on me and visited every chance that they could. We barely had any classes together this year, so I

CHAPTER ONE

don't see them as often as my mother thinks while at school.

Suddenly a horn beeps from out front, promptly causing me to jump from my seat. "There's Oliver," I told my mother, offering her a smile before pushing another piece of French toast into my mouth. "Gotta get to school."

"Make sure that you check in with Joyce at the nurses office when you first get there."

I walked over to the front door, grabbing the multitude of bags that I was required to carry with me. "Yes, mother, I know." My backpack, medical supply bag, back up ventilator and a suction machine. I had practically become a pack-mule since I could carry my own things.

The medical bag was heavy, as it included literally everything I needed in case of an emergency and my mother watched me with sadness in her eyes. I hated the look that she was giving me right now and it wasn't a second later before she was scrambling to her feet to help me with the door.

As she pulled it open, my best friend and neighbor, Oliver, was standing outside waiting with a huge grin on his face. His sage green eyes shined back and the sun poking through the clouds illuminated his inky black hair.

"Let me carry some of that," he offered, grabbing the ventilator and medical bag from me before I had the chance to refuse. That was Oliver Hart for you. The perfect gentleman who was always there to have my back. "Hey Tank," he greeted Tank as he stood beside me with his tail wagging. Oliver was one of his favorite people too.

Oliver Hart was my partner in crime. His family

CHAPTER ONE

moved in next door when we were both three years old. After our parents met, we had our first play date and we haven't been separated since. He has been by my side through every surgery, medical procedure and hospital stay. If you name it, Oliver Hart has been through it with me.

"You are so sweet, Ollie," my mother beamed at him, completely charmed by him like the rest of the universe. I mean, how could you not be? With those plump lips and perfect smile. That chiseled jawline and sharp features. Oliver looked like he was sculpted by the most skilled artist of all time.

"My mother says the same exact thing, Mrs. Truly," he smiled back at her, hoisting my bags over his shoulder.

"Well, your mother sure did raise a fine young man."

Oliver chuckled, taking a bow in front of her while somehow still holding my things for me.

"We should probably be going," I interjected, smiling sweetly at two of them. "Don't want to be late for my first day back."

"Of course not," Ollie nodded. "Have a great day, Mrs. Truly."

My mother stepped up to me, giving me a hug and a kiss on the cheek before sending me on my way. It killed her every time that I was out of her sight and I understood her fear. Medical issues or not—you never knew when it was the last time you were going to see someone.

"Bye Tank," I told my dog as I bent down and gave him a hug. Since I had a nurse at the school who was there just for me, I didn't feel it was necessary to bring in my

CHAPTER ONE

service dog. He was a little bit of an inconvenience there and I already drew enough attention to myself without him, but I felt bad every day I left. Tank looked up at me with his sad brown eyes and I knew he wasn't happy to be left behind.

I followed after Oliver to his black Subaru STI and paused behind him as he opened the backseat. His muscles flexed through his heather gray t-shirt as he put my things in before turning to me for my backpack. After handing it to him, I took my seat in the passenger's side before he walked over and got in behind the steering wheel.

"I'm glad you decided to come, even if there's only a few weeks left," he offered quietly as he pushed in the clutch and released the hand brake before shifting seamlessly into first gear.

I glanced over at him as we pulled away from my house and out onto the street. "You can thank my mom."

"Well, I'll have to make sure to do that when I see her this afternoon," he replied, flashing his perfectly straight teeth at me. He directed his gaze back to the road as he took a left turn onto Main Street. "Are you excited for prom this weekend?"

A groan slipped from my lips as I tilted my head back against the headrest of the seat and closed my eyes. "I can't believe you talked me into it," I admitted as I lifted my head back up to look at him. "Are you sure there's no one else you'd rather go with? I know that there were a bunch of girls hoping you would ask them."

Oliver looked over at me and the different shades of

CHAPTER ONE

green danced in his eyes from the sunlight. "There's only one girl that I would want to go with and she's sitting right beside me." He paused and winked as he held out his pink to me. "Always and forever, Luna Truly."

My breath hitched, catching in my throat and I fought the urge to rip off my speaking valve to breathe easier. As if I hadn't already struggled to learn the art of breathing, when he said things like that, it made my lungs struggle even harder to get the oxygen that they needed.

I hooked my pinky with his. "Always and forever," I murmured back to him.

You see, Oliver Hart was my best friend and my partner in crime.

But he was also the one that my damaged heart belonged to.

Even if the feelings would never be reciprocated.

ABOUT THE AUTHOR

Cali Melle is a USA Today Bestselling Author who writes sports romance that will pull at your heartstrings. You can always expect her stories to come fully equipped with heartthrobs and a happy ending, along with some steamy scenes.

In her free time, Cali can usually be found living in a magical, fantasy world with the newest book or fanfic she's reading or freezing at the ice rink while she watches her kids play hockey.

ALSO BY CALI MELLE

ORCHID CITY SERIES

Meet Me in the Penalty Box

The Tides Between Us

Written In Ice

Dirty Pucking Play

The Lie of Us

WYNCOTE WOLVES SERIES

Cross Checked Hearts

Deflected Hearts

Playing Offsides

The Faceoff

The Goalie Who Stole Christmas

Splintered Ice

Coast to Coast

Off-Ice Collision

STANDALONES

The Christmas Exchange

Tell Me How You Hate Me

Made in United States
North Haven, CT
22 June 2024